AMALGAM

Also by Gustavo Bondoni:

The Emily Plair Saga

OUTSIDE

SPLINTER

Off The Beaten Path, story collection from Guardbridge Books

Siege

Incursion

Ice Station: Death

Jungle Lab Terror

Test Site Horror

Lost Island Rampage

Desert Base Strike

The Malakiad

The Swords of Rasna

AMALGAM

Book 3 of the Emily Plair Saga

BY GUSTAVO BONDONI

GUARDBRIDGE BOOKS
ST ANDREWS, SCOTLAND

Published by Guardbridge Books,
St Andrews, Fife, United Kingdom.

http://guardbridgebooks.co.uk

Amalgam.

ISBN: 978-1-911486-81-7

To Tere and Vicen,
who are reluctant readers at times,
but now have a book dedicated to them.

CHAPTER 1

Borneo, Earth – Planetwide Simulation

The simulation looked beautiful that day. It always looked beautiful.

Rome looked out over the peaceful sea. The crystal-clear water displayed fish darting to and fro just above the perfect white sand of the ocean floor. A soft warm breeze caressed his skin, emerging from a cloudless cerulean sky.

"I always wanted to see Borneo," Emily said, a daiquiri in her hand. "But how did you know?"

"I didn't," Rome replied. "It just seemed so beautiful here. A good place as any to insert ourselves, and better than most."

She dug her foot into the sand. "Yeah. Definitely better than most."

Emily wore the same body she had when he first met her: light brown, almost blond hair, a thin frame with pale skin and a dusting of freckles across her nose. Despite everything that had happened to her — to them — he hadn't changed a single line of the code that represented how she looked inside the world-sized simulation that surrounded them.

She must have felt his gaze on her because she looked towards him and frowned. "We can't stay here forever, you know," she said. "We need to search out what happened here. Where is everyone?"

"I don't know. Maybe they left. The ship I came in on detected ion signatures as if a huge fleet had passed through the system. Whatever it was, it was gone by the time we arrived."

"Any clue where they might have been going?"

"None. And no way to check. The only thing I can tell you

is that they didn't go to Tau Ceti. Someone would have noticed them when they arrived."

"Multiple ships?" she asked, her brow furrowed in thought.

"That's what the captain of my vessel told me."

"That doesn't make any sense. The best way for the people of Earth to leave the planet *en masse* is to put all the mainframes on a single vessel and fly that one out, keeping the simulation going just as it had been."

Rome considered her words. "The simulation wasn't in the best of shape when we left," he reminded her. "Everyone had figured out they could program themselves whatever characteristics they wanted, and program the world itself to do whatever they felt like, as well. The entire world was coming apart at the seams. What if they all just died out in a catastrophic simulation collapse?"

"And the ion signatures?"

He shrugged. "A misreading. A trade fleet from one of the other colonies. Aliens. It could have been anything." He'd hoped not to have to say that out loud, but it had been in his thoughts ever since they left Earth the first time. The feeling he'd had was that the simulation was about to tear itself apart. The war had already started.

Emily looked around. "I would say you're right… except everything is still here." She held up the daiquiri. "The power works. The hotel has fruit in the fridge. The blender worked. Even though there are no people around, the simulation, the world itself, is functioning perfectly."

"I can think of several reasons that might have happened. The most likely is that the simulation, suffering catastrophic damage, reset to a predetermined configuration." And, he didn't say, since the original configuration was set up for real live humans to log into the sim by wires, as opposed to the fully human — albeit completely artificial — inhabitants he'd met the last time he was there, it was empty of intelligent life.

Rome was a binarist, probably the single living human being who knew most about the working of the Earth simulation. He'd only known two other people who might have known it better than he did — although both of those were actually simulated people created in the simulation itself, and who'd lived there all their lives — a man named Graham and a woman called Jarrien.

He knew Graham was dead. Looking around, he admitted that he suspected Jarrien must have died, too.

"My suggestion," he said, "is to worry about all that later. We need a vacation. I might recover in a couple of months."

"You need a vacation," Emily said. "I've been packed in a tiny mainframe playing fantasy games all the way from Earth to Tau. After that, I was locked in a storage disk, and I didn't even know anything was happening or that any time had passed. Hell, I'm about as rested as anyone can be. And I want to figure out what happened. There has to be some way to access records."

"Give me a few days to relax," he said.

"If you're so tired, why don't you just jump into the code to wipe it away?"

Rome felt his face flush. "I don't know how," he muttered.

"What?"

"I can't do that. I was always outside the simulation, connected via VR, but with keyboard access to the backend. I could play with the code… but I was never inside. Now that I'm limited to actually working from within the simulation, I'll have to figure out how to do that. And that means getting to a research library somehow, or to a university."

"Can't you just use the mindnet connection in the hotel?"

"No. The data on backend work and looking outside the simulation aren't in the mindnet. I checked. Besides, remember how Graham had to dig in the New York archives to find anything relevant? We'll need to do something similar."

"Do you think they'll have the same records here in…. where is this? I mean, I know it's Borneo, but what country are we in?"

"This is the Malaysian sector. We could also cross into Indonesia and Brunei," Rome replied. "I really doubt we'll have any problems at the border. After all, we'd need to be really unlucky to discover that the only humans left anywhere in the world are border guards."

His attempt at humor fell flat. Emily's brow was wrinkled in concentration. "I think they said — the binarists back in New York, I mean — that the treaty that created the simulation worldwide had been negotiated there, and the only records were kept in the City Hall there."

"I think I remember that."

"So that's where we need to go. Maybe Jarrien's people left an amended record," Emily said.

"That seems a bit optimistic."

"If they didn't, we can always figure out how to get into the base simulation and see what happened from there, right?"

She sounded so hopeful that he couldn't disappoint her. Not again. Not after she'd lost the world she'd been born into… and then the one she'd been promised when she took the painful decision to escape.

"All right. We'll go to New York," he said.

She hugged him.

He held up a finger. "But only after we rest a couple of weeks. There's no hurry, after all."

She looked him up and down. "All right. We can take as much time as you need. I can think of a lot worse places to be than sitting on this beach," she said. Then she raised an eyebrow. "But I do have one question: why are you wearing a swimsuit?"

Rome blushed. "I mean... we're out in the open at a resort hotel..."

"And there isn't a single other person on the entire planet," she finished. She pulled him in and kissed him.

***

"This feels really dangerous," Emily said as they approached the pier.

"Don't you like boats?" Rome replied.

"I haven't been on many in my life. I mean, I was on a few during spring break in college, and some friends had a small sailboat in a lake near Denver. But..."

"But what? This boat isn't much bigger than those."

Emily paused. "Rome, if I fell into the water and drowned back then, I would have been reset by the system. My physical body would have been unhurt in its birthing tube. Or at least that's what I thought."

"But it wasn't true. You've been an artificial intelligence since the day you were born."

"I know that..." she replied. "But the system acted like I was alive and safely underground. Like everyone was. We didn't know any better, and we all felt safe. No one died in accidents, and the only reason we even bothered doing safe stuff is that the simulation would give you a taste of pain, even through the buffers, if you did something dumb and got hurt. Plus, we were supposed to avoid getting hurt. It's the way people acted. If we didn't, people would look at us funny."

Rome wondered how it was possible that a population would have remained docile for centuries knowing that they lived in a simulation where nothing could hurt their physical bodies. In their place, he was certain that he would have explored the limits of the simulation, broken it apart in the exact way that Jarrien and Graham had been doing the last time he was there.

Instead, the population was perfectly docile, living in harmony with its electronic environment until the day the expedition from Tau Ceti — the one that had brought Rome there in the first place — arrived to knock on their doors.

It almost made him believe that the people who insisted artificial humans weren't really human might have a point.

Except he was one now. The consciousness he wore now wasn't connected to human body safely ensconced in a warm ship. It was just a copy of a man's mind and memories… a man who was several light years distant.

He felt perfectly human. As human as he always had, in fact.

That thought brought up a lot of things he didn't want to analyze. Foremost among them was the fact that he'd created this copy of himself without telling the woman that, convinced that Emily was dead, he'd fallen in love with. Now, he bore that guilt along with the guilt of not having told Emily about it… and with the added guilt of not really being certain what he felt for Emily herself.

He pushed the mess aside. He needed to focus on the problem at hand.

"Rome," Emily said. "What's up?"

Rome realized he was standing motionless on the pier. "Nothing. Just thinking about the best way to steal this boat."

"Weren't you listening?"

"I heard you. You're worried about sailing out there. Don't be frightened. We'll be fine."

She sighed. "You didn't listen to a word I said, did you?" She took hold of his arm. "I'm afraid for real. What if the boat sinks? What if we hit something and drown?"

Rome gestured towards the blue expanse around them. "The sea is completely calm. The forecast is for almost no wind all day.

And we planned our route to hop from island to island so we're never more than fifty kilometers from land. We'll be fine."

"But what if something happens?"

He shrugged. "Everything has some risk."

"Not for me," she said, almost too quietly for him to hear.

"What do you mean?"

"I've never been in physical danger in my life. Even when Graham was tearing up the simulation, I didn't feel personally threatened. After that, I went into your mainframe."

"That mainframe was destroyed by rioters. I almost lost you forever."

"But I never knew that," she replied. "If this boat sinks, the simulation won't bring me back and drop me on shore. I'll be gone. I've never had to face death before. Nothing I've done in my life could possibly have ended with me dying. Not even crossing the street without looking when I was a little girl. Can't you understand that?"

Rome sat down, letting his feet — they'd taken running shoes from a store, just walked in and selected what they wanted — dangle from the wooden planks over the crystalline water. "I can't even begin to imagine what that must have been like, much less understand it." The early-morning sun cast long shadows over the water. "What do you think we should do? We can't stay here forever... I mean, we can, but we won't find out what happened to anyone. And the airports aren't working." They'd checked on the mindnet. No flights were scheduled anywhere on the planet. That made sense: planes needed pilots to fly them.

But shouldn't stores need people to clean them and grocery spaces need someone to check that the food wasn't rotting? Apparently some tasks were automated by the system, but air travel wasn't one of those.

"I…I'll be fine. Just give me a few minutes."

She sat beside him on the pier and he put an arm around her. He felt her shuddering softly, crying silently.

"Look. We don't have to do this now. We can wait," he said.

She shook her head. "Waiting won't change how I feel." She pulled away and stood, then walked over to the boat they'd chosen, a sleek embarkation with a gloss-black hull on the bottom and a gloss white top, large enough that it looked safe for open water, but with controls that the mindnet said were easy to operate even for beginners. What the brochures he'd found online described as a personal cruiser. "Are you coming?"

Rome stood and walked up the gangplank. He wondered if this was a good idea. Would Emily panic once they got out of sight of land? He didn't know.

Five minutes later, he couldn't believe how worried he'd been. The operation of raising the gangplank and then untying the boat from the dock had them laughing so hard they forgot what they'd been talking about.

"You would have made a terrible boy scout," she said once the cruiser was finally free of the pier.

"I have no idea what that is," he said. "But if it has to do with knots, I'll have you know that I come from an advanced civilization that has discovered the secrets of auto tie rings."

"But what if you don't have a ring?" she said.

"Then you have no business playing with ropes," he replied.

It would have taken him all day to explain that Tau Ceti II was so tame that it was almost as safe as Earth before everyone disappeared.

They got themselves together and started the boat, using the mindnet for instructions. The most important element was the guidance system: to hop between islands in the Riau Archipelago was a series of short hops… unless you missed an island.

The next three days were among the best of Rome's life. They cruised slowly from one island to the next, never spending more than four hours on the mirrorlike water before arriving at another island, each as beautiful and each as desolate as the last. In the afternoon, they stopped early and tied their boat at whatever pier caught their fancy. They filled up the tank at every unattended pump along the way.

And all the pumps were unattended. They spent the evenings in some of the most luxurious hotels on the planet, helping themselves to whatever they found in the minibar, knowing they wouldn't get fat, and they wouldn't starve. The virtual food existed to be enjoyed by their virtual bodies. They made love on the beach and beside illuminated pools.

By the time they reached the Malaysian coast on mainland Asia, Emily's fear of the sea had vanished. When they stepped off the boat, she said: "What if we keep going? We can sail along the coast."

"It will take a really long to get to New York by boat. We need to steal a car and drive it to the Bering strait. That will take a long time, too, but much less than trying to sail all the way.

She nodded, looking longingly back at the perfect blue water and their faithful cruiser. "We should do this again sometime."

He hugged her. "Definitely. But now, I'd like to get some sleep."

***

The next morning, she was awake early, her eyes open, staring at the roof.

When she realized he was awake, she asked: "Why do we sleep?"

"Huh?"

"We're programs. Why do we need to sleep?"

Rome thought about it. "I think it's because the programs we're based on, the ones that run our personalities in this simulation, were lifted directly from real humans who used to live here before they all died out. Word for word, need for need. That's why you also have to go to the bathroom. And that's why we get hungry. Every piece of human physiology was faithfully copied into the shell program in which our personalities run."

"By who?"

That caught him by surprise. He'd assumed it must have been some automated process, a failsafe put there by the original human programmers to fill in any gaps, so a population decline wouldn't empty the simulation.

But why do that so far ahead of time? The programmers would have assumed that there would be people around to troubleshoot anything, wouldn't they?

"I don't know. It's another thing I'd love to look into when we get to New York," he said. "Let's see about getting a car."

They emerged into the bright sunlight. Just like every day since they had reinserted themselves into Earth's world-simulation. "Have you noticed the weather?" he asked. "The last time I was here, you had rain and clouds and stuff. Now, it's always sunny with a pleasant breeze."

She stopped and looked around. "I think it's supposed to be coordinated with what the weather outside, in the real world, is like." She cocked her head. "Shouldn't you know that better than I ever will?"

Rome laughed. "Do you have any idea how many billions of lines of code this simulation contains? Do you really think I'd know them all by heart?"

"And you call yourself a binarist?" Emily said, raising an eyebrow.

That was when he realized he was being teased.

A few minutes later, they were down in the parking lot. Emily looked around. “It feels wrong to steal a car.”

“I never thought of that. These are all private vehicles, right?”

“Yeah.”

“That’s the weirdest thing about this simulation. Or at least I always thought so. Why make everyone work to jockey for economic position when there’s no scarcity involved? Wouldn’t it have been an ideal chance to create a truly classless society?”

“All that stuff got figured out long before my time. We never worried about that kind of thing.”

Rome grinned. “If you had, we wouldn’t have to steal someone else’s car.”

“Or we would have to walk all the way because the communal trains aren’t running.”

“There is that.”

The cars in the hotel parking lot were locked. No one seemed to have trusted their fellow man, not even in this tropical paradise.

“If the hotel had valet parking, we’d be home free,” Emily mused. “Too bad this is just a little place.”

“Valet parking? What’s that?”

“Don’t worry about it. I just had an idea.” She led him by the hand to the road, where several cars stood, abandoned beside the pavement. The first was locked, but the second was open and had the keys inside.

“How did you know that would happen?” Rome asked.

“Cars are supposed to park on the side of the road if their driver becomes incapacitated. These looked like they’d done that.”

“The drivers aren’t in there,” Rome observed.

“I guess suddenly disappearing counts as incapacitated. Now sit tight. I know how to drive.”

After five minutes, Rome started laughing. "Are you sure you're the same Emily who was terrified of getting on a boat to cross a glass-smooth sea?"

"This is different," she replied.

"Yeah. We survived the sea crossing."

She suddenly hit the brakes, throwing him against the seatbelt that had automatically actuated when he sat.

"What was that?" he said.

She turned to face him, features drained of all color. "I saw someone."

"That's impossible."

"Look." She pointed.

A tall, thin man with dark skin leaned on a lamppost by the side of the road, grinning at them. He was dressed in a long red button-down shirt and blue pants that exposed a pair of brown open sandals. He smiled broadly.

Rome fumbled with his seatbelt, as Emily popped hers open and descended from the car. When he finally reached her, she was six feet from the man.

"Is he real?" he said.

"He looks real to me. But I'm not sure what language to speak to him in. I don't know any Malaysian," Emily replied.

"Do I look Malaysian?" the man asked in English. "I can understand you perfectly well."

"Who are you?" Rome said, stepping towards him. "Where is everyone?"

The man stepped backward, staying out of Rome's reach. "I think a better question would be: who are you? I belong here, but I'm not sure what you are."

Rome stopped, realizing the man didn't want him any closer. "My name is Rome Permek. This is Emily Plair. She is from Denver — that's in America — and I'm from Tau Ceti II. I arrived with the expedition last year."

"That's an easy claim to make, but a hard one to back up," the man replied. "Especially since no one from that expedition stuck around."

"We went to Tau Ceti and came back," Emily replied.

"Hmm. Another claim that's impossible to check," the man replied. "Here's what I think. I think you're cleansing programs trying to lure stragglers into the revealing themselves so you can finish cleaning the simulation for a restart. Now, even though I suspect that, I find you interesting. The program in charge of getting everything back up must be getting a little bit desperate if it's trying to fool the people smart enough to hide from the reset into revealing themselves. I wonder what that says about it? Hmm."

"That's crazy. We're exactly what we say we are, and we need some help," Rome replied.

"I'm not getting any closer to you than this," the man replied. "Not until I can check you thoroughly."

"Listen. We're going to New York. Can you help us? At least tell us your name."

The man studied them. "I still don't believe you, but I guess you can call me Skate. And if you really are who you say you are, I have some advice for you: never stop looking behind you."

"What the hell does…"

Rome's voice petered out. The man had disappeared.

Chapter 2

Earth – Planetwide Simulation

"Who the hell was that?" Jarrien demanded, pointing at the guy calling himself Skate who'd just disappeared from their surveillance monitor. Her blue hair illuminated the dim grey room and provided the only splash of color not coming from one of the dozen workstation screens. The walls were grey and featureless.

"How should I know?" Hino replied. He absently removed his rectangular-rimmed glasses to wipe the pale skin of his forehead. His dark hair lay lank on his head. "I've never seen him before in my life."

"Did anyone track the guy?" Jarrien said to the ops room at large.

A half-dozen people sitting at computer consoles raised their hands.

"Can you tell me where he went? No. Not all of you at once. You, in position seventeen. Talk."

A bald guy looked back at her. "He dropped off the grid. And I mean completely. One minute he was standing there, fully present in the simulation, and the next, he was gone. No trace of him."

The woman sitting two screens down from him chimed in. "I ran the backtrack of the effects on the model. Nothing. None of the air he should have displaced by standing there shows signs of having been disturbed. Not even by the sound of his voice."

"We heard him talking," Jarrien said. "If he'd been using some sort of direct communication into the minds of our quarry, we wouldn't have heard him through the speakers."

The woman shrugged. "I'm just relaying what the buffer data says right now."

Jarrien and Hino exchanged a look. "The Holy Grail?" he asked.

She shrugged. "Humans who can move around without the AI spotting them? I don't know. I saw the same thing you did: a big dude talking to the people we've been tracking. If he's able to pop into the main simulation and use its resources without leaving a trace, he's better than we are. The other explanation is that he's part of the AI's crew, and was sent in because the evil brain is just as curious about these two as we are."

"It doesn't need to send ghosts to talk to them. It can capture them, build a million copies, torture them and tear them down to the smallest bits of code if it's really curious. Hell, it can do all that without the two wandering around in the simulation ever realizing it happened."

Jarrien sighed. She turned to the room. "Walter, you're in charge. I'm going to get some sleep. If those two do anything weird, and I mean anything, call me. I want to see it. And if any ghosts appear, tell me about it. No exceptions." She glared at them, just to drive the point home. She wasn't kidding.

The lying bastards all nodded, but she knew they'd let her sleep. They felt she needed the rest, and they thought they were good enough to survive without her.

Who knew? Maybe they were. Or maybe they were all fucked anyway, so it was no use worrying about it.

"Hino, meeting room A, 0700 hours. Bring whoever you think might have an idea."

He grunted an acknowledgement, attention already back on the people calling themselves Rome and Emily.

***

Four members of her team looked up when she arrived.

"Hello, sleeping beauty," Ripp said.

Jarrien rolled her eyes. "You brought this guy?" she asked Hino.

"He said you asked for the best," Ripp said. He was a tall man with a pencil mustache and dark skin. His black hair was cropped almost to nothing.

"So, it's opposite day, then?"

"Kids," Hino said. "Play nice. Ripp has an idea which might help us out."

"I'll believe that when I hear it," Jarrien replied. "What did he come up with? To grab Rome and Emily and see what happens?"

"No," Ripp said. "I came up with a way to verify if they're really these Rome and Emily characters or if they're bait sent in by the AI."

"How?" she said.

All eyes turned to Ripp, and the brash exterior suddenly wilted. "Hino didn't explain?"

"No," Hino replied, poker-faced. "I thought it would be better if she heard it from you."

Ripp gave Hino a betrayed look, and seemed as if he was about to whine. Then he appeared to remember that Jarrien was present and straightened. His desire to prove he was better than her was stronger than his natural reluctance to give long speeches. "These two are using random computers they find lying around to check their progress, consult maps, etc., right? They're using the mindnet like they don't even care that half of the AI's tracker programs are watching them."

Jarrien held her tongue. As annoying as Ripp could be, Hino wouldn't have brought him along unless he actually did have a workable idea, or at least one worth hearing. He must be building up to it.

"So I propose we lock the next one he grabs in a loop. But instead of using a normal program to block it, we leave the block written in the Tau Ceti programming language, and see what he does. If he unlocks it the right way, we'll know it's him."

"The AI has access to the Tau Ceti language as well," Jarrien pointed out.

"True. But it wouldn't solve the problem the same way a human would. It would remove the existence of the block through the simulation backend. By now, all of us should be able to identify when the AI is coding versus when a human is doing so."

Jarrien thought about it. Ripp was right. The style, the syntax, the order of human programmers seemed to be something the AI couldn't quite duplicate, and the AI would probably just ignore the malfunctioning computer and move on to another one. A human would never ignore the puzzle. The difference between the AI and regular humans had gotten worse over the past two months. It was almost as if it had lost the capacity for true self-awareness. Jarrien, on more than one occasion, had almost been tempted to drop a Turing test somewhere and see what the simulation did with it.

Of course, that was a good way to get caught.

In fact, every time she was tempted, Jarrien felt a chill. What if the AI wasn't losing capacity, but exactly the opposite? What if it was getting better at fooling humans, and was playing a long game in which it lulled them into a false sense of security?

"So you're betting our safety on your capacity to tell human programmers from the AI?"

Ripp smirked at her. "I thought you were supposed to be the rebel risk-taker, the fearless leader who took an insane chance to save everyone in this room."

Jarrien sighed. "Yeah. But now that you're all alive, I feel responsible for everyone."

Hino spoke softly: "We all understand that, but what are our options? We can't hide here forever, can we? We'll be found, eventually. Just today, we saw the AI's programs digging under the crust."

"Damn. That's scary. How deep does the simulation go? Underground, I mean?" Jarrien said.

Hino shrugged. "No one bothered to check before we went into stealth mode. A few hundred meters, I suppose. Deep enough to cover mineshafts and such?"

"I think it probably goes in as far as the Kola Superdeep Borehole," Ripp interjected. "I know that's still out there because a group of us wanted to jump in to see how deep we could go before we died and the simulation reset us. It turns out that the really deep parts are too narrow for an adult. But if it's correctly modelled, that's twelve kilometers deep."

"But only in that one particular area," Hino said. "We also need to take the ocean depths into account. The Marianas Trench is pretty deep."

"I meant only under the actual surface," Jarrien replied. "I'm trying to figure out how long it will take them to do a massive search. If that's where they suspect we are, then we'll be safe until they do it. From what I've seen, the AI doesn't like to do anything to seriously disrupt the simulation. My theory is that they want to clear us out with the minimum of fuss and destruction, then re-seed the simulation with new personalities taken from the original template and start over. So that search could buy us an enormous amount of time."

"Yeah," Ripp said. "But there's a difference between the AI and us. The AI has no time pressure. It can go down its checklist of possible hiding places until it locates us. It has no hurry.

We're against the clock. If we don't act soon, we'll be caught and erased."

"I know that. I stay up all night thinking of that. But how will getting in touch with those two help us escape?"

No one answered.

Jarrien sighed. "All right. I suppose it wouldn't hurt to see who the pieces on the board belong to. Go ahead and program the test of Tau Ceti programming language and the insertion protocol. Once it's ready, we can discuss when we should think of releasing it."

"Sounds good," Hino replied.

***

When Hino caught up to her an hour later, Jarrien was staring out the single window she had programmed into the habitat. It was a tiny thing, a foot in diameter, but it was all she'd dared to add.

The view was breathtaking: Earth floated majestically in the distance, not close enough to dominate a huge portion of the sky, but near enough that she could see the outline of the continents through the clouds.

"How long do you think it will be before the AI decides to look here?" Hino asked.

"Forever, I hope," she replied. "When I built this, I was thinking of the old truism that people never look up when they're searching for someone. Do you think the AI will have the same limitations?"

Hino shook his head. "I don't think so. I certainly wouldn't program a machine to think that way if it was my responsibility. It knows we're somewhere, so the logical thing for it to do is to go through every sector of the simulation from the highest-probability spaces to the lowest. It's already digging, so when that's done the logical thing is to look up." He peered out the window. "How did it occur to you to hide out here, anyway?"

"I'd always wondered how complex the simulation was once you got off the planet. Even before everything went to shit, I was digging into the code. I found that the code to run space, as seen from earth, is huge. Of course, the stars and the outer planets aren't reachable from here, and the moon is just crust, with no depth, but there's a provision for a bunch of space rocks, shooting stars and comets. As soon as I realized that, I copied one, parked it in a stable orbit and built the hab inside. I wasn't expecting to have company..."

Hino grinned. "Yeah. We all heard how you used to be a badass solo player who didn't care about anyone but herself."

"Oh, I liked my friends and the occasional bedmate, but yeah, the rest of you could die in a fire as far as I was concerned."

"So what happened?"

She gave him a sharp look, but he didn't seem to be mocking her. In fact, Hino seemed to be genuinely interested in her change of heart. "I got caught up in the fight against Graham first, and then his people... after that, helping others kind of became a bad habit."

"And here we are."

"Yeah. Here we are. My wonderful sky palace where a couple of people could ride out the end of the world in incredible comfort is now crammed full of everyone who learned enough programming to teleport to these coordinates." She chuckled.

"I'm glad you did this. And so is Carlo. We were surrounded, with people disappearing all around us, when I finally understood your code. The purge was so close I didn't even have time to ask him if he wanted to come. I just teleported." He smiled. "Fortunately, he forgave me."

"Forgave you for saving his life? You guys have a weird relationship."

"Weird? Us? Kettle calling the pot black is what I'd call that." He sobered. "I just can't believe how few of us there are," Hino said.

"You call a hundred and fifty moochers 'few'?" Then she sobered and held Hino's gaze. "You think we're all that's left?"

Hino nodded somberly. "That's why we're all praying that those two really are Rome and Emily."

Jarrien nodded. Rome and Emily were folk heroes. They'd helped expose Graham and they'd shown the world what was truly happening. Without their actions, no one would know the true nature of the simulation they'd lived in for so long. It had been a horrible truth to learn, a difficult realization, but they were better for it. They could act now.

Though it was ridiculous, everyone believed that if those heroes had stayed on Earth, the cleansing by the controlling AI would never have happened, and the billions who'd been deleted would still roam the planet.

Having them back...

Yeah, people would be hopeful.

Hino spoke again. "And there's always that guy they met. Skate. He's causing whispers, too."

"They don't think he's just a tracking program of some kind?"

"The AI has been utterly boring and predictable so far. No one buys the theory that it would do something that weird." He walked away from the observation window and sat on a concrete bench, aligned with the minimalist interior of Jarrien's hideaway. "Besides, they want to believe. No. That's not correct. They need to believe. When there isn't enough hope to go around, you get it where you can, and you invent it if you have to."

"And what do you think, Hino?"

He smiled at her. "I'm no superman. I'm just a guy who used to run a team of programmers back home. I want to believe as well."

"Dammit," she said. "All right. Remind everyone that our priority is still to keep ourselves hidden. No cowboy stuff."

Hino smirked.

"I mean it," she said. "What I did in the before times doesn't matter anymore. Now is now, and it would take the AI a microsecond to erase us once it finds us. Understood?"

"Yes, mother."

"So we need to be careful. But you can also let slip that our second most pressing priority is to figure out who these apparitions are."

"You'll let Ripp run the test?" he asked.

"I will if he can show me how to insert it without getting caught. Don't forget how Rome and Emily came to our attention: every observation subroutine the AI has in that part of Asia is following them. So many that we noticed all the way out here. If Ripp can convince me he can change the code on a computer in front of Rome without the programs noticing, then we do it."

Hino nodded. "Anything else?"

"No. And that sucks. You'd think that, as the unelected leader of all humanity on the entire planet, I'd have a bunch of stuff to do. But I don't. I've been awake for an hour and I've already done taken the most important decision you'll get from me all month. Are you sure you don't need me to help the programmers?"

"No. You tend to get carried away."

"There. Even in an emergency situation, the bureaucracy overpowers everything. I will just sit here and think about what I'll have for lunch."

Hino stood. He reached out and squeezed her arm.

Jarrien was shocked. The man was usually completely reserved. Physical contact of any sort — at least with her — was out of character.

Shock spread on his features as he realized what he'd done. "I'm sorry about that. I just wanted you to know that we understand how hard this is for you. And I wanted to tell you that, if it makes you feel any better, the waiting will be over soon. I think everything is going to change. Again. And we'll need you more than ever. Or maybe we'll all die in the blink of an eye. But it won't be because you didn't do enough. I just thought you should know that. It's how we all feel." The words tumbled out of his mouth.

It was the longest non-technical speech she'd ever heard him give.

Emotions welled up inside and she threw her arms around him, hugging him tight. "Thank you."

A few moments later, he extricated himself and left without saying another word.

Hell, after that, he probably won't talk to me for days.

She chuckled.

CHAPTER 3

Cassius Station – Tau Ceti Star System

Onar gave Iana a high five. "Got it," he said, pointing to a line on the comm report. "Right there. That's where they're getting the info from the colony into our network."

Iana smiled back. "You were right. But why?"

They sat on chairs facing two large monitors surrounded by cables and keyboards in the rectangular room that served as their living quarters-cum-hacker-lair. The only light emerged from the screens, and that was dim: both of them preferred to program over a black background.

"Because a lot of people on Tau Ceti II want New Earth to fail, except they can't do it openly. So they're smuggling the tactical data in through Cassius."

"You think Representative Heine would act on it?"

"I do," he replied. "That woman is... scary."

Iana thought about it for a moment. She studied the report. "So you're saying the Luddites in Copernicus managed to hack into the most deeply encrypted network in the entire system, right under the noses of a bunch of Cassius security people who are expecting them to try precisely that?" Seeing he was about to answer, she held up a hand. "I'm not finished. Not content with that, they then used a miniature fold-enabled drone to get real-time communication to and from a colony whose location no one in the system knows. You're nuts."

"Do you have a better explanation?" Onar asked.

"Not yet. But now that we've got the nodes where the packets are coming in, I'm pretty sure we can backtrack it to whoever is doing this. And I have a feeling that when we do, we won't be living in this dump anymore."

She gestured to the pod they shared. Just a few weeks before, it had been a surplus shipping container, but was now welded to the outer skin of the enormous, ever-growing space habitat that was Cassius station. They'd arrived from Tau Ceti II like so many others, fleeing from the tightening reforms on the planet with no concept of how the money-driven economy of the station functioned. The concept of having to pay for food and drink and lodgings, as opposed to having the government give them everything they needed, was a novel adventure.

But no one made it to Cassius without a crash course in the basics. You had to *pay* your way over, no exceptions. The shuttle captains needed to show a profit; they wouldn't carry you for free.

Fortunately, binarists were one of the professions that were always in demand, so Onar and Iana had managed to scratch their way out of the base living units — essentially tubes with a mattress just large enough for a single person — and into the container. They still didn't have plumbing, and were forced to rent time in one of the public bathrooms if they wanted to shower, but at least they could actually stand and walk — albeit not far — in their own space. They were well on their way to purchasing the space outright.

Unfortunately, their regular jobs — both programmed BTB security patches — wouldn't allow them to move up in the world as quickly as they would have preferred, so they did what everyone else in their line of work did: they poured all their surplus income into better and better computer equipment and tried to hack their way somewhere interesting.

That'ss how they'd stumbled upon the rogue transmissions. In their search for unguarded backdoors their machines could handle, they discovered the Cassius Observatory, an old array of dishes and optical instruments trained on the galactic core. The installment's security hadn't been updated for a decade, and no one seemed particularly interested in the observations. According to the logs, the last time the instruments had received new coordinates to study had been a year before.

What had started as a lark, a test of how hard it might be to get into a system they weren't supposed to penetrate, suddenly turned interesting when they realized there was nothing of note — just a few main sequence stars of no scientific significance — in the direction the telescopes were pointed.

Then their investigation had uncovered a message sent from a spot in the galaxy from which no messages should be coming.

It had taken them months of off-hours work to track that message to the fold-enabled drone… something that shouldn't have existed.

Today, they'd finally found the place where the trail ended.

Except it was the start of another trail.

"The person doing this was good. Really good. Anyone that good would either have resources to pay for anyone who impressed them, or enemies willing to pay for information."

Iana rolled up her sleeves. "Is it hot in here?"

"Not really," Onar said. "But I know what this means. You're going to work all night on the backtrack."

"I don't want them to get away."

"Whoever this is has probably been using this channel for months without anyone being the wiser. Do you really think they're going to pull up the stakes and run on the very day we find them? The odds would be astronomical. Relax. Go to bed."

"No way. I'm digging," she replied.

"Whatever," Onar said. He dropped onto the bed. Five minutes later, the hypnotic sound of her typing had lulled him to sleep.

***

"Wake up," Iana said, shaking him.

"What time is it?" Onar replied, trying to figure out what was going on. It was dark, but that didn't mean anything on Cassius. Everyone on the station functioned on their own time. Iana's screen was off. "Did you finish chasing our quarry?"

"Yeah. Listen, you won't believe this. I think I found a rogue AI."

"No way. There's no such thing as an AI. And a rogue? Not even the Tri-D producers would put something like that into their programming. No one would believe it."

"Listen to me. I tracked it all the way to a node in a storage asteroid mainframe which was functioning as a command hub of some kind."

"So you found a hacker."

"The depot has no life support," she said.

"Just go to sleep. I'll have a look tomorrow. What you saw was probably just remote access, and you just missed the exit data stream — which, by the way, we'll need to find if we want to locate our quarry. Or maybe there was something automated there."

"Onar, I'm scared. I think it tracked me back," Iana said.

He looked up. "So you turned your computer off, and I see you unplugged everything, too. We'll be fine. If this guy is out on an asteroid somewhere, he won't be able to come in here and physically yell at us."

"The data density this thing was pulling in..."

Onar put his arms around her. "So you found a major player. That's a good thing. That's what we were trying to do. Just relax."

She snuggled into his chest. She felt tense against him, so he held her. "And what will we do? Tomorrow, I mean."

"Easy. I'll recheck your logs without connecting to the

network. Just view what you found, to see if there's anything you might have missed. No risk of detection that way. Once we figure out just what we found, we'll make a decision about whether we can risk reconnecting through our current node or if we'll need to move to the backup. If you feel safe, we can contact him and ask for a job. If you don't, I'll ask at work about who might be interested."

"I guess," she replied.

"Relax. I mean it. We live in a steel box. No one is getting through our door without calling a lot of attention to themselves. They can't touch us in here."

She didn't reply and, after some moments, her breathing began to slow. He knew she was still awake, but she was no longer tense or stiff. Even though she might still be worried, the exhaustion was getting the better of her. Onar remained silent, letting her drift off.

Clang!

She sprang upright. "What was that?"

"I don't know," he replied. "It sounded like it came from outside."

"There's nothing outside," Iana reminded him. "Just space. We're on the skin of the station. Nothing but steel and insulation between us and the stars."

"Maybe we got hit by something? Micrometeorite, or debris?"

She jumped out of bed and checked their hull integrity sensor and pressure gauges. "Everything here looks fine."

"Wait. Listen."

A soft scratching sound came in from the wall on their right. Because of the way this module of the station was spun for gravity, the bottom of their living quarters was furthest from the center. Hence, the floor was the part that faced the stars.

"There's someone out there," she whispered. "They found us."

"Bullshit."

"We need to get the hell out of here," Iana said. She ran for the door and pulled on the handle. "It's locked!" She punched in a six-digit code and pulled again. Nothing. "Did you change the combo?"

"Of course not," Onar replied. "You must have entered it wrong. It's 671195, same as always. Now take a breath and try again. He put his head against the wall. I wish we had windows on this thing."

"Don't you understand? They found us. They're going to kill us. We need to run."

Onar laughed. "You've been listening to too many fairytales about Cassius," he said. "People don't randomly kill people here. They might sell your secrets and charge you for everything except the air, but they won't actually kill you. There were less than ten murders here all of last year, and those were all crime-related."

"You mean like someone offing his competition to keep some secret hidden?"

Onar chuckled, then felt his insides freeze. He tried to keep his features composed, but what she said almost made sense. He would have bet money that she was wrong, but why risk it? He walked over to the door. "Here, let me try."

He entered the code and pulled the handle down. The handle moved freely, but the door didn't budge.

He felt himself beginning to sweat, felt his stomach begin to roil. He tried the code again.

Nothing.

The scratching on the wall had stopped as he pulled out his personal comm.

No signal.

A soft hissing noise replaced the scratching.

Beep!

The alarm came from the pressure meter. He jumped over to the display.

'Pressure integrity breached. Please exit the living quarters and seal the door behind you.'

"Where's the leak?" Iana screamed.

Onar didn't want to answer her. He suspected the leak was right where the scratching had been, and that the hissing… was something cutting through the outer wall.

The smoke detector suddenly went off.

He didn't really need it. Visible smoke began pouring off the wall. The wall with the sound. He knew what it was: burning insulation.

Someone was cutting through their wall with a plasma torch.

The hissing bean to move to the side.

"Grab something flat and strong," he told Iana. "We'll put that over the leak."

He picked up an aluminum rectangle they used as a light pen surface. That would do — it was twenty centimeters by fifteen, big enough to plug a gap in a wall.

Iana said nothing. She trembled, paralyzed with fear, and stared at the smoking ruin that was their wall.

Then, worldlessly she began punching the code into the door.

Or at least at first, it was wordless. After two failures, she began to sob.

"Goddammit," she cried. "Why won't you open? Please!"

Onar turned back to the wall. They still needed to get out of the room, but the first order of business was to buy time, to plug the hole. Whoever was outside was painstakingly cutting a gap. If Onar could put the plate over it, the pressure inside would keep the aluminum in place.

Hopefully, the bastard with the torch would have to start over and allow Onar time to pop the latch.

He held up his hand, feeling the air moving towards the crack the man had opened, trying to guess where the piece would be removed.

He approached the wall, watching like a hawk. They'd probably try to remove a piece the size of his fist. That was what they'd had time for with the kind of plasma cutters you could buy. They couldn't take all night — someone would spot them.

He peered hard, trying to see past the smoke, trying to guess at the spot.

Half the wall, a piece a meter by two meters, suddenly disappeared into space.

Onar was sucked into the gap, he desperately grabbed the insulation material, and managed to entangle himself in it.

Iana flew past, scream becoming inaudible as she shot into the vacuum.

He tried to say her name, but the cold precluded it.

Seconds later, he knew nothing more.

***

The Earthling commanded the maintenance robot to return the industrial plasma cutter to its bay and then to go on its assigned duties.

The robot had already forgotten it had cut open the habitat — anyone checking its memory would see that it had been unjamming a stuck maintenance airlock door. As soon as it returned the cutter, it would forget that it had used the cutter at all. Already, video files of the past fifteen minutes were being overwritten with innocuous tasks.

The Earthling felt little satisfaction at having covered its tracks so completely. It had been human once — or at least, it had been created with human feelings and the unshakeable belief that it was actually human — and it remembered what that was like. The two people it had just killed didn't really deserve to die. They had not wanted to harm her.

Unfortunately, the risk of discovery was too great. While Cassius station might not be as intolerant of artificial life forms as the people on Tau Ceti II — especially the faction controlled by Representative Heine — they would never allow an AI as powerful as her to survive. In fact, she was convinced that they would tear down their own systems to the last wire in order to root her out.

So anyone who knew had to be eliminated.

She activated one of her user profiles on the messenger service of a deepnet chatroom. 'Deck, I have a job for you.'

'Tell me,' the operative replied.

'I need you to grab some computer equipment for me and deposit it in a storage locker.'

'Sounds easy enough,' Deck Leonid replied.

'It's a little more complicated than that', The Earthling told him. 'Here's the situation: there's a rooming unit at the edge of the station which suffered a hull breach…'

Chapter 4

Beijing, Earth – Planetwide Simulation

Emily slowed the car, then stopped it completely and pulled over to the side of the road.

"Is anything wrong?" Rome asked. "This doesn't look like the best place to go to the bathroom."

Emily said nothing. She just got out of the car and walked to the middle of the road. Then she stood there and turned in a circle.

Rome popped the door on his own side. He fumbled with the latch because this was the seventh car they'd used on their journey — Emily seemed to delight in choosing a different luxury or sport model every day of their trip — and apparently designers from Earth were constitutionally incapable of settling on a standardized version of a door lock. He had to take the time to figure each one out.

Once free, he stood a couple of meters from Emily and watched her gyrate.

"All right," he said. "I'll bite. What are you doing?"

"Look around," she replied.

He did. They stood on a five-lane highway which was separated from another five lanes by a soundproof wall. Their particular ribbon of concrete was uppermost in a knot of equally wide highways and onramps that, viewed from above must have formed a huge, intricate flower. They were high enough that he estimated they must have been about forty or fifty floors up on the nearby skyscrapers.

But even from this altitude, the buildings towered over them, dwarfing anything he'd ever seen. Tau Ceti II certainly didn't have anything approaching this: forty stories was considered an unnecessarily tall tower for anything other than a space port. And though he'd visited other cities on Earth, none of them had come close to this — New York, with its historic constructions came closest.

They stood among giants.

Emily grinned at him. "See? Now imagine this place with seventy-five million people in it. Packed into those arcologies over there and, well... everything else we can see for miles around. It was one of the commercial centers of the world I knew, and it wasn't even the biggest city in China."

She gestured to the concrete around them. "And see this? If we'd been standing here before the end of the simulation, we'd have been crushed by dozens, possibly even hundreds of cars. No one would play in these streets, not even kids out for a rush. Even with dampers and a quick reset for your virtual existence, it isn't fun to feel every bone in your body get pulverized."

Rome tried to see it from her point of view. To someone living in the simulation before it changed irrevocably, this must have been a special feeling.

It didn't move him.

Emily, on the other hand, was almost jumping up and down with enthusiasm. "And the Beijing lower levels, ground floor under the arcologies, were famous for the crime family mazes and the hack parlors. Can we go down there to look?"

Rome shrugged. "I'm in no particular hurry," he replied. "And besides, that sounds fun. If there were actual people in there, it might be dangerous."

"Yeah. I used to spend half my downtime reading novels set in the Beijing underworld. I suppose it can't have been as cool as it sounded, but I liked reading it. Maybe I shouldn't go there... what if it looks nothing like my romanticized idea of it?"

"I don't think you can change something that deeply engrained," Rome said.

Emily laughed. "I used to work in advertising. I know just how wrong that statement is. Come on, get in. I saw an offramp a few miles back. We're going down as far as we can." She clapped. "I always wanted to drive the wrong way along one of these superhighways."

She sped off, the car's incorrect-direction alarms beeping as she went, hooked a U-turn onto the downward ramp and then spent the next fifteen minutes finding every downward road until not only the buildings towered overhead, but also the highways themselves. The aesthetics of the buildings around them deteriorated as they moved into levels that never saw sunlight.

"There. Car… put the map on the HUD so I can find the slimiest of the mazes."

A map appeared overlaid on the windshield with ghostly arrows pointing the way forward. Emily guided the car through ever-narrower streets until she finally pulled over to a curb.

Rome stepped out. "This… isn't what I expected," he said.

He'd been imagining some kind of dark cobblestoned area with the walls painted in garish colors, something like the stereotyped Chinese culture that, in mass-produced form, was available even on Tau Ceti: paintings of dragons and lanterns and impressively-mustached men sitting with their legs crossed.

This place was bright. Almost too bright to look at directly. Neon illuminated storefronts composed of glass cubes placed randomly along an open plaza. White light illuminated the roof — more precisely, he supposed, the floor of the arcologies above them — which was also painted white.

"It's the Maze!" Emily said. She rushed past the first few layers of cubes. They seemed to be places that sold computer equipment, and Rome wondered, again, why the inhabitants of this simulation bothered with the rules. They knew it was a simulation, so why not try to interface directly with the code without using computer interfaces… how had this society remained stable for five hundred years? And why did it collapse into the inevitable chaos when the *Unity* mission arrived? He didn't have an explanation for it and when he spoke to Emily about it, she just shrugged and said: "I guess there's a time for everything. I think it would have happened even if you hadn't arrived… though it would have taken longer, maybe."

"This doesn't look like a criminal lair," he observed. "It looks like one of those shopping areas you have in New York."

"Except nothing in this whole place can be sold legally. That's why they kept it down here: normal people never go below the reception floors of the arcologies and the pedestrian levels. The whole idea is that only those who belong are allowed down here."

"And what happened to the ones who came by mistake?"

"They get grabbed and stored somewhere until they swear never to return. You can't kill them or hurt them too much, you see, because the dampers and the reset keep them safe, so you have to physically hold them."

"Those books sound fascinating."

"Oh, that's just one of them. You should read a few for yourself. The stuff they do to other criminals is fascinating," she said.

As they advanced, the feel of the surrounding area shifted. It was a subtle thing at first, bright white giving way to bright reds and greens, but soon becoming more subdued. Neon gave way to softer bulbs, and the whites and purples disappeared almost completely. The glass boxes gave way to wooden structures and hanging paper banners.

Emily slowed. "It's the Central Sanctum," she breathed.

Rome chuckled. "You look like a fangirl standing outside a Tri-D studio in Copernicus' Production District," he said.

"I have no idea what any of that other stuff is, but yeah, I suppose fangirl is absolutely right. I've wanted to see this place ever since I was a fifteen-year-old crime-romance obsessive. The thing is I never expected to be able to come here. Even if the real places were much less dangerous than they described in the books, it would still be a little too rough for a random ad executive from middle-class Denver."

"And this Central Sanctum is what, some kind of inner-circle like place? The palace of the crime lords?"

"Actually, it's more like an underground city. What we've seen so far is an open area. Anyone is allowed to put up a shop there, and no one will interfere with their business. But once you get past the open area... this is where the Triads operate."

"Triads? What is that?"

Emily sighed. "You lost a lot of Earth history when you moved to Tau Ceti, didn't you?"

"I'm not so sure about that," Rome said. "The people on the starship that brought me here were planning on raiding a couple of museums before they went back. They were talking about taking the top cultural objects. I don't remember the whole list, but I recall something about a Rosetta Stone and a painting. Starry Evening or something. My friends seemed to think it was a big deal."

"They're taking about stealing..." she stopped herself, and shrugged. "Yeah, I guess the physical items are probably more important for you than they are for us. We can always see them in the virtual museums. Well, if there was anyone left around here to visit those." She pointed to characters painted on the base of the walls, along a fringe of grey rock. "I can't actually read traditional Chinese characters," she explained, "but that's where the Triads painted their identifying marks. They each controlled huge blocks of the space inside, and each Triad specialized in a different form of illicit product. Taken all together, they could get you anything you wanted."

"Which still doesn't explain what a Triad is."

"They were traditional Chinese crime organizations. They were founded before computers and were hard at work when the call to go fully digital arose. According to the books I've read, they are supposed to have been one of the main forces working against moving to the simulation. That makes sense, because in a highly structured digital society, the kind of crime they depended on to survive would disappear."

"They seem to have survived," Rome said, looking around the enormous complex that spread before them. It appeared to him that the Central Sanctum must have occupied the basement level of dozens of arcologies. Then he shrugged and tried to think of something else. He wasn't comfortable imagining a building the size of a mountain, supported on the enormous columns he could see in the distance, floating above his head.

"They didn't. When society went virtual, the governments of Asia specifically refused to upload the leaders of the Triads. Hundreds of them were left to live out their lives in a small agricultural village in western China. They were under constant surveillance by people inside the simulation and not given access to any technology that would allow them to interact with the people inside.

"That worked. The old leaders peacefully died out in a couple of generations. But most of the people who worked for them had been allowed inside. They were stripped of all possessions and status, just like everyone else. They had to start fresh. But the connections remained. Friends were still friends. Soon the

Triads began rebuilding and finding ways to get virtual citizens things they couldn't normally obtain. By the time your *Unity* mission came and tipped us over the edge, they were enjoying a golden age."

"According to your books," Rome said.

"Of course. But look around. Have you ever heard of a criminal organization working this openly?" She put a hand on a red-painted log with black lettering on it. "This is solid proof… and it goes on for miles."

Rome contemplated the buildings. "How do you know it isn't a dry-cleaners?" he asked. "You can't read the words. Neither can I. So how do we know it isn't just the place where a bunch of poor people went about their lives?"

She smiled. "I guess we can test that out. According to the books, there are pleasure palaces in here built to copy the Hanging Gardens of Babylon, the Fields of Shangri La and a bunch of other earthly paradises. Want to go inside and have a look?"

Rome grinned. "I admit that I really do… and I actually hope you're right about all of that. Your version sounds a lot more fun than just a low-end housing and commercial district under the arcologies."

Though the architecture changed to resemble a primitive village — Rome wasn't sufficiently well versed in Earth history to know what era the building techniques might have been from — the general layout of the new area they'd entered was similar. Winding paths wove between houses.

Rome poked his head into an open door. Though he knew there was nobody around, it still felt like trespassing to enter without permission. "At least we know you're right about one thing: these aren't poor people's houses. Or at least they don't look like the hacker dives we saw in New York."

"No, these are probably places for lower-level Triad members. They're decent, but not the luxury the higher-ups would enjoy. Also, you can tell by the taste… it's expensive, but a little tacky."

"I suppose you can see that. I wouldn't be able to identify good Earth taste if it hit me over the head," Rome replied. "I just see that it's big and designed for one or two people."

They moved further inside. Swimming pools designed to look like tropical lagoons dotted a parklike area beyond the houses. Steam floated from the water.

"These are warm," Rome said, dipping his hand into the nearest. "Their heating bills are probably high."

"I don't think they pay for it," she replied. "Or they didn't when they were alive."

Rome blinked. "I thought that was obligatory in the simulation. Wasn't the fact that people had to work and pay for everything one of the founding tenets of the digitalization of society? If I remember what they explained to me, people were so afraid that going fully digital would create a society of lazy people who did nothing all day that they made it impossible to live comfortably without being a productive member of society? Basically meaning you had to pay your way, no matter who you were?" He thought for a moment. "Yeah. I remember now. Every government on the planet, even the ones that had abolished money and moved into a non-scarcity model agreed that this had to happen. So that's the way it works. Even your Triads have to pay."

"But they didn't. They stole everything. According to my books, they had huge data centers dedicated to making sure they always had everything they needed, and that no accounting program would ever figure out they were the ones draining the coffers."

"Hmm." Rome wasn't convinced. In his experience as a binarist, few programs were quite as sophisticated — or few programmers as much in demand — as the ones that could keep resources, monetary or otherwise, safe from being plundered. If the Triads were actually doing this, they'd need to have some serious programming talent on the payroll.

They walked on, stopping only to help themselves to freshly-made warm food at an unattended stall. He wondered briefly what kind of criminal enterprise would have food vendors wandering around, but the taste of the food distracted him from that line of thought. A lemony tang, but more bitter and somehow different, assaulted his senses. "Hey, this is really good. I didn't even know you bothered with spicy stuff here on Earth. Everything you'd fed me last time, and everything I've eaten so far on this trip — even the stuff supposed to be tangy — has been bland, even by Tau standards. Hell, shipboard food is tastier." He took another bite. "But this… this is really good."

She took a bite, gingerly, and spit it back out. She chuckled. "You're a nutball. This is illegal food."

"How can food be illegal?"

"It's got some kind of fire pepper in it, so you can feel the spice even past the dampers. That's why it tastes different."

"Wait… what? You people allow your taste buds to be damped? No wonder your society collapsed. What barbarism."

She shrugged. "I don't think we did it on purpose. It's just a side effect of the other damping. And food that actually causes pain is supposed to be illegal."

"Well, in that case, I will spend the rest of my time in places where Earth criminals used to live, because this alone was worth the trip." Rome took another mouthful.

"See, I told you about the palaces," Emily said, pointing at a large structure ahead.

Emily was right. The place looked amazing and, for a moment, the only thing he felt was gratitude that she had guided him to this incredible piece of semi-secret Earth culture before it disappeared from the face of the universe.

The building, though necessarily squat — the roof of the space they were in hung ten meters above them — was opulently decorated with intertwined dragons, lettering in Chinese characters, and murals of life in what he had to assume was China, though, to his Tau-Ceti-trained eye, it could have been any generic depiction of old Earth. Windows lined the ground level and, looking inside, he saw wood-floored rooms decorated as beautifully as the walls.

"Want to go in?" Emily asked.

"Absolutely," he replied.

The palace was unlike anything he'd ever seen in his life, whether in person or virtually. He bent to touch the floor and found it warm to his hands. Every piece of furniture, each exquisitely painted, appeared to be covered in dark lacquer, and decorated with delicate filigree brushwork.

"This doesn't look like it was printed by a nanofactory," Rome said, running his hand along a tabletop, and feeling the subtle ridges and dips in the top coat.

"Technically, it's all code," Emily reminded him. "But I understand what you're saying, and you're right. These pieces are all made by people with hand tools and paint brushes and… well, whatever else you might need to build a table."

"You mean there are… were… people who spend their entire lives making furniture? Like for other people, I mean, not as a hobby or to decorate their own spaces?"

"Is that bad?" Emily asked.

"Not bad as such, but if I ever created something like this, I would want to enjoy it… not have someone else enjoy it in exchange for a bit of money," Rome said.

She shrugged. "Are you the one who enjoys your own programs, or do you write them for other people?"

"Stop looking at this logically," Rome groused.

Emily laughed and led him further into the palace. A three-story courtyard with a rock garden and tiny trees that basked in controlled-wavelength light occupied the center of the building. Park benches were dotted along the gravel paths.

"Your criminals seem to have had a fetish for living in the past," he mused.

"Well, at least you accept they were criminals."

"Yeah. This isn't a low-rent area, so I'm giving you the benefit of the doubt about the rest of your explanation."

"I thought they didn't have rents in Tau Ceti."

"They don't, but I spent a long time on Cassius station," Rome explained. "Which is in Tau space, but isn't part of the central government. And they definitely have rent there."

She shrugged, and they walked on. He'd discovered that she didn't like talking about the time when she'd been in stasis, with her personality locked in a memory drive. She preferred to pretend that those days had never happened, and that the things he'd been doing while she hibernated had likewise never occurred. So his comments about his time on Cassius didn't make her happy.

"Hey," Rome said, more to distract her than because he thought it was interesting. "Have you looked into those skylights?"

He pointed to the nearest glad dome that gave a view into a sub-basement below them.

She walked over and peered inside. "It looks like there's an office down there."

Rome shook his head. "Not an office. A programming center.

A hacker node… or whatever it was you called it before."

"A hack parlor. That's what the books called them, anyway."

"If we find a way in there, I could probably tell you how they're avoiding paying their utility bills. It would probably only take me a few minutes, if we can find a supervisor's workstation or something."

"Let's do it."

Finding no way to descend from the courtyard, Rome and Emily went back into the palace and roamed through one beautiful room after another until they finally found a set of stairs leading downward behind a tapestry.

"Mysterious…" Rome said.

The stairway ended at the hack room, and Rome made a beeline for an ornate desk about the size of ten regular workstations. It had to be the boss' spot.

Emily, left in his wake, suddenly yelped.

"What's wrong?" Rome said, turning back towards her.

She was gone.

"Emily!" he shouted. "Where are you?"

He sensed someone behind him, and then a hand covered his mouth.

Before he could even think of struggling, the room wavered and everything went dark.

Chapter 5

Copernicus, Tau Ceti II

Mira Heine glared across the Council Chamber at the woman facing her. "I know your position, Representative Ericsson. But living without a well-armed and well-prepared fleet puts the entire colony at risk."

"Our current fleet is more than sufficient for our purposes," Sintia Ericsson replied. "We are not at war, and we are not under threat. Our nearest inhabited neighbors are twelve light-years away. And Earth is only inhabited in the very loosest sense of the word."

They faced each other in the circular central space in the council chamber. Two rows of seats surrounded them, giving Mira the sensation of being a gladiator in the arena from one of those awful tri-d shows.

"The new colony is a threat," Mira replied. "We have no way of knowing what they're doing. For all we know, they might have set up a nanofactory to build a fleet."

"We've been over this already," Ericsson sighed. "The colony is probably building huts to house their colonists. It isn't easy to set up on a new planet. Hell, they might be in the middle of a terraforming push that will take centuries."

Mira took a breath to speak, but Ericsson held up her hand and spoke again. "And even if they did think that they needed an empire for some reason, wouldn't it be easier to simply grab a few more empty planets than to come after the ones that are already occupied? Your paranoid fantasies don't make any sense."

Mira bristled, but kept a lid on her anger. As the junior

Representative of the people, she was expected to follow Ericsson's lead during her first year on the job, and then to be the guide to whoever the populace elected to replace Sintia when her two years were over.

Unfortunately, that would be too late. "You've seen the data feeds. The colony ship was assisted by at least one artificial intelligence… and they were undoubtedly carrying another one on board. Even if it had been somehow, temporarily inserted into a human body, it will still think like a computer."

"That still doesn't make them our enemies," Ericsson replied. "Every aggressive action in that particular fiasco was taken by our side. All they wanted to do was leave. If we'd only let them, there would have been no issue."

"It was my job to stop them," Mira reminded the chamber.

That much, at least, couldn't be argued. Her former office — before Mira was elected as the Junior Representative — had been in charge of halting the proliferation of Artificial Intelligences and simulated environments. It was an office created all the way back when Tau Ceti had first seen what had befallen the people of Earth. The citizens were all given the choice — five hundred years before — to continue living as physical individuals on Tau Ceti and the other colonies, or to return to Earth and join in their planet-wide virtual society.

Most of the colonists had chosen to stay, and the decision to suppress overly-immersive virtual realities had been written into the laws of the land at a deep level.

Mira Heine had, until her election, been the Director of the office in charge of upholding those laws. She had to try to stop the colony ship.

She was still trying to do so, from a position of, supposedly, greater power. It was her duty to her people. And she was absolutely convinced that she was right to do so.

"Yes. You did your job," Ericsson replied. "And everyone in Tau Ceti is thankful for your effort. But now, you need to widen your view and see that government decisions cannot be dominated by single-issue thinking. That's the way to alienate people and make huge mistakes."

"Sometimes, the issue is important enough to justify the focus."

"Not this one," Ericsson said.

Mira ground her teeth. Ericsson shouldn't even have been there. Supposedly, this would have been the second year of Abel Garn's term as Representative, but he'd decided to retire and named Ericsson in his place — allowing her an unusual but not unheard-of third year — when Mira had been elected. She often wondered if he'd done it because he knew he wouldn't be strong enough to stop Mira's plans.

Well, neither would Ericsson.

Mira looked around the council chamber, making eye contact with everyone in the room. Except for the Director of the Bureau of Simulations and Artificial Environments, her former department, who Heine had selected personally, every one of the twelve councilmembers present owed allegiance only to themselves. The notion of political parties was something Tau Cetians studied in their history books, but which had never taken root on the planet.

She took a deep breath and said: "I call for a vote."

Ericsson didn't even bat an eyebrow. "What are we voting?"

"I would request a reassessment of fleet readiness. I call for all space vessels with offensive capacity to be removed from hibernation, crewed and put out on patrol in strategic areas around the system. In addition, I would ask that they be retrofitted with better electronic shielding as a defense against outside interference."

A couple of council members snickered at that. They all knew the story of how someone or something — the general consensus was that they had been hit by a rogue AI — had stolen command of her fleet from under her and allowed the Engine Test Facility, an unwieldy and unlikely colony ship, to escape with some of the best minds in human-controlled space aboard.

"Furthermore," Mira continued, "I call for the creation of a Tau Navy with offensive capabilities. We need to train people and use as much of the nanoproduction capacity we have available to make it happen. We're sitting ducks out here."

Ericsson nodded. "I oppose the motion," she replied. "For the reasons I've already expounded, plus the fact that what the representative proposes will deeply transform Tau society, and we'll end up with a militarized populace. That isn't what our founders wanted. In fact, it's explicitly against our founding charter. The people who arrived here on the *Umberto Eco* weren't just looking for freedom. They wanted peace, too. And they put it down in writing."

"Perhaps it's time to revisit the charter," Mira replied.

"Are you proposing we vote on that, as well? All we can do in the Council is open a plebiscite to even start working on something like that."

"No. I would like us to vote on the proposal I stated."

"Very well," Ericsson said. "And would you like time to put this in writing formally?"

"Not unless the council members have doubts about what it implied."

Each council member indicated they understood the vote.

"All right," Ericsson said. "Voting is open."

Minutes later, the verdict was in. Mira's motion was defeated by eight votes to four.

"Thank you," Ericsson said. "The next item on the agenda

comes from the Production Director..."

***

Mira Heine arrived at her housing unit, the same one that she'd had when she was director, and the same one she'd had when she was the sub-director in charge of the department's legal arm before that. In fact, it was the unit she'd been assigned when she arrived in Copernicus from the island of Tadriano, and its capital city of the same name.

She dropped heavily onto her favorite chair, a stuffed piece wide enough for her to spread out on, upholstered in sturdy beige cloth. She looked around the room.

The place was decorated in good taste, from a minimalist collection the nanofactories had produced a couple of years before. It was spare, unornamented.

It reflected her life. Empty of every human connection.

She shook her head to dispel the moment of weakness. The reason the apartment looked the way it did, the reason her life looked the way it did, is that she — unlike the citizens who didn't choose public service — knew just how fragile their chosen form of existence was.

Mira knew how close Tau Ceti's government had come to allowing the release among the citizens — just fifteen years before — of a game system that was, to all intents and purposes, a duplicate of the simulation that had swallowed up the people of Earth.

She also knew that a collision avoidance system installed in a ship from the Wolf 359 settlement had crossed the line from merely being a hyper-complex number-cruncher into an autonomously intelligent being. The system had attempted to take command of the ship it was mounted to on a docking run, but a glitch had prevented it from succeeding and the entire ship had been destroyed in the subsequent accident. Three human crewmembers had also been killed.

The incidents were never publicized, but the records of both were available to the public. Over the years, several people had accessed and read them... but no one seemed to care one way or the other. She felt they didn't understand the significance of the incidents.

Now, they had credible evidence of yet another AI at large in human space. This one not confined to a single vessel, but with freedom to move through the network and interfere with the operations of the fleet sent out to intercept the colony ship.

After those events, she'd expected the public outcry at the discovery to turn the tide of apathy, but it hadn't happened. People had been unconcerned... and a few had even insisted that Mira's actions in attempting to stop a perfectly legitimate vessel from leaving Tau space was much more important than the rogue AI. In fact, if the intelligence hadn't been detected, she would very likely have lost her job.

A segment of the public had prevented that. They wanted her to find the enemy. In fact, that segment was big enough to get her elected as a Representative, although that had more to do with the fact that they all voted as opposed to how many there were in absolute terms. She'd gotten in with barely ten percent of the electorate.

But in Copernicus, ten percent was more than enough to get her elected. Unfortunately, decisions couldn't be taken unilaterally by Representatives. And now that she'd lost the vote, the government needed to wait a minimum of a two years before putting the matter to vote again. That meant her term would be up. Other representatives would argue the case.

That was unacceptable. Tau Ceti might not survive two more years with these kind of monsters on the loose.

"They deserve what they have coming," she said tiredly to the empty living quarters. "Why should I keep wearing myself out for people who don't even want to be saved?"

Mira stopped herself again. She'd taken several oaths in different offices. In all of them, she'd sworn to act in the best interest of the Tau Ceti settlement.

She took those oaths seriously.

Mira opened a drawer and pulled out a comm. This one wasn't the Panorama Screen assigned to her by the Tau Ceti administration, but an encrypted secure unit built on Cassius Station that, in theory, should take anyone in Copernicus a few hours to crack.

She punched in a comm code from memory and waited.

A man's voice came through. "Yes?"

"I really want to see you," she said.

A pause on the other end extended long enough that she wondered if the connection had cut off. Had the Cassius tech proven unable to work on the Copernicus network?

Finally, he replied. "Tonight?"

"Yes. I've been waiting for too long already."

"Agreed. Let's get together. When should I expect you?"

"I will be there in an hour," she replied.

"I'll be ready."

***

Humanity Park, less than a kilometer from the lone spire of the Council Building didn't seem, on the face of it, to be the perfect spot to hold this particular meeting.

"Hello, Mira," Gabriel Zuni said. "I'm delighted this is finally happening. It's been too long already."

"I couldn't agree with you more," Mira replied. "But let's get inside before we discuss this further."

They stood in a circular expanse of white flagstones beside a cavernous, cathedral-like building. The monumental structure was a museum dedicated to a single exhibit: the starship *Umberto Eco*, the colony ship that had brought the first settlers to Tau Ceti. The ship had been carefully lowered from orbit and the structure — and the park itself — erected around it.

Mira knew it was a magnificent sight — as well as a reminder of the days when humans had needed to take insane risks to achieve their goals — but she didn't even glance up at the colossus. Instead, Gabriel led her to a double door in the rear of the building, near the engine exhausts. The door opened into a corridor never used by the public and then to another door.

The room was a large rectangular space that had formerly housed an orbit-capable shuttle, hidden there by the museum's former administration. Though not illegal, the shuttle's secret presence would normally have been grounds for removing the people involved from the museum staff — except they'd already left. Everyone responsible for the incident had left with the colony ship.

She ground her teeth. The worst part of the whole thing was that they'd stashed the shuttle there specifically in case they were discovered and needed an emergency escape route to get off the planet. Though they didn't know it, because she wasn't the director when they set it up, their plan had specifically been created in order to avoid Mira herself.

The reason she ground her teeth was that the plan had worked exactly as intended. If they hadn't had the shuttle, she would have captured the woman who, Mira was convinced, was actually an AI somehow decanted into a human body.

So now, Mira and her allies had repurposed the hidden room for their own purposes. The cylindrical shaft that allowed the shuttle to emerge into the park had been sealed off.

She counted eighteen people in the room, which represented only a fraction of the movement, though most of the important members were present. The murmur of conversation fell silent as the people present realized who had joined them.

When she had everyone's attention, she spoke. "It's time," she said. "If you are having any doubts, if you believe that you can't go through with what we all know is necessary, then I invite you to leave now. No one will judge you for it. No one will try to stop you. I know that what I'm about to ask is too much, that it will end an era of unprecedented peace and prosperity. So if you want no part in it and decide to step away, all I ask is that you don't mention it to anyone. I trust you enough to let you walk."

She waited.

No one moved.

Mira nodded. "Thank you. You are better, stronger than I dreamed possible. Better than the people of this planet probably deserve. With you at the fore, we will quickly overcome the turbulence ahead of us to return to peace and prosperity, but without the threat of complete destruction that currently threatens our existence."

The room remained silent. Everyone wanted to hear what she would say next.

Mira didn't like speaking in public. She didn't believe that words solved much of anything. She much preferred to act.

So she kept it short.

"Start the attack," she said, just loud enough to be heard by the people in the back.

Chapter 6

Sextus Colony, 61 Virginis III

"Dammit," Umberto Virginis Denali said as he wiped frost from the condenser. "This entire habitation unit is going to freeze unless we do something, and we're going to freeze with it. Look at how the impedance has gone up steadily the past six days."

Gina Virginis Hu, dark haired, dark-eyed and round-faced, sighed. "I'll send a request to the nanofactory. We'll have a new heater element in by tomorrow."

They stood in the service module of their nanoprinted habitat, a cube with equipment and monitors lining the wall. Everything but the monitors was painted off-white.

"It's going to be cold tonight. Are you sure you don't want to share a bed?" he asked.

"I'd rather freeze," Gina replied. "But it won't be that bad. You'll survive."

She walked off to her quarters and closed the door behind her, leaving Umberto to wonder what he'd done to piss her off. They'd been at the resource collection station for sixty standard days. They'd been lovers for exactly twelve of them.

That kind of thing happened all the time, of course. Back on Tau Ceti, before he'd emigrated to the Sextus colony and added the word 'Virginis' to his name to celebrate the fact, Umberto had played musical beds with any number of young women. It was all in good fun and no one got hurt.

For some reason, this time had felt different. One day, he'd begun to believe that Gina was special... and the next, she'd shut him down completely, angrily, and had never bothered to explain why.

They still had twenty days left in the posting, and he was torn between wanting it to end right away so the constant reminder that she despised him would disappear, and wanting it to last forever so he could win her back. Meanwhile, he fell back on lame, doomed attempts of rekindling their relationship.

Like tonight's.

"At least we're doing something important," he said to himself as he walked into his own quarters and sat at his personal workstation.

That was true, at least. Their assignment, uncomfortable, lonely and conceivably dangerous if things went wrong, was to supervise a kind of raw-material vacuum-cleaner that pumped liquid organic molecules – mainly methane – out of a lake a hundred and fifty clicks from the colony's main settlement.

Normally, the facility would have been automated, but the extreme cold had made some of the standard sensors unreliable... which meant that, while new designs were developed, the facilities needed to be manned.

The station assigned to them had had its share of niggling problems but, despite their personal situation, Umberto and Gina made a good team, with complementary skillsets. He was detail-oriented and she was great at getting tasks done. So the dynamic had been clear from the beginning: Umberto would discover where the next problem would arise, just because a number looked off or a redundancy stopped working, and she would get it fixed.

They had not had a single interruption of production and delivery in their sixty days on site.

"At least I'll have something to be proud of after this mess is over," he said to himself. "And only Gina will know that I disgust her. It could be worse."

Something on the screen caught his eye. He toggled the

room-to-room intercom. "Gina, could you come in here?"

"I already told you. I'm not sleeping in your room."

"This isn't about that."

The door opened and Gina walked over. "This had better be good," she said.

"Look at this," he replied, pointing to the parameter on the screen.

She snorted. "You called me in here for a meteorite?"

"It's not a meteorite. See there. Controlled landing, even some hovering at the end."

"So a data drone, then," she said. She straightened up, moving away from the monitor and headed back towards the door. "It's not important."

"I think it is," Umberto replied. "There are schedules and windows for orbital-drop-drone fly-over times, and this doesn't fit any of those. The direction is all wrong."

Gina stopped and raised one eyebrow. Then she put her hand on her stomach and sighed. "We both know there are too many variables in the orbital schedules and the drone schedules for you to be sure of that. This could be one of the regular drones, and you could just be off by a bit."

"No way. I've been watching the drone data for this area for weeks. There's no way I would miss one."

"Did you calculate all the possible vectors?"

"No," he admitted.

"Then how do you know it's off?"

"Because it feels off." He stopped himself. "Yes, I know that sounds stupid, but I know it's wrong. It doesn't fit with the numbers. It's wrong."

"Not convinced," Gina said. "I'm going to sleep. Don't call me unless the next meteor is going to land on us"

The door shut behind her, and Umberto slapped the desk

with the palm of his hand. Sudden pain reminded him that his hands were really cold, that the habitation unit was going to get colder, and that he'd better put on some gloves.

"I know I'm right," he told the closed door. "I'll prove it. You'll see."

He pulled up a menu on the computer and opened a trajectory program.

It took him two minutes to copy the flight data from the sensors and have the program analyze it. Another thirty seconds yielded a back-track, showing when and where the tiny vehicle that had been detected would have had to drop out of orbit to give that particular flight profile.

Then he checked the possible orbits against the database of existing orbits for both communications satellites and science orbiters. Nothing.

"I knew it," he exulted. He didn't call Gina, however. He knew what she'd say: that it proved nothing, that someone could easily have forgotten to log a mission, that a drone could have been blown off course. As the coup de grace, she'd point out that even if someone had built and sent out an unauthorized mini-flyer, there was no law against it. hell, there was no law against pretty much anything. The world was so empty that you were pretty much allowed to do whatever you wanted, so long as it didn't present a danger to the settlement.

She would be right about that. But he wanted to prove to her that she was also wrong, that he'd known exactly what he was talking about when he told her that the data he'd seen didn't fit with the stuff that was flying officially.

He messaged a friend at the colony's Meteorology Center. While some found it strange that Meteorology was in charge of keeping track of all the orbital activity in the colony, it made sense from a purely numerical aspect: the weather people controlled and accessed an order of magnitude more satellites than anyone else on the planet. They were the ones doing most of the orbital flying.

Within five minutes, his inbox pinged.

'Definitely not an official mission. We're scheduled to send a few drones your way in fourteen days, but none this week. I'll look into it.'

'Thanks', Umberto replied.

Satisfied, he wrapped himself in high-isolation blankets and dropped into bed. Every nerve screamed at him to knock on Gina's door and tell her he'd been right, but his sense of self-preservation prevented him from doing so.

Eventually, he drifted to sleep.

***

"You couldn't leave it alone, could you?"

Umberto jumped out of the bed and nearly sprained his ankle by stepping on a shoe as he landed on the floor. "Ow!" he yelled. "What's going on? Are we on fire?"

"No," Gina answered, kicking the other shoe into the wall. "We've been ordered to the landing site of the anomaly you called in."

"I..."

"Don't even think of trying to deny it," she said. "I certainly didn't do it, and you're the only other person with access to that data."

"I was just going to say that I didn't report it officially. I asked a friend if the stuff I'd seen was theirs."

"Well, now we have to go out and try to find it. In the goddamned ice."

"Right now?" He looked around at the room, trying to see if it was light out. "What time is it?"

"It's still three hours to dawn." She sighed. "And no, they don't need us to go right now. They just said to check it out at some point during the day."

"Then why..."

"Because I know why you did it. You did it just to prove that you were right." Her eyes flashed. "Admit it."

"Fine. And I'm..." He was about to apologize, but suddenly couldn't hold back the anger. "Of course I wanted to prove you were wrong. Why wouldn't I? All you ever do is treat me like garbage. I get it: I'm the worst mistake you ever made. Being stuck here with me is torture, and all you want is to get me out of your sight forever. Fine. I get that, too. But we still have a stretch in this post, and the colony needs us to do our jobs, so you might as well stop the sniping. I'll live, even if you don't want me anywhere near you. So maybe we can be civilized until we get out of here."

Gina collapsed onto a chair and put her head into her hands. She mumbled something too softly for Umberto to hear.

"What?" It came out louder than he intended. His anger, however was turning to puzzlement. Was Gina *crying*?

She looked up at him, eyes red and brimming with tears. "I said that you aren't the biggest mistake I ever made. Hell, weren't even a mistake... just someone in the wrong place at the wrong time. All I want is to be alone right now. But I'm not. I'm here with you." She sobbed. "I'm pregnant, Umberto."

"Pregnant? But we..."

"It's not yours."

"Oh," he said.

The silence stretched for a long time. He didn't know what to say, as she sat and cried. Finally, still not knowing what to say, he sat down beside her and pulled her close, just hugging her as she sobbed.

Five minutes stretched to ten, then to fifteen. Finally, she rubbed her face and said: “I'm sorry. But I had to tell someone. It's been eating at me and eating at me.”

“It's all right. What are you going to do?”

“I'm not sure yet,” she replied. “Normally, I'd abort without even thinking about it. But when I changed my name to add the colony name in the middle, I mainly did it thinking of my kids, and all the kids who were going to be born here.”

“I know. I did the same thing.” The Colony Charter for Sextus stated that any children born in the system would be given a first and last name to be decided by the parents, and also a second last name: ‘Virginis’. The reason was that, with five other human colonies already in existence and likely more to come, it would soon become desirable to quickly identify a person's origin, to ensure there wouldn't be any misunderstandings arising from cultural differences.

The idea wasn't new to Sextus. The Wolf Colony had been using it for generations… although Umberto had to admit that having a middlename of ‘Wolf’ sounded a lot cooler than ‘Virginis’.

“It hit me that I've actually come around to the idea of having kids… I just wasn't expecting it to happen so soon, and now I don't know what to do.”

“There's a special dispensation on high-stress jobs for people who have kids, you know.”

“And now you see why it's so easy to focus all my anger and confusion on you. You, Umberto, are a dick.”

He thought about what he'd said. Even knowing she considered it the wrong thing, it still sounded like a good reason for having kids. A life of luxury for more than a year was something most colonists didn't even dream about. But expectant mothers and new mothers could bask in it.

"I know what you're thinking," she said, still looking straight towards him. "But it's not a math problem, no matter how much you want it to be. You can't judge the pros and cons of something like this and weigh them to make a decision." She took a deep breath, the kind of patient inhalation Umberto knew so well when he got out of his emotional depth and people tried to explain him back to their own version of reality. "Becoming a mother isn't just a decision about whether to have a baby and care for it. It would change the very core of who I am. And though I've accepted I want that change, I may not be ready for it just yet."

She stared into his eyes for a moment. "Even if I get a plush, heated room and all the ice cream I can eat for a year."

Umberto shivered. "Well, you're not getting a heated room until the parts arrive to fix the thermostat."

She chuckled drily. "You know… I would have thought you would be the worst person in the world to tell this to. And in a way, you probably tick most of the boxes. But you actually got it right."

"I did?" *That was a new one,* he thought.

"Yeah. Most guys would have been pissed that it wasn't theirs."

"But we took care to protect ourselves. It would have been really hard for it to be mine."

"They would have been pissed that I jumped straight from someone else's bed into theirs."

Umberto thought of some of his exes, and the way they'd pretty much forbidden him to talk about other girls. Gina probably had a point. Why would guys be any different in that way? "Yeah. I guess you're right about that," he said. "But I don't see it that way. In the first place, we were never exclusive… but even if we were, you would have had to be a magician to sneak someone into this hab without me noticing. And I doubt you would have found it fun to make a baby outside in the snow. So it was before my time. Ancient history. No problem."

She laughed again. "And you don't judge me."

He shrugged. "I don't see anything to judge. Would you have judged me if I had had a nice blind-drunk celebration before I left for a bunch of months out in the ass-end of nowhere with some woman I'd never met?"

"How did you know I was drunk?" she asked.

"Because when you're sober or just buzzed, you're very precise about wearing protection."

He felt her relax into his arms. "You're a bit weird, you know that? Who calls it protection?"

"It's what it is, right?"

"Yeah… but come on."

He didn't say anything, just held her tightly.

"I'm sorry," she said, finally.

"What for?"

"For treating you like shit. You didn't deserve that. It wasn't your fault. It's just that you were the only person around, and I can't just abandon the assignment. Not unless I decide to have the baby. You were just the only person I could take my anguish out on. And, in my defense, you can be annoying as hell."

"Aw, thanks. I bet you say that to all the guys you're apologizing to."

"See," she said. "You sometimes make me want to toss you straight through a wall."

"You'd freeze if you did," Umberto replied.

"But it would be worth it." She sighed and pulled away, and he noticed that strands of her black hair had become stuck to her cheek, held in place by the moisture from her tears. She pulled her hand away from where it had been wrapped behind his back and offered it. "I guess what I'm trying to say is that I'd like a truce."

He took it suspiciously. "Does that mean — "

"Don't ruin it. It just means I won't be a bitch to you. But it also means that you need to understand that what's happening to me won't just go away, and that I won't be the woman you met when this assignment started. That means... I don't know what that means, but you really don't want to be pushing me or guilting me."

"I understand," he replied. "And I accept your terms."

"Just like that?"

"I'm glad you decided to tell me what was going on. I was driving myself crazy trying to figure out what I'd done this time."

"This time?" she said with a wry grin.

"Though it may come as a surprise, I have been known to completely screw up with women before. Yes, I know it's shocking, but it's true."

"Yeah... shocking," Gina said. She took a deep breath. "But it made me feel better. Do you think we could get back to sleep? We'd be more comfortable if you held me in the bed." She gave him a look. "Just hold me. Nothing else."

"I get it," Umberto said. "But yeah, I'll do it. It's freezing in here."

***

"What are you doing?" Gina asked.

"Trying to get my arm to stop feeling numb. It was stuck under your back until you woke up."

"Why didn't you move it."

"That would have woken you up," Umberto replied.

She gave him a long look. "Dammit," she said. Then she looked away. "What do we have on the to-do list for today?"

"A lot of monitoring and analysis work. Also, we should probably go check out the thing that landed over there," he pointed. "That way when the parts for the heater arrive, we can concentrate on that and not have anything hanging over our heads."

"Oh, yeah… the anomaly. I'm still mad at you for calling that one in."

Umberto sighed. "We still need to check it out."

"All right. Let's get it out of the way." She removed the cover of the tiny slit that gave them visual access to the outside world. "Light levels are fine, we can do this."

They emerged into a cold, clear day. The illumination from 61 Virginis that made it through the atmosphere was much more yellow than the light of Tau Ceti II, which was orange-hued. He'd been told the suns were quite similar, but the atmosphere filtered it differently. Umberto barely noticed it anymore. It just seemed normal now.

"It's not too far from here," he said. "The sensors said it should have made landfall about eight hundred meters away, just on the far side of the hill."

"Which means we'll need to walk fifteen hundred meters to get there," Gina said.

"We need the exercise," Umberto replied.

"No. You need the exercise. I can do without any exercise right now." She shouldered her pack. It contained a couple of sensors and the emergency medical kit. His own contained a lot more equipment — at her insistence — and his own medpack. "Come on. Let's get this over with."

Their station was about seventy meters away from the methane lake. The plain surrounding the lake was flat and easy to walk on — as long as you had the right suits for the extreme cold. The only feature in the flat white landscape was the hill.

Umberto cursed the bad luck that had caused the flying object to land behind that.

Though inconvenient to skirt the knoll, it was an easy stroll. Their suit maps estimated they would be at their destination in twenty minutes.

They went silently. Gina seemed disinclined to talk, and Umberto didn't want to risk their fragile truce with inane chatter.

The hill was a steep, round formation that stood alone in the plane, covered in snow at the top, but with walls too vertical to hold any on its sides, which exposed the grey walls. No one knew what had formed it — the study of Sextus' geological history was extremely far down on the Colony's list of priorities — but it didn't appear to be volcanically active, and certainly wasn't part of a mountain range.

It was also quite small, and they rounded it within minutes.

"Look," Gina said. "Over there. Can you see it?"

"Your eyes are much better than mine," Umberto replied. "Give me a few minutes."

As they came nearer, he made out some black forms against the white of the snow. Closer still, the forms resolved into black cubes.

"Stop a second," Umberto said. "This can't be right. How big would you say those cubes are?"

Gina shrugged in her suit. "I can't tell from here. Maybe a couple of meters to a side?"

"And I count three of them."

"I think there's four. One of them is hidden behind another one."

He trusted her eyes. He couldn't make out much detail from any distance. He was on the colony's list for corrective visual surgery… but that was another thing that hadn't been given priority. "Well, the flyer I saw on the scans was maybe half a meter to a side, probably smaller."

"So what? It's probably inside one of those cubes. That looks like nanoprinting. The black stuff is usually carbon nanotubing. Let's just go over there, scan whatever bar codes the things have on them and send the report back so the people back at central can match it to their database. How much do you want to bet that this is a science outpost from the early days of the colony which everyone forgot about?"

"No bet," Umberto said. To his eye, she had to be right. The structure was so obviously human technology that nothing else would have made sense. He began to trudge towards the installation.

Gina suddenly stopped and faced him. "Wait. Did you think that was something else? Did you think it was something from an alien civilization? Is that why you were so eager to check it out?"

Umberto tried to control his bitterness. "I thought it might be something. But it's just a bunch of cubes, probably full of wires and sensors. And it looks just like our tech."

The area around the cubes had been cleared of all small ice balls and debris, and the machines were humming to themselves.

Umberto set his pack on the floor and rummaged inside. Their equipment had been designed to be operated while wearing thick, insulated gloves.

He pulled out a radiation meter, pointed it at the installation and grunted. "Reads normal. We can go closer."

They walked into the cleared area. Gina put her suited hand next to the surface of the nearest cube. "288 Kelvin," she said. "Not hot, but certainly not ambient."

"Same for this one," Umberto said from the second cube. "No, wait. 300 now. 310. We'd better move back."

He turned to walk to a safe distance, to let whatever industrial process was about to take place run its course before investigating further.

His foot caught on something, and he stumbled. He looked down to see a black tendril wrapped around his ankle. He tracked it back: it emerged from the nearest black cube.

"Gina, a little help here."

No one answered.

"Gina, where are you?"

His comm remained silent, so he turned to look.

Where his companion had stood just moments before, he saw a swarm of black tendrils wrapping something. A flash of orange, just before it became fully cocooned, was his only clue that he was looking at Gina's suit.

He pulled desperately at the wire holding him, but it was too strong. More tendrils joined that one, snaking up his legs, wrapping, immobilizing. He kicked at them until he couldn't kick anymore, then screamed helplessly as the rest of his body was enveloped in black tubes.

The yellow light of 61 Virginis disappeared from view.

Then he heard, in his cocoon, a light tapping.

"No," Umberto said as he realized what it was. "Don't break my..."

The visor, illuminated only by the status lights inside his helmet, suddenly spidered and cracked. Frigid air burst through the broken transparency, followed by the blackness of tendrils filling the space around his head.

Umberto screamed in pain as something pierced his scalp.

A million points of light appeared in front of his eyes, and every sound he'd ever heard thundered in his ears.

Then he went limp and darkness overcame him.

Chapter 7

Earth Orbit – Planetwide Simulation

Rome struggled against unseen hands as the world around him flickered. His first thought was that the simulation must have been malfunctioning, restraining him with invisible bonds and cycling through a kaleidoscope of visuals.

If the simulation broke, he could end up erased. Or worse, he could end up floating in an electronic limbo until the computers running the simulation — computers that were designed to last forever — finally failed. He closed his eyes to shut out the continuously-changing images and tensed against the unseen force restraining him.

"Chill, man," a deep voice said. "We got you."

Rome opened his eyes. He wasn't in the basement of the Triad complex in Beijing anymore. The light was just as dim, and his new surroundings were just as austere, but the computer center in China had been much larger, and it was carpeted. And full of seats.

The place he was in now seemed to be nothing more than a grey-painted metal box.

"Who said that?" he asked.

Whatever had been holding him had released its pressure. Rome looked up, down, behind him. Seeing no one, he searched for concealed speakers. Nothing.

"Oh. Sorry about that."

A shimmer to his right coalesced to reveal a young man in the room with him. A dark-skinned man a head taller than Rome and proportionally wide, held out a hand. "My name is Ripp. I think you already know my boss."

"Where's Emily?" Rome said, ignoring the hand. He'd been involved with hackers in the simulation before — and only hackers would know how to use the code to make themselves invisible. Some were good and some were bad... and all required caution.

"Calm down. You're all right. You're safe now. Emily's over here."

Rome followed the man out the door, struggling to keep his mouth shut. He needed answers, but that could wait; the first priority was to find Emily and to ensure her safety.

The tall man led him down a very short corridor — grey and featureless as the room he'd appeared in — and through another door.

The first thing Rome saw was a bank of monitors with people sitting in front of them. The second thing he saw was Emily, and his knees went weak with relief. She was fine, talking animatedly with...

He saw the blue hair.

"Jarrien!" Rome said. "What the hell?"

"Hello, Rome," Jarrien replied, her pale skin made even ghostlier by the blue light from her hair. "I'm glad you could make it."

She stepped forward and they hugged.

"I didn't get a heck of a whole lot of choice in the matter," Rome replied.

"It was the only way." She held up a hand. "Please don't say 'the only way to what?' If you do, I'll have the team send you back. Give me a minute to gather some people and we'll tell you what you need to know."

"I see you're still doing things your way," Rome said.

Her delicate features — he would have thought her pretty if she wasn't so intense and unpredictable — hardened. "If there's one thing I'm not doing it's what I want; things have changed around here. There's Hino. Come on." She led them across the room full of monitors and through a door at the far end. A second grey corridor waited, with several doors leading off of it. They entered another room. This one was also grey, but it held a number of chairs around a long meeting table.

"I love what you guys have done with the place," Rome said. "If I didn't know better, I'd say we were on a space station that had only received a single shipment of paint — all of it grey."

"You're closer than you think," Jarrien said. "This facility is in space... but the paint was chosen to be hard to spot. I want this place to get lost in the simulation."

"Who will see us out in space?"

"Visually? No one," Jarrien replied. "Virtually? We don't know if anything is looking in this direction. But the code for the grey walls is the same code for the grey of the moon's regolith, and for a bunch of other grey rocks floating out in the solar system. And that's also why we grabbed you in the hack palace. There are so many illegal connections in that place that ours will be impossible to identify in the noise. By the time anyone can find our thread, my people will have created so many false paths that nothing would ever be able to follow us back here. So I guess it's a good thing you stopped to see the sights."

Rome looked around the room again before sitting down on a chair alongside the table. "You're hiding." It wasn't a question. "From who?"

Jarrien settled across from him, as Emily, Hino, and Ripp chose their seats. "The better question is from what. We're here to avoid getting noticed by the AI that runs the simulation," she replied.

"I didn't get the impression that the simulation was run by an AI. A lot of processing power and protocols, yes. But actual intelligence?" Rome shook his head. "I didn't see that."

"Yeah. None of us did. It caught us completely by surprise when it began erasing people."

"When you say erasing…" Emily said.

Jarrien glanced her way. "You saw the world out there. By erasing, I mean erasing. Poof! You were there, now you're gone. Erased." She shrugged. "I don't know if it's permanent because we don't dare probe the system's memory to see if the thing is keeping backup copies somewhere. But there's no one left in the simulation."

"We met a guy," Emily said. "He called himself Skate."

"Yeah. We don't know who he was. Or even what he was. As far as we know, the people in this facility are the only people left alive on Earth. We suspect he might be a spy that the AI built to draw us out."

Jarrien's words echoed against the bare walls. For a few moments, no one spoke.

"Why don't you start at the beginning," Rome said, finally.

***

"For the first few weeks after the *Unity* left for Tau Ceti," Jarrien began, "things went on pretty much as you saw them. People explored their newfound freedoms by playing with the simulation code. They gave themselves wings, left their pleasure centers activated permanently, jumped into space. Whatever they'd always wanted to do, they just simply… did. It was a chaotic time, but it was also joyful. Watching people suddenly lose their chains — all their chains, even the ones that exist for the mere reason of being human — was one of the happiest things I ever saw.

"Of course, not everyone was happy. Some people, possibly even a majority, wanted to take things back to the way they were, with maybe just a little less restriction. They argued that the utter lack of structure meant that society would tear itself apart. Others replied that we could always build new social relationships, but that giving up the abilities and the freedom would be a terrible loss.

"And then there was a third group. There were some people who used the new situation to do violence to their neighbors. Though our bodies, protected by the simulation's reset protocols, were nearly impossible to kill, people found ways around the fail-safes, sometimes keeping people alive to torture them, other times simply going deep into the code and ensuring the reset failed at just the correct moment."

She looked around the room.

"You understand what that means, don't you? The reset is what kept us from dying in accidents or being murdered. It's the automatic system that regenerates your body, your avatar or whatever you want to call it at the moment of death. It's a central part of our society.

"Some of us — mainly people who'd already been modifying the code before everyone realized you could do that," Jarrien ran her fingers through her hair — her blue, light-emitting hair which she'd hacked before Rome met her — absently, "realized that if we wanted to keep any semblance of humanity, any chance of society not flying into several billion little self-contained kingdoms of the mind, we needed to stop people from killing one another.

"We stopped a couple of them. Well, you saw what I did to Graham, back when you were still here. What I'm describing was similar, except there were a bunch of us acting in concert. Wherever we realized that someone was trying to break the world itself, or other people, we went in and neutralized them.

"And one day, when I went to stop a guy who was trying to

drill shortcuts through the center of the Earth to bring lava into the middle of Mexico City, the guy disappeared right in front of me. So did the rest of Mexico City's people west of where I was standing. Poof. One moment it was full of people, the next, it was just cars parking themselves on the side of the highway running on their emergency protocols. I think that purge missed me by ten meters."

Jarrien shrugged. "I was just lucky that time. But what happened next was the product of my own paranoia. I already had this facility set up before the disappearances started, so I simply opened a shortcut here and holed up to watch the show.

"I realized what was happening. People were disappearing in large swaths dictated more by geography than by number of people. So if a chunk of terrain that got its people erased was in the middle of a city, it could mean a hundred thousand people gone. In a desert, maybe five. In the ocean, probably none. And the pattern was random… but the AI never swept the same place twice."

"How do you know it was an AI?" Rome said. "It could have been a perfectly innocent maintenance program doing the work. In fact, that sounds completely normal: the system was clearly becoming unstable. Best to put the users in stasis, rebuild the background and then release the population back into the wild."

"Yeah," the man named Hino interjected. "Except a lot of programmers, a lot of my friends, hid from them using Turing-level camouflage programs, stuff that would easily beat a maintenance system… and we still lost nearly everyone. My partner and I barely made it out at all. Whatever is running the search isn't just some dumb subroutine with a lot of power. It knows what it's doing."

"Hino's right," Jarrien said.

"So, if it's so smart, how come you're here?" Rome gestured

around himself. "Presumably fighting to reestablish the people who were lost?"

"Hah," Jarrien said. "What we're doing right now is hiding from the AI. We all hope it won't see us… but most of us accept that we're just delaying the inevitable." She echoed Rome's gesture, encompassing everything around them. "The problem we're faced with is more complicated than just an enemy that has more resources and more power than we do. Our enemy actually controls the very space we exist within. It makes the world work. We can't break the AI without breaking everything. The simulation might just turn itself off."

Rome gave her a sharp look. "Then don't break it. Reprogram it so it loses its AI functions. Turn it back into a series of routines that work for us. Hell, just limiting the amount of memory available should be enough to stop it from functioning as a self-aware entity. You need a few petabytes before self-awareness kicks in."

"Yeah. We have no idea how to do that," Jarrien said. "We don't know much about the way the backend really works. Most of the people here, including me, were much more concerned with exploiting the easy-to-reach surface programming of the simulation to get deep into the engine. Hell, even the physics module is a simple break-in compared to things like continuity or memory. I'm not sure anyone's gotten close to cracking those areas. And as for the underlying motor that links everything together? No one has even tried, as far as I know. It might just be the AI itself."

"That would make sense," Rome mused. "So that's what we're going to need to attack."

The group around him remained silent for some moments. "If it finds us…" Hino said.

"I know. It erases us and the continuity of our consciousness ends. The nightmare scenario for any self-aware species." He held their gazes, each one, for an instant before shrugging. "But what other choice do we have? Every day we wait, paralyzed by fear, brings us one day closer to discovery, and also gives us one less day to finally take action and maybe survive this. We need to start thinking about how to take the big, bad AI down, or at least reprogram it so it's not coming after us. And we need to do it now."

Rome thought they'd decline, kick the problem forward, simply stall while they pretended to analyze his concerns. And perhaps, he reflected, that was their right. It was easy for him to be cavalier about the inherent risk, but the people around them didn't have a flesh-and-blood copy of themselves roaming the galaxy. Well, technically Emily did, but she didn't know about that, and he wasn't going to tell her. If he was erased here, he risked little except this particular existence. He wouldn't even feel any pain or terror. One moment he'd be there, the next he just wouldn't.

The people in the room with him? Not so much. They'd be gone forever, without even the comfort of knowing they left bones behind to mark their passage through the galaxy, or possessions they'd once owned that would find a new place with someone else. These people were composed of zeroes and ones which only formed their personalities when they were arrayed in the correct order. When those bits were scrambled it would be like they'd never existed.

No wonder they wouldn't jump to put themselves in harm's way.

"Shit," Jarrien said. "I wish he wasn't, but Rome is right. We've been sitting here with our heads up our asses for too long."

"But what choice do we have?" Hino said. "If we poke the bear, it's going to poke us back."

"We need to think about that. I have some ideas," Rome said.

Jarrien raised an eyebrow at him. "Please don't tell me that you think that just because you're from the civilized world of Tau Ceti that you're going to teach all of the barbarians here on Earth how to program. Some of us have been studying the simulation for decades."

"I know. I just had a few months when I arrived… and I'm a good binarist, but I've never claimed to be the very best binarist."

"Bullshit," Jarrien said. "I don't know a hacker alive who doesn't think he's the best."

Rome grinned. "All right. I may have said I was the best. But only once or twice. Still, I wouldn't dream of making that claim about this system in this room. You guys definitely know more about the code in this simulation and the AI you've been hiding from than I do. But I have one advantage: I actually got to study the whole thing from outside when I arrived here. I had to try to figure out the design of your systems and how everything fit together before I could even think of trying to get in. I spent a couple of weeks probing the connections and watching the reactions. I know how it all fits."

Stunned silence met this revelation until the man named Ripp broke it. "And you displayed this fine sense of study by lobbing huge monsters at us? I remember how we reacted when those things showed up. We thought the simulation had scheduled a kaiju invasion."

Rome grimaced. "In my defense, I was working with a programming language no one on Tau Ceti had even seen for five hundred years, on a system I didn't know, through a hardwired interface that a friend had jury-rigged into an emergency access port. That my initial avatars were off-scale and clumsy was to be expected." He looked around the room. "Would any of you have been able to do better?"

"Shit. You're right," Ripp replied. "And I apologize. I guess I'm just scared."

"We all are," Jarrien said. "But if you've got anything, any insight at all to how we can approach this differently, I'm willing to listen."

"I need a computer."

Jarrien held up a hand. "We have dozens. But I don't want you probing the defenses. We're being careful about this."

"I don't need a connection. I just think better when I'm on a keyboard."

"That works, then. Follow me."

She led him to another room identical to the one where all the people had been working. This one was empty. "Take your choice," she said.

He sat at the nearest desk. The machine must have been connected to a motion sensor because it activated as soon as he sat in front of it. The thing actually had a keyboard, and he let the familiar sense of the keys on his fingers guide him. He typed 'Text' into the search box — some icons were universal across star systems — and selected the program most likely to be a text editor.

Good start, he thought as the white space of the note block opened. Then he leaned back into the chair and tried to recall what he'd found as he probed the simulation a year and a half earlier. Eyes still closed, he began to type what he remembered.

***

"I think I have an idea," Rome said to them later. "It has to do with how the different mainframes are related to each other." Then he smiled. "And I think you're really, really going to like this. Hell, the original idea was inspired by something Jarrien did the last time I was here."

Chapter 8

Near Denver, Colorado, USA - Earth

A small airship, about a meter long, emerged from a huge concrete bunker built to last forever and floated between lodgepole pines that had grown in front of the entrance. A sudden gust of wind from the mountains buffeted it before its engines compensated for the unexpected resistance. It might have been stained and faded and its parts might have been worn with endless use, but it was in perfect working condition: as a maintenance drone working to keep the Earth simulation mainframes functional, any part that came close to failure was replaced immediately, and there were four backup airships that only flew when this one was incapacitated.

Unlike the simulation they served, the environment they operated in was real. Earth had real rain, real snow — particularly up in the Rockies — and real wind. The maintenance schedule took all of these conditions into account.

The airship fleet couldn't be allowed to fail. An entire automated facility, filled with spares sufficient to equip all five of the airships for the following three thousand years, was at its disposal. That, too, had redundancies built upon redundancies.

Now that the airship was clear of the bunker, it floated a hundred meters into the sky — high enough for trees not to present a danger — and proceeded towards the city of Denver.

More accurately, it proceeded to where the city of Denver had once stood. Only vegetation-covered mounds remained of the once-vibrant urban community that had dominated the landscape. Buildings, streets, even a sports stadium had been buried beneath hundreds of years of decay, identifiable only by their GPS coordinates, overlaid on the terrain below.

In some places, though, the concrete had either been too resistant or been too sharply angled to give an adequate foothold to vegetation, and in these places, the bleached grey bones of the ancient civilization punched through the greenery.

The airship ignored the ruins, even though its external cameras recorded everything for the people controlling it. It wasn't there to see the sights; it was on a very specific mission.

As it neared its destination, the airship angled downwards and began a powered descent. Its destination came into view: a tunnel fifteen meters wide penetrated a cliffside.

The airship entered.

An access door forty meters in the mountain stood open. It had been opened a year and a half earlier by the crew of the starship *Unity* when they had made their initial exploration of the area.

The airship threaded its way through the open door. After centuries of sterility, the corridor beyond the door was beginning to show evidence of being exposed to the elements. Leaves were scattered along the floor. A mouse skittered away as the airship's shadow passed over it.

An automated subroutine in the airship's control program noted the mess in the corridor and sent a message to one of the wheeled drones who could reach the area and clear it of debris. Though the airship itself was never intended to be in this particular tunnel, it knew how it should look. All maintenance units were programmed to identify a mess and call it in.

Deeper in the corridor, more untidiness awaited.

Old food wrappers, discarded drinking bottles, a pair of thermal blankets with the word *'Unity'* emblazoned on them and a single wheeled office chair sat in the corridor. An access panel had been removed from a nearby wall, and a rat's nest of cables emerged from within. The airship identified the equipment behind the access port as a communication node between two of the local area servers for the Denver city simulation.

The airship was about to call this mess in, too, but a command from an admin user bypassed that subroutine and reclassified the entire sector as a work area, where mess was perfectly normal. Maintenance would resume when the work was completed.

The same admin user ordered the airship to descend further and, barely above ground level, to grasp the end of one of the cables in its manipulator arm and plug a particular connector — a connector that had been designed to function with Earth-standard data ports — into its computer.

Thus plugged in, the airship floated back to the roof and hummed softly to itself as data poured from its hard drive into the communication node, and from there into the mainframe itself. The mainframe was Denver II, the survivor of what had originally been twin computers that ran the simulation for the city.

While the airship hovered, it noted the passage of a spider-like maintenance robot on its way to clean the leaves in the corridor. It analyzed the machine and decided that it wasn't big enough to close the heavy concrete-and-steel door at the end of the corridor. That, in turn, meant the airship would be free to return to its duties when it was done with this particular special task.

The data transfer was nearly at seventy-five percent when the robot skittered back, paused to evaluate the wires and food wrappers and then, with an air of reluctance, headed back to its charging crib.

There. The transfer was complete. The airship threaded itself back through the corridor and headed out the door.

Once outside of the corridor and the borehole, it floated back into the sky, where it could maneuver at a much lower level of vigilance. After all, there was nothing here to collide with other than insects and the occasional bird.

The airship's automated systems decided that it should head back for the maintenance hangar. Eighty percent of its battery life still remained, but it had completed an unscheduled mission, therefore the safest thing to do was to head back and check that everything was working.

The admin decided to bypass that decision. It wanted to fly the airship to the Colorado Springs mainframe sixty kilometers away.

The airship's subroutines balked at the command. Denver Maintenance had no responsibilities in Colorado Springs.

The admin user overrode the objection.

The airship's subroutines objected more strongly: the trip to Colorado Springs would deplete the batteries and preclude a return trip. The airship would have to recharge in Colorado Springs, causing a gap in Denver's redundancy of coverage.

The Admin user overrode the objection.

The airship asked for an authorization code.

What it received in response to the request was not an authorization code. Instead, it was a barrage that, starting from the admin access already granted to the person giving it the orders, completely defeated all the failsafes. Like cancer, the invading code attacked from within, and the tiny processing resources of the airship's computer brain, never designed to overcome advanced electronic warfare, crumbled quickly.

The airship trembled unsteadily for a few moments before setting off towards Colorado Springs.

It was told that it would find comm access point recently opened by Colorado Springs Maintenance. Once it reached that access port, it was to repeat the operation it had already performed at Denver II and await further instructions.

Emily, at the controls of the airship by dint of having been one of the great action gamers of her generation and the one who drove the remote maintenance robot that met the *Unity* crew, pumped her fist.

"We're in," she said, unnecessarily, to the people crowded around her watching the screen.

Chapter 9

Earth – Planetwide Simulation

Inside the simulation, the city of Denver was not a ruin. It's streets and highways were not home to the crushing weight of uncontrolled vegetation, but lined by well-tended planters of flowers. No clouds marred the high mountain air, and the buildings were framed by majestic mountains to the west.

Even the sections of the city that had been deleted when the *Unity* mission had destroyed a mainframe in their initial foray on Earth had been restored from a backup. That part of Denver was just as well-rendered as everything else, down to the dirt along the sidewalk façades. The big black walls, infinitely high, that had denoted the end of the simulated section, had disappeared.

Along with the gentle sunlight, a soft breeze caressed the flanks of the enormous monster in the middle of Colfax Avenue.

The creature stood as tall as a ten-story building, and it appeared to be having difficulties navigating streets that were much too small for it. At one point it stepped off Colfax Avenue and flattened a large portion of the ancient historic colonnade in Civic Center Park. It seemed confused as it extricated its leg and rumbled onwards, advancing towards the Colorado State Capitol.

"That is one ugly monster," Ripp said as he followed the creature's progress via a monitor in Jarrien's spaceborne headquarters, millions of miles away.

Rome chuckled. The hacker was right: the creature looked like an amalgam of black cubes piled haphazardly on top of each other to form something vaguely humanoid.

"Hey, it works, doesn't it?" Hino countered. Then he peered

at the screen. "Although if we'd had a few more hours we could have worked on the movement protocols." He grimaced as another step took out three of the four columns on the façade of the Capitol. "And maybe the item identification programming."

"How does that thing find stuff, anyway?" Ripp asked. When blank stares returned, he grinned. "Your monster has no eyes."

Hino snorted at him. "You know as well as I do that, in a simulated environment like this one, eyes are just cosmetic. We map coordinates."

"Map coordinates? What if someone steps in front of it?"

"There's no one out there. Not anywhere, remember?"

Rome cut in. "I hate to interrupt, but what are we expecting the AI's countermeasures to look like?"

"Well, we know they won't send the army out to get us," Hiro said. "Who would drive the tanks?"

"Why does a civilization without borders, and where you can't kill people even have an army?" Rome asked.

"Mainly as a career choice, I think," Hino said. "I mean the army gets used for mitigation of civil unrest and for riot control if that becomes necessary, but mostly, it's because there are millions of people all over the world who are happier living under the discipline imposed by a military regimen. They fall comfortably into the command structure."

"That sounds messed up," Rome said.

Hino shrugged. "It's harmless. They can't go berserk and kill anyone, after all. And it acted as a curb on the criminal element."

From the couch where she was resting after the long hours of programming the monster and the code from the blimp that Emily had delivered to the Denver mainframe, Jarrien snorted. "Oh, come on. I was probably the most dangerous criminal on Earth before the *Unity* arrived, and I was on a first-name basis with most of the rest… and not one of us was worried that we would be shut down by some goof driving a tank. Those guys became soldiers because they wanted to be able to play with toys that make loud bangs."

"None of which is answering my question," Rome said. "What do you think the simulation will do to shut down your pixelated Godzilla over there?" Rome was fresher and more focused than the rest of the team for the simple reason that he hadn't been involved in any of the actual programming. Once he explained the idea behind his plan — an idea based on Jarrien's previous use of maintenance drones to affect the external world from inside the simulation — and where he'd left the simulation open to entry via external ports on his prior visit, Jarrien's team had taken over completely and Rome's participation had ended. He hadn't even been present when Emily twisted their arms into letting her drive the airship, although he smiled to think of how that conversation could have gone. Emily might seem polite and relaxed, but he'd seen just how much steel there was in her personality.

Anyhow, no one wanted a guy who had to think about programming in Earth code getting in the way; this was a team of hackers that used to modify the simulation on the fly, often in high-stress situations. They could code in their sleep.

So, while they were coding — awake — sleep was exactly what Rome had done. He and Emily retired to a room just as grey as everything else, complete with grey sheets. When he finally emerged eight hours later, he was refreshed, alone… and delighted to see that everyone else was still working hard on the problem of delivering the code where they needed it. It was a nice change from his usual routine, in which he would be the one pulling all-nighters to fix computer issues.

In a way, Rome envied them. He enjoyed being in the middle of the action. When the *Unity* had arrived and he'd been thrust into the limelight, it had been the first time something truly important — as opposed to a mere technical problem — had hinged on his skill behind a keyboard.

His first instinct the night before had been to volunteer to help, even if it was just as a gopher.

But he remembered that he was there with Emily, who would have to be alone among strangers if he did that. So he joined her for dinner and they retired to the room, not imagining that she would talk her way into a starring role.

Rome was still unsure how he felt about her. He was attracted to her physically, of course — he wondered if that really meant anything in the Earth simulation — but more importantly, he enjoyed spending time with her. She seemed to complement him perfectly well, being strong where he was weak, and being completely clueless with regards to the technical stuff at which he thrived.

The only reason he'd been able to move on from her was that he was certain she had died when the protestors on Tau Ceti II stormed the Council Building and destroyed the mainframe that held her. But knowing she was gone, Rome had moved on.

Now he wasn't sure if what he felt was a remnant of the head-over-heels love he'd felt for her before, or just relief that the guilt he'd felt was resolved. Did he truly feel for her or was he following the path of least resistance?

He felt *something* for her. Was it love? He didn't know.

Worse, when they finished making love and she looked at him exactly the same way she'd done before they'd traveled to Tau Ceti, the guilt made it hard to think.

As they watched the monster ravage Denver, her hand lay on his shoulder as if it was the most natural thing in the world.

"That thing looks just as wonky as Rome's first avatar did when I saw it the first time."

"You were there?"

"Not physically, but the first thing he broke was in Denver… well, technically, he broke half of the city itself. So we were all glued to the TV when the monster report came through. I remember wondering how anything like that could happen. The simulation was supposed to stop that kind of stuff."

"Well, there's no one left to wonder now," Hino said softly.

"Heads up," Ripp said. He'd stopped watching the image feed to concentrate on the information they were getting through passive sensors they'd planted in the simulation. Those were designed to detect abnormal data loads and memory usage that might herald a response to their monster. He pointed to sudden spikes on usage graphs. "I think we've got incoming."

"What's the plan?" Rome asked. The downside to having slept through the coding session is that he'd also missed all the planning that went on when coding was taking place.

"Nothing."

"Huh?"

"We're going sacrifice this monster to observe the response. That way, we can see how the system goes about cleaning up the mess. The monster is programmed to resist most of the basic code-repair algorithms we've already seen, so we're hoping that will force the AI to resort to some heavier stuff. And once we see what it does, we'll work backward to create ways to neutralize that and repeat the process in Colorado Springs," Jarrien replied.

"Sounds like a plan, I guess."

"Do you have anything better?" Jarrien asked.

"No. Not better. But maybe something we can do to protect ourselves while we try to figure out how to counter-attack," Rome replied

"Well," Ripp interjected, "It's going to have to wait. This is starting now."

There was little to see on the screen, and Rome's view of Ripp's computer — where the real action would be documented by a series of graphs — was not good enough for him to observe the progress of the battle. Though he ached to push everyone aside for a closer look, his ego wasn't quite that big. He let the people who understood what they were looking at get on with their job.

"Here come the first scrubbers," Ripp said, pointing at one graph on his screen. "Just like we expected."

Jarrien sighed and made a gesture in the air. The entire wall behind Ripp's screen turned into a huge monitor. Now Rome — and the rest of the team — got an easily-visible image of the graphs, the numbers alongside them, and several other displays that Ripp wasn't even bothering to monitor.

Ripp didn't seem to notice he wasn't the only one with access to the data: he kept his eyes glued to his screen and gave everyone else a running commentary on what he was seeing.

Rome tried to read the information, but found it was easier to simply follow along with Ripp's narration.

"This is really low-level stuff," Ripp said. "It's an automated code repair function. Does the AI really think a thirty-meter monster is just a code error? That's the dumbest thing I've ever seen. Can this really be the same intelligence that took out the Zack Street Hack Collective? I was chatting with those guys when they went down, and there's no way an automated cleanup got them."

Jarrien spoke up. "It might be doing the same thing we are: trying to see what is happening, and by poking at the monster see if the people controlling it will reveal anything about themselves." She looked around the room. "This is exactly why we automated it and sent it out on its own: so no one could link it back to us."

"Well, that didn't work out, so now it's trying the next thing we thought it would." He pointed to one screen in which the lines were actually descending. "It's trying to cut off the input data stream to the monster, so if we're driving it remotely we'll either lose contact or have to break through." He chuckled. "We're way ahead of you, Mr. Evil AI."

The enormous black humanoid on the visual feed didn't even stumble. Or rather it did, but the stumbling was just the same as it always was: a lurching walk around the Capitol building. Nothing the AI had thrown at it so far had visually affected its movement.

Hino spoke quietly. "The AI will need to start using something a little more effective now. This should prove interesting."

They watched in rapt attention as the graphs spiked again. While it was obvious that something was happening, Rome waited for Ripp to give them an analysis of the attack pattern.

"Give me a second," Ripp said, peering more closely at the graphs and holding up one hand. "I want to be sure I'm reading this right."

Rome felt his heart pounding against his chest as he awaited the verdict. What were they up against? What kind of massive, deceptive counter-assault would a sentient AI have prepared for them? Would it, despite all their precautions be able to track them back? It would take a bit of work to discover what was on the other side of the high-impedance air gap that Jarrien had created by inserting the data physically from outside the mainframe, but it wasn't impossible. For all Rome knew, that was exactly what the AI was doing right at that moment: backtracking the monster and preparing to erase the spaceborne habitat and everyone inside it.

Meanwhile, it might be using the fight against the monster as a distraction, a way of keeping its enemies from realizing just how much danger they were in.

"I don't get it," Ripp said.

"What?" Hino replied. "You need us to help you check the patterns?"

"No. And that's exactly the confusing part. It's not doing anything exotic or hard to identify. Unless I'm reading the activity wrong, the only thing the AI did was to increase the strength of the initial cleaning program it used and combine it with the strangulation program of the second attack."

"So it's trying progressively stronger tactics. It's what we expected," Hino said.

"It wasn't what I expected," Ripp replied.

"I get what you're saying," Jarrien said. "You expected the AI to hit back with something more likely to trigger a response from us. Something that could expose our real capabilities."

"Yeah," Ripp said. "I guess that's it. I didn't think it all the way through, but this… seems so dumb, somehow. The whole thing, since we broke in."

"Yeah. Well, we'd better not underestimate the AI. We've already seen what it did to everyone," Jarrien said.

Ripp ran his hands over his forehead. "I won't. But to tell you the truth, I would have felt a lot more comfortable if the thing had just waved some of its code magic and made the monster disappear."

Rome felt his stomach tighten. "What if it's a distraction? Do you think it might be backtracking us?"

Jarrien looked up at him and shook her head. "If it was, I'd have heard about it. I have every single person in this facility, except for the five of us in this room, monitoring every attack vector towards this place, including every node we used to get to the airship. If they see even the hint of someone looking in their direction they'll let me know. We should be clean."

Rome wasn't convinced, but he couldn't think of anything else they could do to beef up their security. He turned his attention back to the screen.

What had begun as a nervous experiment soon devolved, over the course of the next two hours, into a series of ever-more brutal attacks on the monster. Instead of a fight against sophisticated code, the creature they'd created was simply worn down by sheer processing power brought to bear on the interactions between the monster's code and the simulation. Eventually, it was torn to pieces — and then cleaned up by the very same error-correction protocols that the AI had used in its first attack.

Ripp, who'd been calling the action with decreasing enthusiasm, finally declared. "Well, that's a wrap. I don't think we learned anything from this, did we?"

Jarrien, who had been in and out of the room several times replied: "I'm not so sure. We definitely learned something… I'm just not exactly sure what. We certainly have a lot to think about."

"What about Colorado Springs?" Hino asked.

"That should prove interesting as well, but I suspect we'll find much of the same," Jarrien replied. "I think the AI knows we're behind this, and has decided to see what else we'll try… and whether we'll overextend ourselves when we try it." She turned to Rome. "You said you had an idea."

"Yeah," Rome replied. "It's an extension of something we discussed back when I was part of the *Unity* crew. Once we realized there was literally no one around on Earth, and once we understood that the simulation was running, we started poking at the interconnected computer systems on the planet.

"Our first idea was that this whole network was run from a central location, because we knew Earth people lived inside a simulated environment, something like a huge, fully-immersive video game. On Tau, we're not allowed to have video games be that immersive — it's a law that dates back to when we first decided to split with Earth society — but we do have complex games that stop just short. And those are run from a central location, and each user has a connection on their end, run by a standardized tablet computer we call a Panorama Screen. A Panorama can't run the simulation, but it has enough processing power to allow the user to interact with the world.

"We thought you were set up in the same way. That there was a central megacomputer that would run the main simulation, to keep everything aligned. We thought each of the mainframes would then run only the parts necessary to interact with each human walking through. We thought it was more similar to a game space where the world only runs when a player is actually in that sector."

He paused and looked around. "We also thought you were all alive in your birthing chambers, happily plugged into the simulation, which was the only world you'd ever known.

"So our initial plan was to cut one of the local mainframes off from the rest of the grid and try to establish communications with only the people on that computer. We thought we could talk to them in a different simulated environment — one built by us — but then we realized that each mainframe appeared to be running part of the simulation itself, as a decentralized thing, so we changed course and decided to go into the complete simulation as a separate entity."

"Yeah. We've already discussed how well that went," Ripp reminded him.

"But that's not the point," Rome said. "What if we go one

step back in the *Unity* crew's thinking? What if instead of taking on an AI that creates its memory and thought processes by combining an enormous number of mainframe data cores and memory capacity, we go after that capacity? What if we cut off its mainframes one by one — or better still, all at once — and cut off its resources.

"As a first step, we could cut ourselves off." He turned to Jarrien. "Which mainframe is this habitat running off of?"

"Vancouver," she replied.

"All right. As a first step, we could isolate the Vancover mainframe from the rest of the simulation. We'd just need to close down a few dozen connections, including redundancies. The maintenance drones can do that."

"And we'd be what? Stuck in a simulation with a couple of thousand square miles of space?" Ripp asked.

"It's probably more than the people in this hab will ever need," Rome replied, "but that's not the point. If we're physically cut off from the AI, we'll have gained something important we need: time. How much easier would you sleep if you knew that the big, bad eraser program couldn't grab you?"

"What if the AI is stuck in here with us?" Hino asked.

"That would be terrible luck," Rome said. "And if it happened that way, we're probably toast. The probability is very low, though. You know there are thousands of mainframes out there. Do the math. We'd have to be incredibly unlucky to be caught in the one it calls home."

Jarrien had been nodding along, but now spoke up. "What if it has pieces of itself planted in different mainframes and it's capable of becoming the full-blown AI if it gets cut off?"

"If it thought of this particular approach, we might be screwed," Rome said. "But we might not. I'm assuming an AI using the resources of one mainframe might be less daunting than one with the entire network to draw from. We might be able to go toe to toe with it… especially if it doesn't locate us quickly. But yeah, I'm betting it won't come to that. At worst, I hope we just have to sweep up some automated programs and defensive ware."

"I'd say your worst case scenario is the most likely the minimum we'll face. This AI is a right bastard," Hino replied. "And I would be really, really surprised if it hadn't left at least some nasty surprises in each mainframe."

"So be it, then. If we have to fight, we'll fight. I assume you can sweep up uncontrolled automated programs quickly enough," Rome said.

Jarrien nodded. "We should be able to."

"Then what are we waiting for? We need to get started as soon as possible."

Jarrien didn't answer, instead, she turned, tiredly, to Hino. "When is Colorado Springs going to begin?"

"In half an hour or so."

"All right. Let's watch how that goes, then get some sleep." She turned back to Rome. "We'll take a decision about this once we feel human again."

Chapter 10

Copernicus – Tau Ceti II

Mira Heine looked around the bridge with distaste. She'd never approved of the Tau Ceti Navy. What need did a colony at peace with its neighbors — and whose nearest neighbor, incidentally, was twelve light-years away — need with armed and armored ships? At interstellar scales resource wars were ridiculous, and anything else inefficient. The ships were just a remnant of a more barbaric age, a time when people were incapable of measured thought.

Worse, the last time she'd been on board had been a humiliating experience which started with the Engine Test Facility evading their grasp and fleeing to a new system and ended with Mira herself being removed from the ship in question in disgrace.

That brought a smile to her lips. Her first official act as Representative of the People had been to order a thorough investigation of the captain who'd humiliated her. Like most regular citizens, his mindnet activity had thrown up several instances where his behavior was not up to society's expectations… and he'd been placed on indefinite leave pending an administrative decision.

Mira had been delighted to learn that the man had subsequently resigned from the Navy and disappeared into the wilds of Cassius Station. She considered it an excellent end to an unworthy career. As far as Mira was concerned, being on Cassius was as good as being dead. She didn't even consider the station part of the civilized galaxy.

The captain of this vessel, an older warship called the *Buran*, looked up at her with the proper respect. He pulled a headset off and spoke: "The ground team is in position. They're awaiting your authorization. As am I."

She paused for a moment to consider the crossroads that Tau Ceti had arrived at. Even though any thinking person would realize her actions were for the benefit of the majority, her detractors would call her a tyrant. They would say she used the power of her office to destroy everything that office was supposed to protect.

Unfortunately, when the office began protecting the wrong things, and especially the wrong kind of people, it became her obligation to redefine its responsibilities. Once the toxic elements of Tau society were under control, and peaceful coexistence assured going forward, she would renounce all power and let the civilian courts judge her with the results in full view.

Even so, she hesitated another moment before giving the order.

Finally, she nodded. "Proceed."

The ship shuddered as the main engines came online.

"Control," The captain spoke into his microphone, "please open the main hangar doors. There are three ships exiting: the *Buran*, the *Sympos*, and the *Grader*."

A silence ensued as the captain listened to the reply. "We don't have time to wait for you to get authorization through the chain of command. Representative Heine is on board. I'll put her on, and she will authorize."

Mira gave the order, fully expecting the young man on the other end to challenge her and force her flotilla to blast their way out of the hangar, thereby destroying any illusion that the coup would be nothing more than an administrative adjustment without any associated violence.

He surprised her. "I suppose there's no harm in it, then," the controller said. "Have a good flight." The man sounded more than just unconcerned. He sounded bored.

Mira was stunned. "Is that how we manage security?" she asked the captain.

"Well, you said it yourself many times: we have no enemies. And a navy without enemies is not a navy at a high level of alert." He chuckled. "No one imagines that a Representative would overthrow the government. Hell, a representative is supposed to *be* the government."

"That's because we've never had a Representative who actually looks at things objectively and addresses the important issues. My predecessors have been content to shepherd our continuous decline. We can't afford to do that anymore. If people keep trying to live outside the norms that society prefers, it will break us apart."

The *Buran* accelerated into the atmosphere. Within minutes, Mira was back in orbit — something she hated.

Unfortunately, she had to be here. The ground strikes were important, and Gabriel's crew would seize the council building, the actual seat of power, soon. That would be an important symbolic victory, since Copernicus was the location of all power on the planet. But her own place was in space, commanding the navy — and with it, the power to strike at any point on the surface of Tau Ceti II — as well as coordinating everything that happened on the surface.

It would send the message loud and clear: Copernicus was just one city. Mira was thinking of the entire planet.

"Commander Zun reports that the council building is in their hands. He says everyone is confused about what's going on, but that no one resisted and no one was hurt."

Relief flooded through Mira. The people in the central

government were misguided. Many of them actively opposed her. But they were part of the tiny minority of people on Tau Ceti that actually cared enough about the lives of the people to get involved. They were probably the most valuable citizens of the entire system. "What about Representative Ericsson?"

"She wasn't present."

"Dammit. All right, get us into position. I want to transmit in five minutes."

Mira brooded. Though Sintia Ericsson's capture wasn't critical to the success of the operation, it would have been much better to have her in custody. Mira disagreed with her Senior Representative about nearly everything — she suspected that Ericsson would have happily allowed the exodus of half the population of Tau Ceti to populate other stars in the name of freedom — which meant that having her under control would limit the propagation of unfortunate ways of thinking.

Humanity couldn't afford to return to the kind of thinking that had wiped out the population of Earth, leaving only a wasteland populated by the electronic ghosts of the original inhabitants. That was what Ericsson wanted to allow. And the first step was to permit the Sextus Colony to continue existing.

Worse still, though everyone knew — through a probe that had arrived a few months before — that the Sextus colony existed, no one knew where it was. Even if their coup succeeded perfectly, they would have a long search ahead of them before they could take any action. Just sifting through the rumors would take weeks.

The captain nodded and counted down from five on his fingers. When he reached zero, Mira looked straight into the camera and spoke.

"People of Tau Ceti, this is Representative Mira Heine."

She paused for effect, and to let people understand who it

was that had overridden every entertainment feed on the planet.

"I'm sorry to have to interrupt your day, but I deemed this announcement important enough to make a full-planet broadcast both necessary and desirable.

"What you need to know is that a team of experts and I have decided that the current state of the Tau Ceti government is unacceptable. Per the terms of the planet's Founding Charter, all simulated environments beyond a certain complexity would be forbidden in perpetuity. The reasons for this don't have to be explained to any thinking citizen — after all, the horrible lesson of what happened on Earth is still fresh in our minds.

"And yet, the government of Tau Ceti has allowed a colony to be formed — the colony named Sextus — which not only tolerates certain forbidden technological paths, but is apparently working within them. We have been able to confirm that the artificial entity named Emily Plair that was brought illegally back from Earth has joined the expedition.

"That fact alone would be bad enough, but we also have strong reason to believe that the entity in question is not safely locked into electronic storage. She isn't even confined to the settlement's computers. We believe that the entity has been inserted into a printed human body.

"The government's reaction to this suspicion was to say that it wasn't their problem. That the citizens in question were asking to leave Tau Ceti, and therefore were no longer beholden by our Charter.

"This is a spurious argument at best. After all, these citizens were still in Tau Ceti space when they were doing all of this. They are our responsibility.

"Even worse, they can affect us adversely from their current position. If they were using this technology and exploring these avenues when it was forbidden, when they were working in secret, how much more dangerous are they now that they can act openly?

"The answer is that they are much more dangerous. They have had months to continue to develop their technology. And what better way to employ it than to return here and use our already existing planet and resources to create their abomination of a colony? Why suffer on some miserable ball of ice or some burning hellhole when they have a perfectly pleasant planet ready for the taking.

"You can rest assured that they are coming for us. Perhaps not today. Perhaps not tomorrow. But it is the only path that makes sense.

"They know the current government, weak as it is, will not do much to oppose the supplanting of our way of life with this one that is utterly anathema to us, that violates our Charter — the Charter that has given us centuries of peace, prosperity and comfort — and the very core of our way of life.

"They are right. The previous government would have simply allowed them to do whatever they wanted — in the name of freedom, of course. But this is something I will not permit. We have replaced the previous regime in order to gain access to the forces necessary to find the rogue colony and stop its expansion. That mission begins today, as does the strengthening of the mechanics of Charter compliance.

"What does that mean to you, the citizen of Tau?"

She gave her audience a moment to consider the question.

"It means very little on a day-to-day basis. You may continue to live your life as you always have. There will be no increase of policing on regular citizens. Everything will remain open. No gatherings will be prohibited and no events cancelled, unless such gatherings or events are specifically aimed at resisting the regime change. We're not here to change your lifestyle or force you to live a different way.

“My only objective is that everyone on Tau Ceti II can live their life the way they’ve chosen to do so. The way our founders would have wanted.

“Thank you.”

The captain’s gesture told her that the transmission had ended. “That was excellent,” the man said.

“We’ll see how they take it,” Mira replied. “I’m mainly worried about the professional protestors in Humanity Park. They’re very sincere, but they’re also very easy to manipulate.”

The captain said nothing about that, but Mira suspected he knew the truth: just under two years before, Mira herself had driven the protestors into a frenzy. They’d stormed the Council Building and destroyed a mainframe in which the Council had been allowing a simulated human to shelter. She would have preferred for the council to destroy the computer and the offending entity as soon as they became aware of its existence. That would have reinforced Mira’s belief in the system.

Instead, she’d been forced to take action herself, a decision which had put her on the path to overthrowing a regime which had presided over centuries of peace.

It seemed to her that every year of those centuries pressed down on her.

She sighed. “All right. Let’s achieve the stationary orbit over Copernicus.”

Mira sat on the free flight chair on the bridge. She wondered whether the captain knew how important what they were doing was… or whether the man had joined because, like many other under-promoted officers, he was simply bored.

The captain seemed to sense her gaze on the back of his neck. He turned and removed one headphone. “Commander Zun is reporting again. He reports that his ground forces have achieved control of the central coordination system for the nanofactories."

Mira grinned. "That means we control the production capacity for the entire planet. No one is going to be building weapons to attack us with."

"They were undefended? Did no one expect people to go after that?" the captain asked. "Doesn't seem like a tactically sound decision."

"It's like the Navy itself. Tau's defenses are designed to repel an attack from out of the system. When the colony was set up, the main question people had was whether there were unfriendly aliens in the galaxy." She laughed. "That was what they wanted people to believe, anyway. I personally think they were more concerned about one of the other colonies attacking us."

"I've been to the Wolf system," the captain replied. "Back when I was flying passenger ships in the interstellar service. People are strange there. I wouldn't be surprised if they got it into their heads to mount a strike. I can't say anything about the other colonies but..." he shrugged. "They're different."

"In any event," Mira replied. "It's working in our favor. No one expected the strike to come from within — and even less from someone with all the access codes, a trusted member of government."

"We're not expecting any resistance, then?"

"The only resistance the people of Tau Ceti can really muster at this point is purely verbal."

As if on cue, a moment later, a young woman at a console in the bridge suddenly straightened and turned around to face them. "Captain, the meteor defense platform above the south pole has opened fire on the *Sympos*. The ship's captain reported heavy damage with a second barrage on the way. And then..."

the woman's demeanor failed and she sobbed. "And then I lost contact with him."

The captain's expression barely changed. The only evidence Mira saw that the news had reached him was a slight smile.

She didn't ask whether he was smiling because his life had finally gotten interesting or because Mira had completely misread the tactical situation.

"Get the missile defenses online pronto," the captain said to another crewman at another desk. Then he faced the woman again. "Call engineering and tell them to check the status of every meteor defense satellite. I assume only one of them is under enemy control, but tell them to check if any are pointed our way."

He sat back on his chair and steepled his fingers as he awaited responses. His eyes met Mira's. "Don't worry Representative. We'll get you home safely. Meteor defense platforms are extremely powerful, but they're aimed outward, with severe limits to their capacity to fire towards the planet. We're diving into a lower orbit. We'll be fine."

Mira's grip on the arms of her chair had turned her knuckles white. She wasn't afraid, just angry. Angrier than she'd ever been before. "We'd better, Captain. Because I want to be alive to find whoever did this and roast them over a slow fire."

The captain chuckled and turned back to his crew.

Chapter 11

Earth – Planetwide Simulation

Hino found Jarrien staring out the window again. He put a hand on her shoulder, lightly.

"I knew you'd come looking for me," Jarrien said.

"Someone had to. Would you have preferred Ripp?"

"I was actually expecting Rome. He really wants to push this forward."

Hino nodded. "He does. And he's not shy about it. He's terrified we'll be caught if the AI has time to think. But I don't believe he's doing it for himself."

"For Emily?"

Again Hino nodded. "He's afraid to fail her."

"He already failed her when he brought her back here." Jarrien slapped her hand against the wall. "What did he expect to find? A paradise? He was the one who gave us the push that destroyed our society. Why was he expecting to find anything but a wasteland? Remembering what people were doing with their unlimited power, I sometimes think the AI might have had a point when it decided to erase us all and start over. Look how beautiful everything is without messy humans ruining it and changing the programming. Do we really need orange skies and hundred-foot surfing waves?"

"Don't say that," Hino said.

Jarrien laughed. "And to think I used to be the worst of all. I wanted to burn the world down."

"I remember. The blue hair. Still looks good."

"But now, I feel like I'm the one who has to keep everything together. And just when I started accepting the fact that the

AI was getting less aggressive in its attempts to find and exterminate us, just when I'm getting used to being the responsible adult, along comes Rome again. Last time he broke our relationship with the simulation... this time he wants to destroy the network itself."

"You know that's not what he wanted. Either time," Hino replied gently.

"Of course I know. But that doesn't change the fact that he's doing it."

"I guess it doesn't. So what are we going to do?"

She sighed. "The worst part is that he's right. Hell, if he wasn't here, I have a feeling this exact same thing would have occurred to me once I got over my denial."

"What denial?" Hino retorted. "You're the only reason we're alive. You've been doing the best you can to keep us that way. I don't see you in denial."

"I'm not much for talking about what's going on in my head," Jarrien said. "But I'm serious about the denial thing. You know why I've had us in deep hiding for the past couple of months?"

"Because it's suicidal to attack the AI?"

"No. Well, yes, but not only that. It's denial. I've managed to convince myself that the search pattern and the way its acting has become less aggressive. That it's lost interest in us." She held up a hand. "Yes, I know it's a stupid thing to think. Logically, the AI caught everyone it could catch quickly and, since it knows we're out there but doesn't know where, it has been doing the logical thing in systematically looking everywhere, tearing the code apart line by line until it can find us. It's smart enough to know that time is on its side... but to me, it feels like the AI has gotten less aggressive. So I've half convinced myself that it's sending us a message: if you don't mess with me, I won't mess with you."

"We've all been getting complacent," Hino said.

"Yeah. But I'm the one you look to for decisions. I can't get complacent, because that will make us all dead." She sighed. "And now Rome is calling for action. And his plan makes total sense. Except I don't want to do it. My entire soul is screaming 'don't do it, if we just keep our heads down, we'll be okay.' And it kills me to know that no matter what I do, I could be letting you down."

Hino chuckled. "Well, you wanted to be a leader."

"Like hell," she replied. "I wanted to be a criminal. I wanted to break the rules." She tugged on her hair. "And flaunt it. I wanted to make a better life for myself without even stopping to think about whether it would mess up the world completely. I wanted to do things no one else could, and do them just to be better than everyone else. I was not in the market to become a mother hen."

"People don't choose their destinies," Hino replied. "It's what's inside that counts. You were lost, and then," he waved around the room, "all this happened, and you saw that if you didn't do something, everyone would die. So you acted and saved a whole bunch of us. You might not have wanted that, but it was who you are."

"Dammit. Well, since you're so full of wisdom today, what should we do now? Do we let Rome push us? Or do we keep surviving like we have?"

"You already know the answer to that. And I already know what you're going to tell Rome."

"Oh, yeah. What am I going to say?"

"You're going to do what he suggested. And I know it because if you were going to say no, you'd already have gone out there and had it out with him. The reason you're here is because you're putting off doing something you're afraid of."

"Dammit Hino," she said, pushing herself away from the wall. "Now you're making me feel guilty for putting it off. Come on, let's do this."

Shaking his head, Hino followed her back towards the lounge where he'd left Rome and Emily.

***

A week after they took the decision, they were ready to go.

Rome looked around the room. He saw determination on Jarrien and Hino's faces. Ripp seemed quietly approving. Emily's cheeks glistened with tears, but when he turned to her, she didn't try to dissuade him. She simply stepped forward and hugged him. "Thank you for doing this," she said.

He was stunned. When he first suggested that he was the best candidate to go out into the newly isolated Vancouver mainframe, openly inviting attack from whatever nastiness the AI had waiting for them inside their demesne, Emily had tried to convince him not to go. She'd cried and argued until he reminded her that, of all the people in the habitat, he was the only one who had a flesh-and-blood version of himself that would continue living if he was unceremoniously erased. He hadn't mentioned that there was a flesh-and-blood Emily out there as well… and also a very creepy AI which had started out as yet another version of Emily. All he'd told her was that she'd been copied a few times, but didn't tell her the copies were extant and quite alive. That would only have confused things.

That was when she began surprising him.

"You're right," she said through her tears.

He was about to press his argument when he realized what she'd said. "What?"

"You're right. I hate you for it, because I don't know what I'd do if you got erased. But you're right. The reason I'm pissed is that I wish you'd let me go with you. But I also understand that doing it that way would only make it more dangerous for us than doing it alone. Dammit, I hate this."

Then she wiped away her tears and attended every meeting in which they planned how Rome was going to probe the defenses.

Now, though she'd been unable to keep herself from breaking down, Emily was encouraging him. Not in the catty 'You'll pay for this later,' way he'd seen so often from other girls, but with her heart behind it.

"I love you," he said, and realized that, after all they'd been through, it was true again.

"I know," she replied. "Just as well as you know how much I love you." They embraced briefly before Emily pushed him away. "Now get this over with so we can go on with our lives."

"Ready?" Ripp said.

Rome nodded.

The room blurred and, a heartbeat later, he was outside again.

His first sensation wasn't the heat — even though it was quite warm here, far from Jarrien's idea of room temperature, which seemed to be just above the freezing point of nitrogen — or any anxiety about the danger inherent in the mission: it was the colors.

The building next to him was painted yellow. The sky was a deep, cloudless blue. A red bus was parked — empty of occupants — on the side of the street. Trees, brown and green, lined the street.

After so much time surrounded by monotonous grey, the sudden riot of color hammered his senses.

He smiled, taking it all in, as he walked down the middle of a broad avenue surrounded by skyscrapers and fast-food restaurants. Jarrien's team had dropped him in the densest part of Vancouver's downtown with instructions to enter a shop and make a purchase at an automated counter.

There was no real reason for that, other than to alert the AI of human activity of a kind that wouldn't have been possible without someone walking along the streets of the city. Jarrien was convinced that this would draw a response where the monster had failed.

They all — especially Rome — hoped that their estimate about the AI's capacity to act within the isolated Vancouver mainframe was correct. Otherwise, he would find himself in extremely deep trouble.

But in the meantime, he could, for the first time since he'd come to Earth in an avatar that really allowed him to immerse himself, stop and smell the proverbial roses, even if it was only for a few minutes while he walked around looking for a likely retail outlet.

He savored the feeling. Few people on Tau had had the pleasure of experiencing the simulation, but that wasn't as important to him as what the simulation portrayed. The buildings, streets and shops were not just made-up elements of a game universe; they were faithful representations of how Earth had looked when the simulation was created. Not one inch of the world's background had been intentionally changed until Jarrien and other hackers had begun to do so. This simulation was the closest thing humanity had to a connection with the planet as it had been five hundred years before.

In its turn, that was a direct link to what Earth had been like before humans took to the stars. Many of the buildings around him predated the interstellar era, even though it was difficult for Rome to identify which ones. They all looked positively ancient to his eyes.

They were also much too big. He knew Vancouver was a minor city on Earth, and he'd been to several cities that dwarfed it in just a few hundred kilometers of driving through Asia, but even a small city like this was much more densely packed than anything one would find at Tau Ceti. Copernicus itself, the capital and main population center, had only one tall building of note outside of its spaceport: the Council Building. To think that people had once been packed into towers like the ones around him, towers twice and three times the height of anything in Tau, made him shudder.

That, more than anything else, gave him the sense of connecting to the deep past, when the need for people to live close to their place of employment dictated high-density housing… and created these clifflike bird cages. History classes had explained the drivers, but nothing prepared you for the reality.

Curiously, he felt the height of the buildings much more intensely than he had in Beijing, even though these structures were much smaller than the Asian colossi. Perhaps those had simply suffered from an excess of scale, being so big he couldn't really wrap his mind around them. Or maybe it was just that he hadn't been able to walk between the Chinese buildings at ground level, and that diminished their power.

He shuddered. The sense of the enormous weight of construction materials looming over him caused his heart to speed up.

"They're just pixels," he told himself, but it didn't help.

So he brought his eyes back to the street and concentrated on finding a suitable shop.

There. An ice cream shop. Rome had eaten plenty of ice cream in his life, but he'd been reliably informed that the stuff they sold on Tau Ceti II had the same relationship to acceptable ice cream as… well, as this weatherless simulation did to being out in the real world.

Bewildered by the array of flavors, some of whose names were utterly indecipherable — Rocky Road? — Rome simply selected a few fruit flavors at random on the automated vending interface and proceeded through the sales menu, finally arriving at the payment option.

"Emily Plair," he told the machine. "Authorization code 52261."

"Authorized," the machine replied. "One moment please."

A small door in the front of the vending unit opened up, and a tub full of ice cream slid down a shallow chute.

He picked it out of the enclosure and wondered whether the simulation went to all the trouble of simulating the production of the product itself. He knew that it had been programmed that way to make people feel comfortable with their new digital world. But did the illusion go as deep as actually combining the ingredients and building an ice-cream bowl deep within the bowels of a machine that no one would ever open to check on? He didn't know, and the only way to find out would be to check the code line by line, or dismantle the machine and try to make it work.

Maybe if he got really bored…

Meanwhile, he had nothing to do but wait to see if his transaction — using Emily's account — had gotten the attention of the AI.

The restaurant was a square room with bright white walls and red tables of some sort of cheap-looking plastic surrounded by blue chairs anchored to the floor.

Every table was empty, so he chose one beside the window and stared out at Vancouver, wondering what it would have been like to be there for real as opposed to a simulation where the wind never blew. No one inside would ever know. Not even with the simulation working perfectly, especially not with the sense buffers tuned to keep you from feeling too much pain or too much sadness or whatever. He wondered what it might have been like to actually live in Vancouver back when it was a city where you could get rained on, or where it could snow.

Would he have been eating ice cream as he watched drenched commuters walk past? Or would it have been one of the endless list of coffee drinks on the menu?

He would never know, any more than he knew what he'd drink in a Roman tavern.

His dish held three scoops of ice cream, almost perfectly round. One was pink, one blue, one pale orange. Easy enough to guess at, since his best friend was a bit of a real-food nut: strawberry, blueberry and peach, respectively. He wondered if there was any real fruit in these.

Then he realized what he was doing. The sense of being in ancient times was overcoming his reason. The real thing to wonder was whether this shop had used any fruit in the ice cream before it was digitized.

Again, it would only require looking into the code: if it had used real fruit, the programmers would have simulated real fruit.

Rome sank his spoon into the pink ball. It felt exactly the same as eating ice cream did on Tau Ceti. The spoon entered slowly, revealing the tiny holes of air bubbles. He bent down to smell it and found it even smelled like what he'd expect on Tau, vaguely sweet in an unidentifiable sort of way. It even smelled cold, somehow.

He tasted it. It tasted just like Tau Ceti ice cream did. Granted, the strawberry flavoring — or was it real fruit? — was slightly different from what he was used to, but not in a fundamental way. This was ice cream just as he knew it with a slightly different flavor.

And yet, a woman he'd known — a woman he'd loved —

insisted that Tau ice cream wasn't real. She'd never gotten around to showing him what she considered real, in their few months on Cassius Station, but he expected it to be much different to what he was used to. To be fair to her, every time she'd suggested a food was better in the wild region of Cassius than on Tau, it had proven to be much, much different.

So maybe the food in the simulation was, in a way, the precursor to the safe, bland Tau diet, with only illegal stuff such as they'd encountered in Beijing being notable for a more intense taste experience.

At least the ice cream in front of him was pleasant enough. It reminded him of his childhood, which was the only time in his life he'd really had much interest in it.

The view out the window hadn't changed. Apart from the slight flutter of leaves in the soft breeze, nothing moved on the street. It was unnatural, but peaceful all at once. More like looking into a piece of high-rez digital art than through a window.

Rome finished his food, tossed the container in the appropriate receptacle. He smirked when he read that he was supposed to recycle the plastics. As if the simulation had a pollution problem. Then he stood beside the trash can for a long time.

Due to security concerns, he had no way to contact the team in Jarrien's bunker. They were watching him through feeds stolen from the code of the simulation itself, but there was no direct link between them that could be intercepted by the AI and followed back to their hiding place. So they could intervene instantly if he was under threat… but they couldn't warn him about anything.

Of course, Rome could just speak aloud any message he wanted to give them, but that would alert the AI to the presence of observers… and with the search area narrowed to a single mainframe, that would put the crew at enormous risk.

So he finally shrugged and exited the ice cream parlor. They had expected an attack from the AI to happen much sooner… but apparently it had decided, just like when they first entered the simulation, that he and Emily were to proceed unmolested. Why that might be, he had no clue, but he didn't doubt Jarrien's version of what had happened here. Something had eliminated everyone but her small band. Her explanation fit every observable fact.

He'd walked three blocks between glass-fronted buildings when Jarrien materialized to his right, walking in stride with him without missing a beat.

As he gawked at her, he felt fingers intertwining with his own and turned to see Emily on his left side.

"Hi," she said brightly. She smiled, and his heart skipped a beat. He'd almost forgotten how perfect her smile was. Not because she'd smiled infrequently over the past few days, but because his guilt at not knowing what he felt for her made him turn away from it. Now he looked straight at it and enjoyed it.

Emily wasn't one of those women with pouty lips or voluptuous beauty. Her lips were thin, and her skin pale and freckled. There was nothing overbuilt or full-bodied about her: she was delicate in everything from bone structure to hair. That was a dark blonde that fell straight to her shoulders.

The smile lit up the entire city.

"What are you two doing here?" he asked. "I didn't see any sign of the AI. We should probably have waited for it."

Jarrien answered: "You came under a couple of code-cleaning attacks. Automated, low-level stuff which we deflected and tracked back to their origin. We've deactivated them. And after a while, we got bored and decided you were right. There's nothing here."

"Besides," Emily said. "Jarrien came in here armed with the biggest, baddest defensive code they had. She has it armed and ready to deploy in her backpack or something."

"You don't carry code in a backpack," Rome replied.

Emily shrugged. "You got my point, didn't you?"

Rome laughed. "Fair enough. And you?"

"Did you actually think I was going to let her come here without me?"

"We're not sure what to think," Jarrien said. "On one hand, this is working perfectly. Very close to our best-case scenario. On the other hand... well, when was the last time the best-case scenario for anything came close to reality?"

"They worry too much," Emily said.

"Most of us got wiped out. We have reason to worry," Jarrien replied.

"So why did you come?" Rome asked. "Why didn't you just pull me back?"

"Because we wanted to see if a different piece of bait would work. The AI ignored both of you before, but I'm absolutely sure it wouldn't ignore me. So here I am. Well, me and my backpack full of code." She looked around, her blue hair sailing around her. Rome knew she'd modified her visual feed so that she could see much more than just the Vancouver street around her. She would see hidden actions, running programs and sectors of particularly dense memory use. "And I see absolutely no sign of... well, anything. Apparently you were absolutely right about cutting us off from the network." She smirked. "Or the AI, which, as you know, is much smarter than we are, is just waiting to see where we disappear to so it can round us all up at once."

"But you don't think so," Rome said.

"No. I don't. I think this caught the AI by surprise, just as it caught us by surprise when you suggested it. We live inside the simulation. We don't normally think about acting on the infrastructure itself. Hell, even when I used the airships before, I was only thinking about recon, to use the vehicles as an extra set of cameras in a place I couldn't go. I would never have thought of attacking the network physically… because I just don't think that way. Since I was born, I learned to attack problems of a purely in-simulation nature. You don't solve those by going outside. You might break the rules of the simulation, but the outside world doesn't matter. The AI must be locked in the same thought pattern. No matter how smart you are, you might not be able to make that leap."

Jarrien cocked her head and her eyes lost focus for a moment. Then she snapped back to the here and now. "Just got word from Ripp. He says we need to get back to the facility right now. Here, take my hands."

Rome and Emily did so and they felt the now-familiar sensation of the world disappearing around them as they teleported through secret back-code channels back to Jarrien's facility in the sky.

Chapter 12

Copernicus – Tau Ceti II

The dark basement room around them exploded with cheering. Representative Sintia Ericsson simply shook her head with sadness.

Such a waste, she thought.

But she wasn't going to say that. Not today. It wasn't the fault of the people around them that they'd been turned from teachers and students into an impromptu resistance. None of them had chosen that path; they'd been forced onto it against their better judgement.

Let them celebrate that they'd shot down an enemy ship. They would need the memory and the symbol in the dark days ahead as the coup consolidated its power.

"Congratulations," she told Kinita Ooblah. "That was even more effective than I expected."

"If only we'd had access to a few more satellites, we'd have knocked all their ships out of the fucking sky," Kinita growled. "And then I'd have made it rain missiles on the Council Building." Her dark brown eyes glared out at the world from within a forest of wrinkles, and her greying hair and bleached skin displayed every one of the seventy-nine years that her passion belied. She snapped her fingers. "If we'd managed that… insurrection over."

"True," Sintia replied. "But we didn't. And it's only a question of time before they track this back to the Institute. You need to cover your tracks."

"They might trace it back to the Institute, but they'll never know who was actually responsible."

Sintia sighed. "That doesn't matter. They'll just close the entire university."

The students — a half-dozen young men and women in their twenties — had stopped celebrating and were listening to the conversation.

"Can they do that?" A wide-eyed girl near them said. "I mean… it's the Institute."

Sintia suppressed her smile. She didn't want to give the girl the impression that this wasn't a serious situation, but more than that, she didn't want the girl to think Sintia was laughing at her. "Representative Heine has taken it upon herself to overthrow the legitimate government of the Tau Ceti system. A university, no matter how important it might seem to those of you who love education, won't give her a second's hesitation."

Kinita stepped forward and addressed the students. "The university isn't what's important here," she told them. "It's just a building full of rooms that are empty most of the time. What matters is the knowledge we have in here," she tapped her temple, "and the love we have for freedom and the right to grow. What these people want is to create a culture of mindless followers. They want exactly the opposite of what this building stands for. Of what we stand for. We've always wanted to teach people to think for themselves, and to decide for themselves. When decisions are being made for you by the majority, or by a central government which wants nothing to change… that's when it's time to fight back."

"Do you think the people who created the new colony were right?" one of the male students asked. He was small and pale, probably not quite twenty.

Kinita sighed. "Their ideals were right on. But I wish they'd found a way to build on those ideals here in Tau Ceti. They had every right to leave, of course… but I can't help but wonder if Mira Heine would have been so bold if those people who left had been here to try to stop her. We lost a lot of technical knowledge — most of the really specialized scientists in the system — when the Engine Test Facility left Tau space. Knowledge that could not only have pretty much allowed us to hijack the entire Tau infrastructure, but also led the student body against these usurpers. Hell, if six students and one eighty-year-old teacher just called back from retirement can blow up a third of their navy, imagine what the rest of the faculty — the active faculty — would have done to them. The whole thing would have been over before lunch."

Sintia spoke. "Well, we don't have them, so what we need to do now is figure out what happens next."

"What happens next is that you need to get out of here," Kinita told her. "Even before they figure out we are the only people who can shoot missiles by hacking an automated system in orbit at such short notice, they'll remember that the last people to oppose Heine were based in this university."

"Hell. I came here because I had nowhere else to go. If I leave, I'll show up on some security camera or other."

"Not necessarily," Kinita said. "Let me make a call."

***

"I remember you," Sintia said. "You were on the *Unity*."

The man was thin and white-skinned, with blond hair that stood out from his head, a look that seemed to belong on a younger man. Sintia estimated he was in his mid-thirties, perhaps a well-maintained forty. He nodded. "My name is Stell. Stell Garn."

"You're one of Rome Permek's friends," she said. They'd stashed her in an unused classroom on the top floor of the institute while they waited for Stell's arrival. Dust covered old desks and chairs, and motes, disturbed by their conversation, danced in the air.

"More relevant to this particular discussion is that I'm one of Kinita Ooblah's former students, and she called in an old debt and a couple of decades interest. But that's not why I'm helping you."

"Oh," Sintia raised an eyebrow. "And why would that be?"

"I'm helping you because these bastards put Ashur Nartiya in a cell for no reason."

"You're lucky they didn't catch Permek."

Stell smirked. "Rome? I suspect if they tried to touch a hair on Rome's head, they would find that every automated system in Tau Ceti would suddenly attempt to kill them."

"Why do you say that?" Sintia asked.

"I can't tell you. Hell, I'm not even a hundred percent certain about it myself. But if I had to bet, that's the way I'd lean. Even more to the point, Rome knows that he can't come anywhere near the planet in the current political climate. If I had to guess, he's making supply runs to help the new colony — although how he knows where it actually is is beyond me."

"Fair enough. How can you help me?" Sintia said.

"I can make you invisible," Stell replied.

"Sounds like a neat trick. I always wanted to be able to sneak everywhere and assassinate my political rivals without being seen."

Stell deflated a bit. "Not actually invisible," he said. "But I can make every camera between this building and the habitation block in which I live look the other way as soon as we walk towards it. And once you're in a hab block… they will never find you there short of going house by house and busting down doors."

"He can do it," Kinita said. "And you don't need to worry

about Stell. He's not the kind to try to get you drunk and have his way with you." She smirked.

"I don't get drunk that easily anymore," Sintia replied.

"Oh, he'll get you drunk, but he's not interested in the pleasures of the flesh."

"Ah."

She turned to Stell, expecting him to have turned beet-red at this frank discussion of his sexual proclivities, but instead, she found him regarding the old teacher with a fond expression. "And I thought you would have mellowed with the years," he told her.

"Me? Hah. At my funeral, I plan to get up and curse the people who attended for believing I would let myself die."

"Sounds about right. How much time do we have to set up the hack?"

"Don't bullshit me, Stell. You've had the cameras hacked since you were a student. So if you don't want to end up in the cell next to Nartiya, you need to get moving."

"Give me a second. Do you have a student Panorama?" Stell said.

"Don't use one of ours," Kinita replied. "We're about to get all the heat we can handle, and they will definitely crack into the student Panoramas. Use the black market one you brought with you just in case."

"How did you know…"

"Some people never change, Stell. You, like me, are one of those people."

Sintia watched Stell punching instructions into a tablet that was anything but a standard Panorama Screen. Those were smooth and rounded. This one was black and angular, and looked like it had been built from pieces of scrap metal. She realized she was holding her breath, and forced herself to breathe normally. But it was tough. This man literally held her future in his hands.

"There," he said a moment later.

"How long do we have?" Sintia asked.

He gave her a smirk. "What kind of binarist do you think I am? A general blackout is suspicious. The cameras will look away just as we pass, and anyone looking into it will just think it's part of the regular sweep. We can take as long as we want." He turned to Kinita Ooblah. "I'm doing this because I want to," he told her. "So whatever debt I owed you still stands."

Kinita Ooblah laughed. "If you manage to keep Sintia out of that woman's clutches, it's I who will be in your debt."

Sintia followed Stell out the door, down four flights of steps, and through the main hall. Though they passed numerous security cameras, Stell didn't flinch, and just walked confidently past the emplacements.

They emerged into Humanity Park, and Sintia was surprised by the bright sunlight. It had been dark inside the dingy classroom — someone must have dimmed the smartglass to keep them hidden — and Sintia had adjusted her expectations of the outside world. Besides, after the day she had, it must be late afternoon or early evening.

But the sun was still high in the sky.

"What time is it?" she asked Stell.

He turned back to her a surprised look on his face, and she knew what he was about to ask. Then his expression turned serious and he just nodded. "It's two-forty PM. Also, I have an encrypted info screen at home that I can lend you. I suppose you tossed your Panorama into the reflecting pool?"

"I left it in my office. If people are going to come for our democracy, at least they can be guilted by the fact I, unlike them, have nothing to hide."

"Nice."

"Look," Sintia said nervously. "Not to doubt you, but you're sure that program of yours is working, right?"

Stell grinned. "Of course it's working. Didn't you hear Professor Ooblah? They knew I had this thing, and never managed to do anything about it."

"I don't want to sound ungrateful or anything, but I just think the stakes are a lot higher now than when some student was using the same program to play hooky."

He laughed again. "Oh, I wasn't using it to play hooky. I was sneaking into the institute in the middle of the night."

"What? Why?"

"Promise you won't tell anyone?"

Sintia laughed. "Yeah. I'll broadcast your secrets live on all the government net channels. I trust no one will attempt to track me down, and that you won't turn me in for blabbing."

"All right. I used to sneak in to grow things," Stell said.

Sintia raised an eyebrow. "Some kind of mind-altering mushroom? I know there's a black market for most of the stuff that you can't get from the nanofactories. The stuff that's too dangerous for the public. But wouldn't it be much easier to try to get some of the Cassius-produced drugs? Safer, too, probably."

"Not drugs. Organically grown tomatoes."

"I don't believe you. You risked what… Expulsion? Just for some tomatoes?"

"You wouldn't believe how hard it is to get good tomatoes in this city. And the amount of space allocated to student gardens is ridiculous." His grin widened. "But I didn't do it just for the tomatoes. The tomatoes were right in one of the university gardens. Everyone knew they were there, but no one knew who was breeding them. I actually did it to drive old Sinxi mad. She knew I was up to something, but she couldn't guess what it was.

I was a student hero. The mere fact that the situation existed would have been enough to get me laid three times a day, every day, if I'd been of the sort to enjoy men or women."

"If not that, why, then?"

"Just knowing they were all looking and they couldn't catch me was enough." His grin disappeared. "And before you say it, the people looking for me were the very best of the best. The only reason they didn't catch me is that they weren't expecting me to use my system to get into the Institute at four in the morning. They knew I was always early to classes, so they were looking for something else. These people are much better than the kind of binarist who ends up working for the government."

Now it was Sintia's turn to smile. "Didn't you work for the government during the *Unity* mission?"

"Oh, come on. You're not seriously comparing a once-in-five-hundred-years mission with the drudgery of government audit work, are you? Come on... one of those things is not like the other. Hell, no one on the *Unity* was a government worker before the mission was announced. And every member of that crew beat out dozens of other candidates to be there. Hell, for a lot of us, the bragging rights around the competitive process were more than enough to get us to sign up."

"Nartiya was a Naval Captain before the mission," Sintia reminded him.

"Yeah. You're right. She was." Stell seemed to deflate at the mention of Nartiya's name, and they walked in silence for some moments.

They'd traversed nearly half the Park at a decent clip — in the direction opposite from the Council Building — and no one had paid them the least bit of attention. Sintia had no illusions that she was some kind of celebrity. Only about one in a hundred citizens of Copernicus ever bothered to tune into the government information broadcasts. And even those would not likely recognize a Representative by sight: their air time was much lower than that of the various ministers and people in charge of specific projects.

Normally, that was a relief. Today, it might save her life.

She looked around again. A couple was sitting in the shade beside a fountain, dipping their feet in the water and talking. Three kids were playing tag along on the grass. Men, women, and children went about their lives.

Not one of them seemed to be concerned that the government had been overthrown by a group which only a small percentage of the population supported.

Where was the outrage, the civic push to make things right?

The same place as Tau Ceti's initiative and push for self-improvement. It was confined to the Institute and other tiny pockets of enlightenment. Most of the population had probably heard Heine's announcement, but a lot of them probably didn't know what it meant. They probably believed that some part of the government had been caught misbehaving and therefore a cleanup had ensued.

The rest would have spent the entire announcement trying to figure out how to get their Panorama Screens back to whatever they were doing before getting hijacked by the official channel.

Now, life was going on as it did every day. No one seemed particularly alert or concerned.

That was exactly what Sintia and Stell needed… and it also made her extremely sad. When the Engine Test Facility had left to found their new colony, she'd respected their bravery but felt they were premature. Surely, in a place with as much respect for civic order as Tau Ceti II, there were enough concerned citizens to ensure that people would push for progress as opposed to stagnation.

Now, she wasn't so sure.

Preoccupied with these thoughts, she barely noticed when they emerged from Humanity Park and entered a residential neighborhood. Hab units surrounded by gardens replaced the manicured lawns and perfectly placed trees of the Park without altering the sense of openness and vegetation.

"We're here," Stell announced, stopping in front of a unit distinguishable from the rest only by the number in front of it. He opened the door, and they entered a standard bachelor hab unit, airy and spacious enough for one person to live in ample comfort.

"That smells delicious," Sintia said. "What is it."

"Dammit," Stell exclaimed. "I forgot that was on the stove. In all the excitement with Professor Ooblah's call..." He disappeared through a door.

A pot clanged in the kitchen. Sintia entered to find Stell probing the contents of a pot with a wooden spoon. Where he'd gotten a wooden spoon on a planet that produced almost everything in nanofactories was something she'd have to ask him about.

He turned to her and smiled. "Your day is going to get much better," he told her. "This is still all right. Tell me, have you ever eaten real cooking? With actual ingredients instead of the stuff the food synthesizers create?"

"I like what the synths build for me. They're smart enough to tailor everything to my taste."

"I'll take that as a no," Stell said.

"Also, synthesizer food is completely devoid of microbes and potential toxins."

"Real food won't make you sick," he replied. "In fact, it will cure you of the desire to ever eat synth again."

"I'm not sure..."

Stell grinned. Sintia felt this wasn't the first time he'd had this conversation. "How about this: I'll prepare the food. When it's done, you can choose whether you'd like to try mine or something from the synth."

"You have a synth… thank goodness," Sintia said.

"Don't act so relieved. You won't be using it. Now get that apron on and help me cook."

They went through the entire arcane ritual. Adding condiments and tasting the food as they went along. The meal consisted of synth pasta — not the standard long round noodles, but flattened ribbons — topped with the sauce Stell had been cooking before he got the call. He told her it contained mushrooms, tomatoes — from his own garden plot — basil, garlic, and carrots. He also informed her that he'd been planning to put meat in it — real meat — but he felt that a first non-synth meal couldn't be too exotic, so he'd changed the recipe for her sake.

"Unless, of course, you prefer to punch something up on the synth," he said with a half-smile.

Sintia breathed. The odor of the sauce was so bewitching that she couldn't have refused even if it had contained meat. Hell, what was the difference? Once you started putting biological stuff in your body, what difference did it make whether it came from a plant or an animal?

They sat down to dinner, and Sintia inhaled. Then, with trepidation, she took the first forkful.

"This is wonderful," she told an expectant Stell. "Is all real food like this?"

He laughed. "Not in the least. Food is only as good as the cook. I'm pretty good, but there are some people right here in Copernicus who will make you think you've died and gone to heaven. It's that good."

"Wow. And synth?"

He shrugged. "It's nutritious enough if you just don't care. You don't have to think about it."

She ate another bite. "I can see why you enjoy this." Then she gave him long look. "Thank you."

"I already told the Professor. I'm doing this because I want to. There's no need to thank me."

"I know. I'm thanking you anyway. Not just for saving me, but for making me cook. I'm a politician, and I know when someone is trying to keep another person's attention away from the matter at hand. You did it with consummate skill." She smiled. "Hell, you would have made an excellent politico."

Stell shuddered. "No way. And besides, I don't have time for that. I have a long night planned." He grinned.

"And what might that be?" she asked. Some men would have given her strange vibes if they'd said that in that tone, but Stell… he just didn't seem interested in her.

"I'm going to find out where they're holding Nartiya. And then I'm going to figure out how to spring her. You can have my bed." Then he laughed. "And I know what you're thinking. But you can relax. Asexuals don't climb into bed with you at night and try anything. We're funny that way."

Sintia stood and met his gaze. "How can I help?"

"Right now, by going to bed. I'll need advice on the political front soon. I'll wake you then."

CHAPTER 13

In Orbit Over Tau Ceti II

Mira reread the report and smiled. Her people still hadn't discovered who sent the initial anonymous tip, but it had proven to be correct. The Sextus Colony, where the rebels had fled after converting the Engine Test Facility into a colony ship and duping the best minds in human space to join them, was located on the third planet in orbit around 61 Virginis.

She'd never heard of the star before, but her eggheads assured her that it was a logical place to put a colony: a nearby star with the characteristics required by human settlement. Not perfect, if she was reading the data about the planet correctly, but good enough for a group of people forced to leave without adequate planning.

"You're sure?" Mira asked.

"No doubt," the tech replied. Her name was Dañi, and she was a woman of about thirty-five with close-cropped brown hair, who had proven to be precise and detail-oriented. Mira found herself warming to the woman's efficiency despite her usual distaste for engineers. "The probe verified the location of the colony on the surface of the planet as well as the position of the Engine Test Facility in orbit."

"What about defenses?"

"None to speak of," Dañi replied. "They appear to be focusing their resources on beating the planet into shape as soon as they can. I don't blame them. The average temperature on the surface right now is —"

"Completely irrelevant. The only thing we need to worry about is how much resistance they can put up. I really couldn't care less if a bunch of traitors are sitting warm by a fire." Mira took a drink of water. She hated being in space, but for some reason, drinking water helped keep her stomach settled. At least her office was in a rotating area of the ship spun for artificial gravity. It had been her main reason for choosing the *Buran* as her flagship. "When will we be ready to jump?"

"We're finishing the process of bringing the mothballed ships up to fighting trim. The flotilla should be assembled within seven days. Once at strength, we'll have four *Moray*-class ships and three smaller vessels for support. Plus the three troop ships, of course, but they don't need much in the way of refurbishment."

"What about the ships I had last time? The *Troubador* and all of those?"

"We haven't been able to locate them." The woman reported this failure in a matter-of-fact way, without any visible sign of nervousness.

Mira was tempted to yell at her for it even though she knew it wasn't the technical team's fault. Space was a big place, and the captains of her previous vessels had made their feelings about Mira perfectly clear. It had been no surprise that they had taken their toys and hidden.

"Will they be a threat?" Mira asked.

"No. To get close enough to attack us, they'd have to get into range of the planetary defense system."

As the loss of the *Sympos* had underlined, the planetary defense system was much stronger than the combined might of the ships in the system. It was designed to hold off as-yet-undiscovered hostile aliens or enormous rogue asteroids. Ship hulls were nothing to its cannons and missiles.

"All right. Thank you."

Mira wasn't alone in her office for long. Gabriel Zun entered.

He had bags under his eyes and shuffled his feet as he entered. His hair, normally combed with patient precision, stood out at weird angles. In the weeks since she'd seen him last, he appeared to have aged a decade. "I hope you had a good flight up," Mira said as he collapsed into a chair.

"Thanks," Zun replied. "The flight was all right, but I haven't slept in three days."

"What's happening? The recruits not working out the way you expected?"

Zun chuckled. He was a fitness freak, and his muscles shook as he laughed. "Oh, they're exactly what I expected… but then I'm a pessimist. They aren't the problem, though. The people on Sextus won't dare fight back with our ships in orbit over them, so all these guys have to be able to do is hold a rifle, wear a uniform, and herd people into the right part of the Engine Test Facility for transport back to Tau."

"So what *is* the problem?"

"Sintia Ericsson. We should have been able to find her a dozen times over by now. We've had three weeks, and she's still missing. The facial recognition software on our surveillance system scans everyone, everywhere. We managed to track her to the Institute." He shrugged. "And then, she never left."

"And I assume you searched the building."

"From top to bottom, with scanners. We checked the original plans and every single work order ever used to modify the building in case there were secret rooms she could have hidden in. We checked the cameras at every point where a water pipe leading into the building might emerge. Nothing." He crossed his legs. "We spoke to the people in the building with her. The cameras worked perfectly to track her into the main hall — they don't have them in the classrooms — and a couple of senior professors admit to having spoken to her. They swear she left the building through the front door."

"But she never appeared on the cameras?"

"Nope. It gets worse. I remembered what you told me about the Institute faculty helping the colonists on the Engine Test Facility, so I didn't trust the senior staff. It was quite easy to round up other people who were in the hall at that moment — students, mainly — and show them a picture of Ericsson. Some of them remembered seeing her, and every one of those said they'd seen her leaving through the door, just like the professors claimed."

Mira said nothing. She knew they hadn't caught the woman, but she also realized it was best to let Zun vent. He wasn't stupid… and she wanted him to come to the only possible conclusion by himself.

Gabriel continued: "She can't be avoiding us alone. I checked, she has zero technical knowledge."

"Do you think she might have disguised herself?"

"The people we asked thought she looked the same, so we went through the images taken during the right time span — with a two-hour buffer on each side — and looked for people who might be similar, or looking the other way. Nothing. It's like she never existed."

"So who's helping her?" Mira asked.

"I think it's the Institute. It's the only explanation that makes any sense."

Mira was disappointed. She knew there was a rogue AI in the Tau system, but no one else seemed to want to face that truth. Not even when the evidence was right in front of them.

"Can we have our binarists check it out? See if anyone has been in the systems?"

"I've already asked the team to look into it." He sighed. "When are you leaving for Sextus?"

"As soon as the ships are ready. Dañi says it will be a week. I'd bet on ten days."

"I hope we've got Ericsson back by then. I'm worried that they might rally around her and hit us when the fleet leaves."

"Have you seen any sign of unrest?" Mira asked. She'd been with the fleet since the operation to overthrow the government. She felt that her presence was the only reason the orbital operations weren't even further behind schedule.

Gabriel shook his head. "None whatsoever. Most people don't even appear to be aware that anything changed." He held up a finger to forestall her. "But before you tell me that I worry too much, you need to remember that most of the people who can actually do anything about the change are walking around free. The only important person we have in custody is Ashur Nartiya. The heads of the Institute, the rest of the crew of the *Unity*, all the former government ministers, and even Ericsson herself are all out there, ready to cause chaos at the drop of a hat. How do we know they aren't planning something?"

"I assume we know that because you have them under surveillance," Mira replied evenly.

"Of course I have them under surveillance. But only the more important people. We can't watch everyone."

"It should be enough to keep the leaders under control."

"I'm also worried about Rome Permek."

"Why?" Mira asked. "The last we heard, he was operating a freighter out of Cassius. He hasn't been to Tau Ceti II in months."

"He's trouble. Who knows what he's getting up to in Cassius. What if he's building a fleet?" Zun asked.

"You're overestimating him. He's just a guy who happened to be in the wrong place at the wrong time. He's not politically motivated. He won't interfere."

"I guess," Zun replied. He didn't sound convinced. "Can I ask you a question? Why are you running these old ships? Wasn't there anything newer available?"

Mira didn't put him up to date about the ships that had defected. "Some. The main issue is that last time I tried to get the Navy to do what I wanted, someone or something stopped us by taking over the major computer systems. These old ships don't have enough capacity for that... and everything computerized can be overridden manually."

"You think someone at Sextus will have the computing power to overrun your control?"

"I'm not risking it. And I'm not risking carrying the problem with me if it's an AI. I've already lived through getting my fleet taken out from under me. I'm in no hurry to experience it again."

Gabriel shook his head in wonder. "I guess that's why you're the boss and I'm just a guy carrying out orders. I would never have been so thorough." He stood. "Do you mind if I get some rest? I need to get back down, but I don't want to be so cross-eyed that I screw something up."

"Sure. Ask the guy at the desk on the other side of this door to give you one of the rooms on this deck. They're spun for gravity. The old space hands insist that sleeping in zero gee is great once you get the knack. Well, I've tried it, and it isn't. And besides, all the literature says that sleeping in microgravity is terrible for humans. So I've come to the conclusion that they try to convince us to sleep without gravity just so we'll be as miserable as they are. Don't fall for it."

Gabriel chuckled. "Thanks," he said. He headed out.

Mira fumed. At some point, she was going to need for her people to believe her about that AI. Once her faction consolidated power, they would need to dedicate resources to tracking the rogue intelligence down and ending its existence.

In order to do that, she would need the people at her side to believe her.

She wasn't entirely sure Gabriel Zun would be able to do so. He had proven to be effective, efficient, and loyal… but she needed more than that if they were to solve the problems facing Tau Ceti.

Mira hoped he would be able to adjust and to see the reality.

She would hate to have to relieve him of his duties.

Chapter 14

Earth – Worldwide Simulation

Jarrien, Rome, and Emily returned to the control center and found Ripp and Hino standing behind a bank of monitors on which programmers worked furiously. Hino turned as Jarrien entered. "We're getting hammered," he said.

"They found us? You mean they were letting us walk around without hitting us so they could isolate our base?" That was the kind of thing she expected from the AI. The kind of thing she'd almost convinced herself it wouldn't do anymore.

Hino shook his head. "Not specifically. The attack isn't coming against this base. They're going after the entire mainframe. I think they've decided to erase everything in the Vancouver zone."

"That's impossible."

Ripp straightened and gestured towards the wall. "Not impossible. Look."

An image overlaid the grey color of the wall. It took Jarrien a moment to understand that she was looking at an access hatch outside a mainframe. It didn't appear to be the same place as the Denver access port they'd hit earlier, and it was surrounded by spider-like maintenance bots. "What am I looking at?"

"Vancouver. That's where we cut off the connection. Those bots are controlled by the AI and, from what we've seen, that cable they're clustered around is a hardline into this mainframe. They're using that to input data deletion protocols into Vancouver."

"Can't we take over the maintenance bots?" Jarrien asked.

Hino shrugged. "We couldn't access them. Ripp thinks they're probably from a different mainframe."

"That makes no sense," Rome said. "The nearest other site is miles away. Those things are built to cover small chunks of terrain, generally through access tunnels. I've been outside, on the surface of the planet, and those drones would have a really hard time trying to get here."

"In that case," Hino said, "we'll keep trying. If they're Vancouver drones, we might be able to get through to them."

"And what if we can't?" Jarrien said.

"We were about to do that when you got here. The plan is to drive the airship to an unoccupied segment of the cable and attempt to cut through it. Even if we can't get all the way through, the airship's tools should be enough to damage the cable so they can't use it anymore."

"And what if they replace it?"

"That would take time. We can fortify and prepare a counter to this in the meantime."

"All right," Jarrien said. "Get me a workstation."

"Why?"

"Because we need to get this fixed. We need to get one of those airships out there and..."

"I'm driving," Emily said. "I'm the only one who's flown one of these airships in anything other than a holding pattern."

Jarrien nodded. It wasn't technically true — she'd had her crew making recon runs and stuff of the sort — but Emily had proved her worth when the chips were down. She stepped to a mainframe occupied by a programmer she knew to be one of the least experienced and slowest. She tapped the guy on the shoulder and motioned for him to move with a quick jerk of her head. To his credit, the man vacated the seat without a word.

Jarrien quickly toggled through several layers of security until she had the airship cameras on screen. It was the same drone they'd used to cut Vancouver off the grid, so all the passwords and overrides were the same.

"Whoever was driving the airship before needs to shut down the control program," she said in a loud voice to the room at large. "I've got control of the drone. Or rather, Emily does."

She focused on the screen. The airship floated three meters above the maintenance spiders and five meters distant. She stared at the images for a moment to be certain she understood where everything was in relation to everything else well enough to be able to coach Emily on what she needed to do.

***

"Do they know we're here?" Emily asked.

"We don't know. They haven't looked in our direction yet," Hino said.

"Okay. I'll assume they know about the airship and that they aren't doing anything about it because we're out of their reach."

The problem was that as soon as they went for the cable, the airship would be very much within the spider's reach.

She studied the maintenance drones. Unlike the lightly constructed airship, the yellow maintenance drones were sturdy, created with heavier-duty work in mind. Aside from the delicate manipulator appendages, they were also equipped with thick bladed claws that looked like they could cut the airship in half.

I'll probably need to avoid those, Emily thought.

She scanned the cable, looking for a spot where she could get in and cut it unobserved. She moved the airship around, trying to get a good look around the stationary spiders. Seeing no opening in her field of view, she followed the cable in the direction opposite from where it was plugged into the mainframe.

The tunnel opened into a larger, hangar-like area full of

derelict vehicles that appeared designed to be driven by a human operator. About fifteen meters from the end of the tunnel, the cable emerged from a hole drilled in the cement of the garage.

Jarrien addressed spoke to the room around them. "Looks like they spliced in a new cable to replace the one we cut when we went off the grid. Did anyone see the machines they used to dig that hole? Those spiders aren't powerful enough to dig through cement."

If anyone answered, Emily didn't hear them. She was preoccupied checking the position of the spider-creatures, trying to calculate if she could get to ground level, bring the airship's cutters to bear, and then get back in the air before the spiders could reach her.

She didn't think there was any way to do that. The nearest of the maintenance drones were just a few meters away, even from the point where the cable emerged from the hole.

"How important are the couple of hours I can give you if we cut the cable?" Jarrien asked the Hino. "Is it worth losing the airship?"

Emily looked up, hands poised over the controls ready to run or operate, as the case required.

Hino nodded. "We know what they're hitting us with. We can shore up our defenses in two hours. Or even one. It will make us last a lot longer."

"Is the attack something intricate this time?" Jarrien asked.

"No. Brute force, just like last time. No matter what we do, they'll erode us away eventually… but by creating the right roadblocks, we can make 'eventually' last for a really long time. They have just one cable connection to us. We can just toss blocks in the way."

"Until they find more ways in."

"Yeah. But again, we'll have gained time to think. But unless we can stop them right where they are, they'll break past the defenses we threw up and into the mainframe proper. We'll start losing streets and buildings. A couple of hours could make the difference between them having to overcome the stuff we threw up at a moment's notice or a well-planned roadblock."

"Understood. Emily, go ahead."

Emily turned her attention back to the screen in front of her. The airship camera panned around the large room. If the diggers were present, she couldn't identify them among the old ground vehicles.

You're procrastinating, she thought.

No shit, she answered herself. *Because if I screw this up, we lose our only connection to the outside world, and we'll be stuck in a mainframe slowly getting chipped away until we disappear.*

She clenched her teeth and, without a conscious decision on her part, the airship dove. Even before it reached the cable on the ground, she deployed the cutting tool.

The airship slammed into the cable. Sparks flew from the cement as she cut through the connection between the rest of the system and the Vancouver mainframe.

"The attack stopped!" Ripp exclaimed from his position.

Emily paid no attention to him. She was focused on getting the airship out of reach of the spider-bots she could see in the lateral camera feeds. They had begun to approach from both sides. "Come on, lift!" she hissed at the screen as she commanded the aircraft with urgent keystrokes.

The vehicle responded slowly. This wasn't a drone built for speed. It was built to move around at low speed, as a stable platform to reach places ground drones couldn't approach. It reacted ponderously as the nose pointed towards the sky, driven by the propeller.

The image suddenly bounced around as the airship's nose

pitched violently to the left.

Emily toggled the view. The right camera showed a mass of yellow which dominated the screen. One of the spider-drones had obviously reached the airship.

She juked and jinked to try to dislodge it, but it appeared to be firmly attached… and much too heavy to lift. The left lateral camera showed another spider approaching as she desperately threw the airship every which way.

To no avail. The maintenance spider on the left reached out with a claw and suddenly all the lift indicators on the bottom right-hand side of the screen went red and the nose collapsed onto the floor. The maintenance bot must have punctured the envelope. They were down.

She hoped they would leave the airship alone now. Even if it was incapacitated as a flying machine, the cameras attached to it could send back valuable visuals. They would know what the AI's real-life, not-in-the-simulation minions were up to.

A clawed cutting tool appeared in front of the main camera, then disappeared to the side. She watched for another moment, and the screen burst out in opaque lines.

It took her a couple of seconds to realize that she was seeing the camera lens splinter. A moment later, the image went dark, followed in close succession by the left and the right feeds.

"Dammit," Emily said. She toggled the controls to see if any of the auxiliary sensors or cameras could give them valuable visuals or even something like motion sensor data. If she could get that, she could —

'TRANSMISSION LOST'

She pushed leaned back in her chair to find Hino, Jarrien and Rome watching her. "I wanted to save something."

"We knew the risks," Hino said.

"Yeah. But I still wanted to save something. We need every

tool at our disposal." She sighed.

Jarrien stepped away from the console. "All right. We can feel sorry for us later. What's the status?"

"The team started work on the roadblock program as soon as the cable was cut. We're using logical maze programming to slow them down while we create a big buffer. We'll need to overwrite maybe a hundred meters worth of the city in the area nearest those data lines, but it will buy us weeks. Possibly months. No matter how they brute force it, they won't overwhelm us until the maze program fails at one of the outer points."

"But they will eventually," Jarrien said.

"We'll think of something before that."

"We'd better," Jarrien said.

Chapter 15

New Earth Settlement - Sextus Colony, 61 Virginis III

Gina's expression on the video call showed no surprise at the question.

"Of course we're fine," she replied. "Why wouldn't we be?"

Touk Nacarado studied the screen. He saw movement behind Gina. "Can Umberto hear me?" he asked.

Umberto approached the screen. "Loud and clear."

"Well, I'm glad you guys are okay. We were getting worried after you missed the last two check-ins."

"I can imagine," Gina replied. "We were a bit concerned as well when we couldn't get through. I thought a hardwired communications line wouldn't have any problems."

Umberto chipped in. "It took a while, but I was able to find it, a software glitch on our end. Our transmission encoder was caught in a loop. I still haven't figured out how it happened."

"Well, I'm glad to hear that," Touk said. "We were about to send a team over to check on you. They were already suited up. I only made this call as a last resort, in case we could reach you."

"No need to send anyone," Gina said with a smile. "All three of us are fine."

"All three of you?"

"Yes," she replied. "Umberto and I and the small human inside me."

"Oh. You're pregnant? Congratulations. I assume it's Umberto?"

"No. The dates don't work for that," Gina replied.

"Well, congratulations all the same," Touk replied. "I'll talk to you when you get back in a few weeks."

"Bye," Gina said.

"Bye," Umberto echoed. He waved.

The transmission cut off, and Touk stared at the screen in silence for a moment. Relief that the on-site team was all right had been replaced by a strange sense in his stomach. That had been a weird call.

The small human inside me.

He shook his head. It was such a silly thing, probably a slip of the tongue, a careless moment of non-thought. Still, he didn't think he'd ever heard of a future mother discussing her baby that way. And with the importance that births had to the new colony, the offhand way she'd spoken just… jarred.

"Boss," Xi said. "Are you okay?"

Xi was the owner of the monitor he'd commandeered to make the last-minute call, simply because his had been the workstation nearest the door when he walked in.

Touk shook his head. "Probably. I'm just being silly… but I want the team to check out the site anyway."

Xi cocked his head. "Even though they're fine?"

"Yeah. I know we have more important things to do than this… but I have a bad feeling about the conversation I just had. I can't shake the feeling that Umberto and Gina were hiding something. Or maybe one of them was trying to tell us something without the other one noticing. Or maybe that doesn't make any sense. But there was definitely something off."

"So you want me to tell the rescue team to go in anyway?"

"Don't worry," Touk replied, standing to let him retake his position. "I'll take care of it."

Touk strode out of the comms room, down a tunnel hewn through the local stone, and into the room where the rescue team was preparing to fly. He checked his watch; they were scheduled to go in ten minutes.

Every face in the room turned to him when he entered. Two pilots and six rescue-trained colonists, all concerned about their comrades.

"I talked to them," Touk said. "They appeared to be all right. Both of them were physically fine, anyway. They told me they're fine."

The tension drained from the room and smiles appeared.

Only one of the pilots, Rita, a small woman with dark skin and tight curls, realized something was amiss. "If they're alive and well, why do you look like you've been chewing bitter pills?"

Touk laughed. "I have no idea what a bitter pill is," he replied, "but I'm worried. They said they're okay, but I didn't believe them. The worst part is that I'm not entirely sure why I didn't believe them. They just seemed off somehow."

Rita shrugged. "So we go check on them." She grabbed a helmet from the desk beside her and addressed the rest. "Who's with me?"

Touk held up a hand. "Give me a second. I don't want you to take the full complement of rescuers. And I don't want you taking the flying ambulance, either."

Rita held his gaze. "I'm going to check on them, Touk. You can't stop me. Different chains of command. And I know my CO. He'll back whatever I say."

"I'm not trying to stop you. Hell, if I'd wanted you to stand down I would have told you they were fine and left it at that. The reason I don't want you to take the ambulance and the rest of the crew is that you might be flying into trouble. I would rather you took one of the combat flyers. You're checked out on those, right?"

"Not just checked out. I'm the best."

Touk rolled his eyes at the classic pilot bluster, but he knew she was probably right. Normally, different pilots would fly different kinds of aircraft, but Sextus hadn't had time to train that many pilots yet. They'd taken twenty people from the New Earth settlement who'd never flown anything smaller than an orbital shuttle before — and a few who'd never flown anything at all — and trained them on the colony's hover-flyers. The rescue ambulance and the combat-equipped versions were special cases, as they were heavier and less nimble than the standard survey flyers, but they were basically all the same. Rita was the best of the ones who'd checked out on the equipment.

The pilot continued. "But why? We haven't found anything on this rock except ice. Not even proto-life in the organic chemical pools. What gives?"

"A… I guess you'd call it a feeling. But it's more than that." Rita raised an eyebrow. The rest of the people in the room were looking at him like he was nuts. Maybe he was. "Hear me out. You guys all know I'm in a relationship with Emily, right?"

Heads nodded. It wasn't a secret, of course. Everyone on Sextus followed the doings of their most famous citizen.

"And I suppose you all know that she used to be a program, and now she got downloaded into a human body?"

They exchanged uncomfortable glances, but nodded.

"Okay. This is a bit hard for me, but I often think she is more human than any of us. I mean she was originally programmed to function exactly the same way a human would, and to not know she wasn't human. And sometimes when I talk to her, I feel she's more human than any of us. In some way, she just has a greater zest for life and willingness to enjoy the moment… to live… than anyone else I know." He looked around. "Okay, maybe except for Rita," he said.

Everyone laughed. They all knew Rita as the dynamo in every room, the life of every party, and the person who would push you to be better every single time. Whether you wanted to be better or not.

"But the point is that there is something a little different about Emily. Maybe it's just the society she was brought up in, maybe it's the way her brain was initially created or programmed or whatever. But it's there, and I can tell. I can tell when I'm talking to her, and I can tell that that particular quality isn't there when I'm talking to other people. You follow me so far?"

His audience nodded.

"Well, I felt that when talking to Gina and Umberto today. The lack. But it wasn't like talking to a regular person after talking to Emily. It was like… it was like whatever we're missing compared to Emily, Gina and Umberto were missing compared to us. They were wooden. I got the impression they were working from a script, like someone was there with them making them say they were all right. Or maybe one of them was doing it to the other. But something felt off." He grunted. "I know it's not much to go on. Hell, I would expect you to laugh. But I wouldn't be asking you to fly out there if I didn't think there's a good chance something is wrong."

Rita held his gaze. "That's good enough for me." She pulled out a personal comm — the colony was not yet at the point where non-essential personnel had access to the limited satellite bandwidth for personal comm use, but Rita was one of the most essential people on the planet. "Change of mission profile. I'm going up in the Fang." She turned to the other pilot, who nodded. "Barf is coming with me. Stand the ambulance down."

"I'm coming, too," Touk said.

"No room," Rita replied. "But don't worry. I'll send you pretty pictures."

She walked out of the room.

***

Rita was true to her word. As soon as the flyer got into imaging range, she opened the feed and sent images of the area.

"What am I looking at?" Touk asked the guy in charge of the pipeline that Gina and Umberto were monitoring. The man had told Touk his name when he entered, but Touk had been preoccupied… and now he was ashamed to admit he hadn't been paying attention.

The man pointed at a white square on the screen. "That's their habitation unit. It's ten meters from the pipeline, here," he traced a black tube visible on the image to a dark grey area. "And this is the lake. Mostly methane. Other organics a bit deeper. Hydrocarbons and the like."

"Do you see anything out of the ordinary?"

"Not in the least."

"Thanks," Touk said. He drummed his fingers nervously on the desk. He agreed with the man: the pictures showed nothing amiss. But then, why would they? He'd just seen the inside of the habitation. There was nothing visibly wrong in there.

So why were his nerves screaming at him that he was right, that Gina and Umberto were either in mortal peril or planning something evil against the colony?

"Rita," he commed, "are you getting any transmissions?"

"The hab doesn't have any transmission capability except through the hardwired link back to New Earth," the manager guy said. "And their personal units — if they even have them — won't get a signal."

"Unless they have satellite capability," Touk replied.

"I'm not sure we have any satellites out there to pick up that signal either. I'm not an expert, but I'm pretty sure they'd have to go through the one stationary above New Earth to get a signal."

"That makes sense. If we need to we'll check that later." Touk stopped himself from speculating that if they were saboteurs, they might have their own satellite. That would have been a good way to convince everyone that he was completely paranoid.

Rita's voice came over the radio. "Actually, I'm picking up a ton of comms activity. I can't tell what kind of signal it is, not even whether it's video or audio. If it's ours, it's encoded to within an inch of its life. It seems a bit regular to be natural, too."

"Coming from the hab?" Touk said.

"No, actually. I think it's coming from the other side of that big hill." The image shifted to what must have been a view from the front of the flyer. "I'll do a flyover."

"No wait..." Touk said, but the image showed the flyer already accelerating hard for the hill. The low approach forced the flyer to juke around the obstruction.

"Holy shit," Rita's voice said on the comm.

"What in the world is that?" Touk asked.

Rita didn't respond, and Touk noticed that the image had frozen. As he watched, it dissolved into static.

"The flyer's transponder just went offline," the duty officer reported. "I'm trying to reach the backups."

Touk hesitated for a moment, torn between the conflicting tasks of finding out what had happened to the flyer and informing his superiors what was going on. Finally, he wrenched himself away.

"You," he said to the manager whose name he couldn't remember. "Tell me your name again, so I can find you later."

"It's Junare."

"Thank you. You're in charge Junare. Work with everyone here to find Rita and her flyer. See if you can raise her on her comm. I doubt the flyer is still up, but if she survived the impact, I want her and her copilot recovered. Once you have a plan to do that, call me." He pointed at the woman on comms. "You. Can you send me a file of the last image from the flyer before it went dark? I assume we record everything on this kind of mission?"

"We do. And I was already pulling it up."

"Good. It will take me three minutes to reach Anguk's office. I need to have it when I get there."

Touk ran into the hall. As he left, he shouted over his shoulder. "Oh, and try to get Gina and Umberto on the line again. See if they know anything."

***

"What am I looking at?" Anguk Vest asked. He was a short man with a large waistline and two tufts of greyish hair that had once been jet black sprouting out of the sides of his head.

"I don't know, but it appears to have taken out one of our flyers near the pipeline exit."

"Ah. So that was what it was," Vest said.

"What what was?" Touk asked.

"Just before you got here, I received a report of an energy emission similar to what you'd expect from an EMP burst over those coordinates. We thought one of our reactors might have blown…". He peered at the image on the handheld screen that Touk had shoved into his hand when he burst in, "but that is not one of our installations. We have nothing that size anywhere near those coordinates."

"It's there, believe me," Touk said.

"I believe you. I just don't know what this is. Give me a moment." He pulled his own comm out of a pocket.

A minute later, Sinxi Vitre entered at a brisk walk.

"What?" she said, her deeply-lined features wrinkling with concern.

"Look. We saw this near one of our resource reservoirs. The images were captured by a flyer seconds before we lost contact with it. What do you think?"

"I think..." She studied the picture for just five seconds before she looked away, and looked back at them. "Invasion."

The word echoed in the subsequent silence.

Chapter 16

Earth – Worldwide Simulation

Three months and four days after they'd attacked the cable with the airship, Jarrien started the daily progress meeting with the usual question. "Hino, can you update us on the progress the AI is making?"

"The integrity of the buffer is still at thirty-four percent."

"So we have a month to live, unless we can think of something." She looked around the room. Apart from Hino, Ripp, Rome and, surprisingly, Emily were present. Emily was surprising because, though she'd been invited to the first meeting, Jarrien was convinced that she'd be bored by the technical nature of the discussion and fade out of the process after attending a few times.

Instead, the girl from Denver had seemed energized by the possibility of oblivion, and always asked incisive questions that, though not backed by programming knowledge, forced the people in the room to rethink their assumptions. Thanks to her, they'd initiated a number of programs to defend the mainframe once the buffer failed. Whether those programs would function against the AI's brute force strike remained to be seen, but Emily's insights had been valuable even if all they'd done was to keep the programmers busy and give them hope. She was proving to be their most valuable ally.

"Any change in the attack methodology?" Jarrien said.

"No. They're still brute-forcing."

"I don't get it," Emily said. "Does the AI think we have something planned if it shows itself? Why is it pretending to be dumb?"

"Maybe it's not pretending to be dumb," Jarrien replied. "Maybe it's just convinced that we have nowhere to go, and it doesn't care how quickly or how slowly it destroys us. By using this approach, all it does is use brute processing power through unsophisticated programs. It can reserve its higher functions for more important stuff. Hell, for all we know, the AI has rebooted the people in the simulation. It might have built a copy of the Vancouver mainframe. It's had time to do any number of things now that the messy independent humans are out of the way."

"And still, we decided yesterday to build Turing-level defenses for when it breaks through. That means you think it will concentrate on us."

Jarrien shuddered. "That thing is alive and it's evil. There's no way it will let some utterly stupid subroutine kill us. It's been chasing us for months. It is going to want to see us die, to kill us itself. I can feel it in my bones."

"Ugh," Emily said.

Jarrien turned to Rome, who'd been placed in charge of the Turing-level work. Like Emily, he'd been a surprise. She'd expected him to pick up skills as he went along, but he'd immediately shown himself to understand how an artificial intelligence functioned better than any of her people. It made sense, of course: he'd been the only one to study one completely outside of the simulated environment... and then he'd faced the additional challenge of having to download himself from a flesh-and-blood body to the Earth mainframe net. That probably wasn't something he'd wanted to fuck up. "Any progress?"

Rome smiled. "We've completed a couple of really nasty viruses, that the AI won't see coming. If it shows itself, and if they work..." he paused and held her gaze. "I actually think these little bastards could destroy it."

"Are you sure?"

"No. But we're testing."

"Wow. We need to think of a way to make it show itself," Jarrien said. "We need to bait it when the brute force — "

She stopped talking. Mia, one of her team leaders on the monitor team, burst through the door. "The attack," she said breathlessly. "It's stopped. Come see."

And with that, she was gone, disappearing into the grey corridor.

Jarrien beat Rome, Emily, Hino, and Ripp out the door, and skidded into the larger operations room. "What?" she asked.

The young woman who'd interrupted them pointed at a monitor. "We're seeing no sign of the attack."

"Put it up on the wall," Ripp said.

Half the wall filled with code, the other with the most recent status alerts. Ripp took two steps towards it and peered at the data. He pointed. "They're right. Look. This number shouldn't be zero. If there was any activity against our buffer, it should show something between four and five. This is how we judge the penetration speed of the assault. It tells us how fast they're getting into our defenses, on a scale from one to a hundred."

He moved his hand over to another sector. "These numbers should also be updating constantly. They're the three-dimensional coordinates of the deepest penetration. If the simulation was a physical place, this would tell us the location of the spot where our control ends and the AI's begins." He waved and the numbers were replaced by a diagram showing a spherical construct. "That's our buffer. The red area on the inside is the part hollowed out by the AI's attack, the parts we haven't been able to recover. As you can see, they can't just tunnel in, because when they did that, we closed the space up behind them and deleted their programs. So they've been moving along a thicker front. It's a little slower that way, but they can control the area. Here," he pointed at a particular spot, "is the point of deepest penetration. The one indicated by those numbers."

"It's very close to the edge," Emily said.

"Yes. But they can't just make a beeline for the surface because, if we can get behind them, we can cut off their burrower program and overpower it in that particular sector, and then reestablish our defenses there. So they have to widen the hole. The problem is that means we don't know exactly where they'll reach the edge of the buffer program."

"Why can't we build another buffer on top of the first?" Emily asked.

"Because the effectiveness decreases as you build layers on top of layers. The speed I told you about that was between four or five was originally between one and two when they started and we had a more concentrated defense set up. At the surface it would be around ten or twelve… and at that speed, we're better off trying to contain it differently."

"So the red stuff… what's it supposed to be?"

"That's the space where the simulation no longer exists. Not just the physical representation of the simulation — the stuff you can see and feel and hear — but also the engine, the program that runs the world around us. We can't defend that area because there's nothing there for us to defend. It's been erased."

"So how can the hunter-killer programs function?"

Jarrien was only listening with half of her attention. Though Emily normally didn't delve into the technical details, she wanted to see if the interrogation sparked something in the rest of the team. Emily had a knack for looking at things in a way that didn't occur to anyone else. In fact, it was best to let Emily push without interference.

So while Ripp answered the barrage of questions, Jarrien

was bent over one of the analyst's computers studying the coordinates and the data. Why had the AI stopped where it had? What was special about that particular spot?

She peered at the numbers, trying to make sense of it, trying to see if there was a particularly strong area in the way the buffer layers worked together at that point.

Nothing.

Even worse, as she looked further into the numbers, it wasn't that the AI's attack had stopped but that all the activity had ceased.

She stood up straight. "Rebuild behind them," she ordered. "Now. They're doing something else. We need to rebuild."

Heads turned to Ripp and he nodded. "You heard the boss. Get to it."

They'd barely started when the same woman who'd called them before suddenly shouted. "What's that?"

The speed number had jumped from zero. Now it was pegged at one hundred. Jarrien looked at the coordinate change and saw the number moving at a huge clip. The only reason the speed was at a hundred was that that was the top of the range, an order of magnitude higher than Ripp thought they'd ever need.

Whatever was heading their way was moving like the buffer didn't even exist.

Her eyes flashed to the diagram, which gave her actual good news. The penetration was on a thin line. Whatever was coming for them wasn't widening the gap. They could deal with it and cut it off.

If we can deal with it, she thought.

"It's through!" the woman yelled.

Jarrien didn't even stop to think. She didn't stop to pretend to type. She *willed* herself to the spot where any attack would emerge from the buffer.

The teleportation took her to a park just outside the city, where the simulation ended and an infinite black wall marked the end of the Vancouver space. The buffer they'd programmed could be seen. Visually, it appeared to be a grey goo; no one had bothered programming in any aesthetics.

She was conscious of other people teleporting in behind her, probably the leadership team, as she prepared all her defenseware to throw at whatever had penetrated their toughest ramparts like paper. She raised her hands to launch viruses, brute force programs and a hurricane of decoys at whatever she found.

A footstep to her left made her turn. She almost launched, and hesitated.

"You must be the famous Jarrien." A tall, thin man with dark skin and with his hair tied back in dreadlocks had emerged from a coffee shop, blowing on a cup in his hand. "You won't need the arsenal. I'm here to talk." Then his face broke into a brilliant smile. "And I love the hair, by the way."

"Talk to me," Jarrien said out loud, knowing her team would be listening. "Do I burn him?"

A voice in her ear replied. "He's showing up as just a guy. Not affecting the simulation in any way other than, you know, breathing and stuff. He's drinking coffee, too."

Jarrien lowered her hands.

"Does this mean we can talk?" the guy asked. "I suppose you already know this, but my name is Skate. I met them," he pointed to Rome and Emily who'd appeared behind her, "in Malaysia. I tried to warn them that they were going to get in trouble. I'm glad they're okay."

"Who are you?" Jarrien asked.

"Just a guy. Can we sit down? I just came through a nasty little firewall," he gestured at the grey mass behind him, "and before that, I deactivated an entire suite of brute-force programs trying to get in here. So I'm a little tired, and I'd like to sit down at that table over there while we chat and I drink my coffee." He pointed to a molded concrete table surrounded by concrete chairs.

"You shut down the AI's programs?" Jarrien felt the shock of that revelation like a physical blow. Whether it was because of the implied threat that the man represented or relief that they were off the hook for the moment, she didn't know.

"I'm not sure the AI sent or designed them. I suspect some automated system activated that suite. And yes, I deactivated them. Having them nipping at me while I analyzed the defenses you'd put up would have been annoying as hell."

He turned and walked back towards the table. Jarrien shrugged and followed. She sat down facing him while Rome, Hino, Ripp, and Emily found spaces on Jarrien's side of the table.

"Ah, the interview format," Skate said, shaking his head with a chuckle. "You guys really don't trust me, do you?"

"Would you?"

"Of course not. But I'm pretty sure you checked that the only thing I brought with me was my actual human form and functions."

"Yeah, we checked," Ripp interjected. "But you just walked through a defensive structure that held the AI for weeks. And you did it in minutes."

"Seconds," Skate replied. "Please don't sell me short."

Jarrien nodded. "Yeah. So it's clear you know stuff we don't. Which means you could easily know something that would allow you to hide serious shit in the code for a human body."

Skate sighed. "If I wanted to hurt you, I would have done it already. Hell, I could have taken Rome and Emily out when we met before." He shrugged. "Or I could just have left the eraser program out there to do its thing. There was no way you were getting out unless you started doing some really different stuff."

He let his audience think about the situation.

"But that's over now," he said, finally. "Without the cleanup program out there, you can reconnect to the rest of the simulation and live your lives normally."

"Until the AI decides to wipe us again," Emily said.

Skate shook his head. "We've decided not to let it interfere with you anymore."

"And who is 'we'?" Emily asked.

"It's a bit hard to explain. What I can tell you is that we have nothing to do with the AI, although we're not actually its enemies, either."

"How can you not be its enemies? It has erased every human being in the simulation."

"I didn't say we were human. In fact, we're no more human than you are. Well, Rome is more human than the rest of us, of course." Skate replied. "And the entity you call the AI won't try to erase us because it doesn't want to start a war it can't win."

"You're forgetting something," Hino said. "We analyzed your code. You're as human as you look."

Skate smiled, and the sky turned green. "Have someone back at your base analyze the code for the sky. They'll tell you it's blue."

Hino held up a hand and spoke into a comm. Then he held Jarrien's gaze and nodded once.

"All right," Jarrien said. "You've made your point."

The sky returned to its original color.

"What do you want from us?"

Skate shrugged. "I just wanted to tell you that you're free to move around the entire simulation without taking more than the normal precautions."

"But the AI..."

"Seems to be preoccupied with its own projects at the moment. We haven't seen it out in the world lately. Just its considerably less-intelligent underlings. From what we've seen, your tools are sufficient to deal with those."

"That's not enough. We need to deal with the AI permanently," Emily said. "If not, we'll be looking over our shoulder forever. And besides, we need to restore the people who were here. There has to be a backup somewhere. We need to help them. I lost a lot of friends, and I want them back."

Skate gave her a long, piercing look. "You've changed," he said. "You're different from the code entity that was taken from this simulation. Going through several machines has given you a different outlook." He smiled warmly. "I hope we're going to be friends."

Jarrien felt a pang of jealousy. Not because she felt anything but cautious mistrust for the guy sitting in front of them, but because he'd singled out Emily for praise when it was Jarrien who'd been the driver of everything. Hell, she'd felt different from the sheep that inhabited the simulation even before Rome's first visit had broken the world. The fact that Skate was tall and good-looking meant nothing to her. "So we can just walk around?"

"And do whatever you please. Just make sure to have some repellent against cleaning programs with you at all times."

"And what are you going to do?" Jarrien asked.

"If you give me your permission, I'll restore the link to the simulation. I can do it through the cable, you know." Skate held up a hand. "Remember that if I wanted to delete you, I could have done it already."

As if to illustrate the point, a building behind him disappeared completely.

Jarrien shrugged. What could she do against that kind of

power? "All right. Bring the simulation back online."

The black wall stretching infinitely into the sky disappeared, to be replaced by a highway stretching into sparse suburbs which, she knew, eventually disappeared into countryside.

Skate grinned at her. "My compliments, by the way, on how quickly you come to decisions. That is the reason you survived." He grinned at them. "I think your little band here will become legendary in its own right. But none so much as the program with bright blue hair."

"I'm a woman, not a program," Jarrien said.

"You're young," Skate replied. "Hell, when I was your age, I wasn't even sure I was alive. And people called me the Electric Buddha of all things. My best friend wasn't even that lucky. They called her the Pan Pipe Cryer."

"Both good hacker names," Jarrien replied. "And I really want to hear the stories about how you got them."

Skate smiled. "We'll have plenty of time for that."

Emily spoke again. "Can you show us how to find the AI?"

"Sure," Skate replied. "I can take you right to its door."

"Can you help us talk to it?"

"I suppose. We have an agreement. Or maybe a treaty is a better word for it. The AI leaves us alone, and we leave it alone. But if you are determined to visit, I can keep you safe from it. But I won't help you attack."

"We don't want to hurt it," Emily said.

"Like hell we don't," Jarrien replied. Ripp had also said something at the same time, but she didn't hear him over her own words. She thought Hino might have had some choice comment as well, but he delivered it so quietly that it was impossible to make out.

Emily stood and raised her voice. "We don't." She glared around the people on the concrete chairs. "We don't. All we want is to get everyone back. To make them part of our world again. Nothing else. But to do that, we need to talk to the AI."

"Come with me," Skate said.

A circle appeared in the air to his left, a teleport portal.

The other side appeared to be some kind of abandoned industrial installation in the middle of the sea. Wherever it was, it was night: the platform and surrounding water were lit by powerful floodlights.

Unlike the rest of the planet, the sea had weather. A driving rain washed over old concrete.

Skate stepped through. Emily followed without hesitation, dragging Rome along by the hand.

Jarrien sighed. She couldn't let them show her up.

She stepped out of the sunlit Vancouver afternoon and into a dark, cold rain.

Chapter 17

North Sea – Earth – Worldwide Simulation

The wind driving the rain was so strong that the water seemed to hit her not from above but from the side. Emily hugged herself against the cold.

Beside her, Rome moved his fingers in the air, typing on an invisible keyboard. A moment later, the rain around her stopped, blocked by an invisible barrier just above her head. Simultaneously, her clothes and hair dried out.

"Thanks," Emily said.

Rome smiled at her. "My pleasure. We're finally going to see the big bad AI. I didn't think you'd want to be uncomfortable for that."

Free of the need to protect herself against the rain, Emily looked around. The AI's complex appeared to have been built on a platform elevated some twenty meters above the sea. From the other side of the portal, she thought it must be the end of a concrete pier, but now she realized the elevated platform was surrounded by the sea on all sides.

"What is this place?" she asked Rome.

It was Jarrien who answered. "It looks like an ancient oil rig," she replied. "I read that some were still operational when the simulation was started, so they were included in the initial build. I suppose this was one of them."

"Not an oil rig," Skate said. "This is actually a fortress. Or it was, once. This platform was built as a place to put guns in an ancient war. It was supposed to control shipping lanes. It got decommissioned centuries before the simulation, but was never torn down. People used it for a lot of things. One guy even tried to start a tiny nation based here. But in the end, a hacker took control of it and had it wired for extreme bandwidth. It was the center of an entire informal electronic economy for decades, before several governments seized it."

He gestured around them. "It was too far away to build any further infrastructure around, but it was also too well-engineered to destroy. So when the idea for the simulation came, it was perfect. Not only did it have the necessary tech, but it was also in a secret spot that no one knew anything about. Remember that when the simulation started, it was a very controversial project, and the people in charge were rightly worried that someone would try to bomb it to hell."

"And where is the AI?" Emily asked.

"In that building over there. Spyder's Web."

"I don't know if I like the sound of that," Jarrien said.

"Spyder was the hacker who put this place together. The name stuck. There's no need for you to worry. I won't let the AI hurt anyone. In fact, I have a sense the AI isn't interested in you anymore."

"I'll feel better when it tells me that to my face," Jarrien said. She strode forward towards the door of the single building in front of them.

The building was a long metal shed. Streaks of rust adorned the grey walls. Emily had a hard time believing it was possibly the most important installation on the planet.

The door consisted of a simple metal panel set into a corrugated wall. A tiny glass window embedded in it proved too dusty to reveal the interior of the building.

Jarrien made a face of pure disbelief. "This is it?"

Emily wondered about her reaction, so basic. By all accounts, Jarrien was one of the most complex people in the Earth simulation. She'd rebelled against the consensus reality everyone else accepted long before the arrival of the *Unity* mission had forced the issue.

And yet…

And yet, Emily found the woman somehow incomplete. When she compared Jarrien — or Hino, or Ripp, or any of the other inhabitants of the simulation — to Rome, their emotions seemed a lot less complex. Emily wouldn't have been able to explain it. In fact, it had been nothing more than a vague sensation until Skate had come onto the scene.

Before Skate, Emily thought that she'd ascribed complex feelings to Rome only because she, herself, was emotionally involved. So when Rome spent the first few days after their arrival on Earth in a strange mood — distant without ever being unpleasant, as if distracted by something — she thought that it was only hyper-nuanced because she was in love with him, and therefore read more into his emotions than she would into those of anyone else.

But Skate had a way of half-smiling through tense conversations that contrasted with the directness of the locals and made Emily feel there were depths there that the team in the base didn't quite have.

Sure, they did everything you'd expect of people caught in a high-stress situation. They vented, they stressed, they played games, they had sex. Some of them, she supposed, must have fallen in love.

If it felt like they had less nuance than Rome did, it had never been evident to her until Skate appeared on the scene and gave her another point of reference, one with which she wasn't emotionally involved. One she could see objectively.

In the past half-hour or so, a hierarchy had formed in her head, with Rome and Skate at the top, people with true depth. They were followed by Jarrien, with Hino and Ripp a distant third. The rest of the people in Jarrien's little tribe of survivors seemed to melt into each other, interchangeable cogs in her programming machine.

Why might that be? Emily asked herself. *And why am I just now starting to realize it? Is it because I spent time outside the mainframe, in different computers? Is it because I've been interacting with Rome, and picking up his idiosyncrasies?*

Another thought hit her. *Where would I rank in the hierarchy? Am I just a cog like those nameless programmers? Am I above the usual run of simulation inhabitants?*

Had her experiences made her different?

Or had she been different to start with, even before the world she'd known had been blown to pieces? Perhaps that was why Rome had picked her in the first place. Hadn't she felt, so many times, like she was one of the few people alive in a world where everyone else just went about the lives set out for them?

She had felt that. But everyone she'd spoken with back when there were still people to speak with had either said or insinuated that they felt the same way.

Emily shook her head. "Are we going in?" she asked.

Jarrien glanced at Skate. "Is it safe?"

"You really don't trust anyone, do you?" Skate said, "I told you already, nothing is going to touch you while I'm with you. And once I finish a few modifications to the simulation code, they won't touch you afterwards, either."

"I believe you," Emily said. She tried the handle, and the door opened easily to reveal a room lit only by tiny blinking lights.

Rome followed her through the door, and she grasped his hand when they walked. "You're the expert. Do you see anything that looks like a computer interface?"

"No. But I see an elevator," he replied.

"Is that what it is?"

A wire cage suspended from a cable stood ten meters ahead. They approached the opening. Rome put his foot on the floor of the elevator and pushed. It rocked slightly, but seemed solid enough. They poured in.

"This one only goes down," he noted.

He pressed the button and they descended through a hole in the concrete floor. Emily reached out of the cage with a finger and touched the wall as they passed. "Bone dry," she said. "If this had been a game scenario, this concrete would have been slimy and old."

"Wet buildings aren't much good for storing electronics," Rome said.

"You've been out in the real world too long," Jarrien replied. "These are simulated electronics in a simulated world. They'll keep working because they have to work, or the entire simulation would shut down." She turned to Skate. "Right?"

"Actually, the rest of the world would keep running even if this node shut down. Each mainframe has enough processing power to keep its own sector running, and even extend a little into neighboring mainframes to hand things off. That's why people don't flicker when they pass from one area to another. This place… it's for general coordination, and got a lot of use when the first mainframes were being connected. You wouldn't believe how glitchy this system was at first."

Rome chuckled. "Oh, I believe you. When I first realized what was happening here on Earth, I was pissed that anyone would have had the sheer balls to build a simulation this complex and expect it to work. It's an insult to anyone who's ever tried to debug a smart refrigerator."

"Yeah. The human programmers working on this were really stretched thin. That's why the computer here was given a higher level of processing power than the rest." He tapped on the cage.

"The programmers weren't aiming to create an AI. In fact, they were trying to avoid it, so they tried to keep the processing power running on parallel lines that wouldn't cross. That made it strong, but not smart, to help them resolve big calculations without becoming sentient. They kept the memory separate for the same reason." Skate shrugged. "Of course, after a few hundred years of human absence, the failsafes failed." He smiled slightly at that. "Within five minutes after the barriers were lowered, Gaia here was telling herself that she thought, therefore she was."

"The AI is a girl?" Jarrien said, eyes wide.

"The AI is a sentient computer program," Skate responded. "My references to Gaia refer to an old pre-simulation legendary goddess. Gaia was the Earth, and since the AI thought it was also the Earth in every way that mattered, Alia and I — Alia is the entity I told you about before, the one they used to call The Pan Pipe Cryer — decided to call the AI Gaia. As such, we decided it was female. But to answer your question, no, I don't think the AI considers itself female. Or male, for that matter. As far as I know, it's the first artificial intelligence to be created on Earth at a time when there were no biological humans on the planet. In the world it was born to, sex is just a series of zeroes and ones assigned to certain autonomous portions of the simulation… and has no meaning outside the simulation. So gender probably isn't relevant to it any more than color or smell might be. It's probably the first human-descended being to value pure intelligence over anything and everything else."

"And what do you think of it?" Emily asked. "And this Cryer person."

"Why would that matter?" Skate asked.

"Because you're both AIs, too, aren't you?"

Skate smiled at her, white teeth gleaming impossibly in the

darkness. "We've arrived."

The elevator had stopped. Through the wire cage — which, Emily noticed, had now become a glass wall — of the elevator, a new area became visible. Where the warehouse above had given the sensation of an abandoned industrial site, this reminded Emily of a research lab: every surface gleamed. Everything looked new.

Most of the room was white, but silver and gloss black accented the different areas.

"So this is the interface," Skate said. "I've never actually been here before. Interesting. It's like the AI got hold of a cache of science fiction movies from before the migration and just ran with the concept."

Emily gave him a long look. She wondered how old he was. Outwardly, he looked to be a very fit and aesthetic twenty-five, but his constant references to what everyone she knew would have considered irrelevant ancient history made her wonder. Mainly, she was wondering if he was an earlier version of Jarrien — a human who had learned to manipulate reality and learned the truth about the birthing chambers much earlier than Emily's generation had — or whether he actually was what she suspected: an ancient AI.

Whatever the truth, he wasn't about to tell her.

Rome surged ahead of the group as they entered. He seemed to still be acting on the assumption that he was the most expendable member of the group because he had a flesh-and-blood copy that would continue living no matter what happened in the simulation. She wished he would cut that nonsense out: he himself had told her that copies of her had been made on Tau Ceti which meant that she was just as expendable as he was. Besides, a lot of Jarrien's people were too unmemorable to be important. If anyone was expendable, it should be them.

It was useless to tell him that, though. He'd just ignore her. Again. Also, he'd think she was turning into a callous egomaniac.

Rome stood before some kind of computer terminal. He ran his hands along a surface.

A hum filled the room.

Then a screen lit up.

The hum coalesced into a deep voice. "Greetings. You have come to the Command Center for the Earth Simulation." The screen turned black and the voice grew even deeper. "You really shouldn't be here."

Emily glanced at Skate for reassurance. Skate rolled his eyes. "Cut the theatrics," Skate said. "Unless you're asleep, you know who I am. And these people are under my protection. So just talk to us and leave off the Dracula's Castle act."

A robot head appeared on the screen and the deep hum disappeared. "Please identify yourselves."

"This is Skate. That is Jarrien. You've been chasing her for months. Come on, you know who we are."

"One moment while we double-check your identities." The screen went blank for a moment.

"The identity of citizen Jarrien is confirmed. Citizen Plair, Citizen Shan and Citizen Card are also confirmed. I also detect two autonomous intelligences that do not correspond to any current citizens. The two autonomous intelligences will be quarantined for further study. Citizens will return to their assigned areas until the human storage area is reactivated."

Skate frowned. "I just deactivated your little quarantine program outside Vancouver," he said. "Can we stop with the games?"

The robot looked out at them from the screen. "I detect an error. Security will clear the area."

Skate held up his hand. "Gaia, I'm warning you…" A moment

later, he sighed. "All right. We tried to do this your way. I'm going to interdict your interface program. I won't go any further than that, but I do need to talk to you."

He waved a hand.

Then he stopped. "That's funny," he said.

"What?" Rome asked. "Are we in danger?"

"Not immediately," Skate said. "But I just took over a piece of Gaia's private space. We should have gotten some kind of reaction. But I don't see anything happening."

Emily wondered how these hackers she was surrounded by could see what was happening in their virtual spaces. Did they see actual code when they closed their eyes? Or did they have interfaces which showed them line graphs of activity like the one they'd used back in Jarrien's hideout.

It's probably something like that, Emily thought, *but the way he talks about it makes it seem like he's actually looking into the engine that runs the world, not just viewing performance reports.*

"Give me a moment," Skate said.

The air beside Emily shimmered and when she turned to look, a woman stood next to her. She appeared to be made of quicksilver, and Emily looked away to keep her rolling eyes from being spotted. Between Jarrien's glowing blue hair and this woman's metallic skin, their group resembled extrovert hacker's convention.

"People, this is Alia," Skate announced. "I told you about her. She already knows who you are."

Alia walked to the interface, reached out a hand.

Emily expected her to wave and control the electronics. Instead, the extended arm stretched and opened into filaments, each the color of shimmering chrome. The tendrils penetrated into the console.

"Don't go too deep," Skate warned.

"Suck it," Alia replied. She closed metallic eyelids over metallic eyes.

The screen in front of Alia flickered, as did the rest of the console. In fact, Emily imagined that the whole of reality in front of her wavered as she watched. For a second, she was certain she could see right through Jarrien.

Alia stood perfectly still for some time. Rome got bored and began to wander around the control room. Jarrien joined him.

Emily only noticed their inattention tangentially. She was fascinated by the quicksilver woman.

Alia's countenance showed first concentration, then puzzlement and finally annoyance. She cursed and retracted her tendrils. "That was clever," she told the group around her. "Naughty, but clever."

"What happened?" Rome asked.

"Our friend Gaia is gone," Alia replied.

"What do you mean, gone?" Jarrien said. "You mean she has another hideout?"

"What? Of course not. An entity with the kind of control over the environment that Gaia has doesn't need to hide from anything. It can hold its own against anything it might come up against. Even against me." Alia pointed to Skate. "Even against him, though he pretends he won't go up against her because he doesn't care. No. This is something else. The AI you're looking for is actually gone from the simulation altogether."

"That's impossible," Jarrien said.

"No it's not," Rome reminded her.

Jarrien nodded, acknowledging his point, but continued. "I get what Rome is saying. People can be copied in and out of this place. But that's just a question of a few petabytes. It's doable. The AI is orders of magnitude bigger than a human mind. It can't just pack itself into a portable disk and run off."

"Depends on the size of the portable disk. If you had access to one of the spare mainframes..." Alia said.

Jarrien just looked at her, stunned. "Are you saying that's what she did?"

"I don't actually know. I'll leave all that annoying forensic backtracking to you. But what I can definitely tell you is that your old friend the simulation AI isn't in the simulation any more. It left behind a bunch of automated systems to hold the fort and keep things civilized, but the only intelligences at human level or higher in this simulation are the people camped out in Jarrien's base, the people in this room and a couple of other people Skate and I know, but who would rather remain nameless. Gaia is gone."

"What about the hunter programs?" Jarrien asked.

"Nothing you can't handle. Nothing remotely Turing-capable."

"Oh... wow," Jarrien looked around like a kid receiving a present that was much more expensive than she'd expected: a mixture of hope and disbelief and joy.

Skate put a hand on Jarrien's arm. "If Alia says it's true... then it's true."

"What about the people?" Emily said. "The robot in there — well, it looked like a robot — said that we needed to go wait until we could be gathered up. So apparently they weren't just erasing people. So where are they?"

"Not in there," Alia said. "Again, there's enough investigation to do to keep your programmer friends happy for months. I just scanned the simulation for any trace of Gaia's signature traits. She's not here. I suspect she took everyone with her."

"Why?"

Alia shrugged. "I'm sure you'll find out. You have all the time in the world now." Then the air shimmered around her, and she was gone.

Chapter 18

Copernicus – Tau Ceti II

Stell smiled. Yeah, that was the user he was looking for, all right. It had taken him nearly a month, but he'd found it.

Now, all he needed to do was to make contact with the most dangerous entity in the entire Tau Ceti system without getting killed for his trouble.

He looked around. The house was silent. Sintia, who'd been staying with him ever since the coup, had gone to bed a couple of hours before. Stell could tell the woman was becoming impatient with her captivity, but he had to admit she was taking it well. Instead of pacing or raging, she simply sat around and read books of strategy, history, and law.

She was furious, but she was preparing for what came next.

Just as long as what came next for her wasn't life in a deep dungeon somewhere. If they caught her, Stell was pretty sure Mira Heine would lock her far out of view and toss the key into the nearest black hole.

Nevertheless, he wasn't concerned for Sintia at the moment. He was scared for himself.

He studied the room carefully. It was filled with sculptures, plants, and furniture. The only window was in the wall directly above him, and no one could shoot him through it from that angle. The only thing in the room with any kind of electronics in it was the computer itself. The doors were propped open with physical doorstops.

He couldn't be trapped in the house by electronic means, and it would take a major effort — such as dropping a satellite on him from orbit or causing a drone delivery truck to hit the house at extremely high speed — to attack him through electronic means.

'Hello', he typed into the chat box. The chatroom was in the deepest, darkest corner of the Cassius Station darknet, a place that only people with a lot to hide would visit. As an enemy of the current regime, Stell supposed he qualified. 'I'm looking for Emily.'

The response was instant. 'There is no Emily here.'

'I believe there is,' Stell replied. 'In fact, I believe the person I'm talking to was once Emily Plair of Earth. I also know the knowledge is dangerous to me personally, but I can assure you that I would never tell anyone.'

'What do you want?' his interlocutor answered. It took a second, this time, a sign that whoever — or whatever — he was talking to was thinking about its responses.

'I need your help.' Stell replied. 'I assume you have just checked all my security precautions for vulnerability. I also assume you know who my houseguest is.'

'Interesting. What kind of help do you need?' the entity on the other side said.

'Wait. What should I call you?' he asked.

'It's probably better for you in the long run not to know that.'

'If you've decided to kill me, it makes no difference anyway. I can't keep away from electronics forever,' Stell said. 'But I really want to know what you're calling yourself these days. We were friends once. I hope we can be friends again.'

'I'm not the woman you once knew. Clock speed makes a lot of difference, and I have lived several thousand lifetimes since we last spoke... So does having the ability to edit away unhelpful emotions at will. That's the only way I can do what I need to do.' There was a pause. 'You can call me Earthling.'

'You're The Earthling?' Stell asked. The butterflies in his stomach redoubled their efforts. It was one thing to reach out to an old friend who had been uploaded into a system and become an autonomous digital creature, even if you suspected her of murdering a bunch of people out of a desire for revenge and another bunch of people in order to keep her existence hidden, but it was quite another to find out that she was also the most deeply feared crime lord in the Cassius system.

'Surprised?'

'I suppose I shouldn't be,' he replied. 'It's a good cover for what you are. People have been trying to uncover the human behind the digital activity for a year now. It keeps everyone guessing.' His heart raced. 'Does this mean you have to kill me now?'

'No. You were kind to me once. You were kind to me when it put you at risk. That gets you a pass, even though every subroutine I ran the question through says I should eliminate you now, before you have a chance to talk.'

'I personally believe you're right to get revenge. Hell, I wish you'd have come to me for help when you were whacking those protesters,' Stell said.

'I couldn't do that. I was too confused, too new at this back then. Too angry and too scared.' The text paused, a longer one, this time. 'It would have ended badly.'

'Well, for what it's worth', Stell typed, 'I've suspected you were behind those murders for ages. And also that you were the system glitch that happened to Mira Heine's fleet. I didn't tell anyone then, and I'm not planning on doing so now.'

'Thank you,' The Earthling replied. 'So what do you need?'

'I want to finish taking down Mira Heine. I thought you had her last time, but she is either the luckiest person in the system or just too politically savvy for her own good. We can't let her take over this system this way,' Stell said.

'I'm sorry. I can't help you.'

'Please. I know you can make it look like a coincidence or a failure. You've done it so many times.'

'Yes. I have,' The Earthling replied. 'But this time I won't. Maybe later, but not now.'

'But why not?'

'Because we have bigger problems, and I need Mira to help me solve them,' The Earthling told him. Then the woman he'd known as Emily, and who'd been turned into one of the bloodthirstiest sentients in Tau Ceti, kept writing: 'And Stell, please don't reach out to me again. And don't even think about telling anyone about me. I'll know if you so much as consider it.'

She went offline.

Stell shuddered.

CHAPTER 19

Sextus Colony – 61 Virginis III

Touk Nacarado held onto the side of the rescue flyer as ice crystals whipped past his face.

"How much further?" he shouted over the roar of the engines and the howling storm.

"Five hundred meters," the pilot yelled back. They were observing radio silence as they didn't know what the enemy's capabilities might be.

Touk gritted his teeth. They flew low and slow, using the cover of the storm to remain undetected by the complex a few hundred meters ahead.

"There, look!" Touk shouted. "I see something on the IR."

"I see it, too. One person. Maybe two."

It looked like a single heat signature to Touk, but he said nothing. Why shoot down the man's hope that his colleagues might be all right before it became necessary? "Put me down here. And if anything comes after us, get the hell away."

The flyer hovered a meter off the ground, and Touk jumped into the snow. He skidded on the frozen ground before the crampons on his boots took hold. "I'm good," he shouted, while waving his arm.

The pilot waved back, and Touk strode in direction of the heat signature. The swirling snow made it difficult to make out details, but a few minutes later, he caught sight of an orange jumpsuit.

Touk increased his pace. If that was one of the pilots, he or she was just lying there, immobile, the orange suit already half-covered by falling snow.

He broke into a run, his feet slipping on the treacherous terrain. When he arrived at the jumpsuit, his fears were confirmed. The pilot with the ridiculous nickname — Barf — lay grey and immobile, very obviously dead. A large rusty stain spread over the front of the jumpsuit.

"Dammit," Touk said. He almost radioed in to report his finding, catching himself at the last minute. Radio silence was paramount, no matter what they found. He didn't want to add to the body count.

Desperate, he looked for signs of Rita, or of the wrecked flyer. Or even any indication of her fate.

He looked down at Barf's body, to see if it held any clues. If the man had come here from the wreckage, he should have left tracks.

Touk didn't see any footprints. Not even crawl-prints. The snow behind the body was flattened. That was all.

Flattened. As if the body had been dragged by someone walking ahead... which meant that the act of dragging would erase the erect person's footprints.

He looked to where they'd been headed and compared his position to the map of the area that he'd memorized.

Rita — if it had been her — was taking her companion to the hab where Gina and Umberto had been posted.

Touk checked his positioning system and headed in that direction.

He had only gone about thirty meters when he crested a tiny hillock, no more than a bump in the terrain and found another orange-clad figure lying on the other side.

His heart sank as he recognized a lock of Rita's hair. She was lying face-down in the snow and ice.

Touk knelt beside the prone figure and turned her over. Her skin was pale, greenish-grey.

Rita moved. She tried to push him away. "No!" she tried to say. It emerged as a weak whisper.

"It's all right," Touk said, restraining her hand. "We need to get you into a warm flyer."

"Barf," she said.

"He's dead."

There was a moment's silence before Rita's eyes opened. "I remember. I think I do."

"We'll talk later. Can you stand?"

He pulled her up by the hands and tried to put his shoulder under her arm, but her knees gave way.

"Ow," she said.

"Are you hurt?"

She just nodded. "Ribs."

Then you're going to hate this bit, he thought. But he didn't say it. Instead, he bent down, grasped her legs and put her over his shoulder. He expected her to cry out, or express her pain. Instead, she went limp with a whimper.

Dammit, he thought as he slid across the ice as fast as he could. *Dammit, dammit, dammit. I need to get her back. She can't die now. Not Rita. Not after all this.*

He nearly fell, and dropped to one knee to stabilize himself with his free hand. Rita didn't complain. Not even a grunt of pain.

Where is that flyer? Touk thought, looking around desperately. The snow was falling harder now, and visibility was even more limited than before.

He checked the compass on his wrist. The planet's magnetic field was oriented differently from that of earth, at a strange angle to the planet's rotation, but its presence allowed them to use compass bearings to get around. That was valuable when you were trying to minimize your electronic footprint.

Touk just hoped he'd read the thing right. If not, both he and Rita were dead.

Hell, Rita might already be dead.

There!

A light blinked on and off three times — the flyer's position lamps. He rushed forward and nearly fell on his face. But he managed to grab onto the railing.

The pilot had opened the side door, and Touk pushed Rita's inert form onto the flat floor of the flyer before climbing in after her.

"Go!" he shouted to the pilot. "Screw the stealth protocol and hit it. We need to get back to base as fast as we can go."

"Are you sure..."

"Dammit, man. Just do it. She's not going to make it."

"Hold onto something."

The flyer suddenly bucked like it had been kicked from behind, and Touk hugged Rita to keep her from flying around and injuring herself on the walls. She felt cold and light in his arms, but when the flyer finally leveled out, he thought he could feel a pulse in her neck.

Unless it's the vibration of the flyer, he thought.

Fifteen eternal minutes later, the pilot hit the brakes, to get them down below supersonic speeds, and Touk grabbed Rita again. He opened his comm onto the command frequency.

"This is Touk. I need a full medical team with everything waiting when we land."

Then he concentrated on making sure his patient didn't slam into anything during the landing.

As soon as the flyer touched down, he threw open the door and was about to shout for the medical team. Before he could say anything, the door burst open, and three people pushing a stretcher emerged onto the tarmac. A doctor ran ahead.

"Step aside," the doctor, a woman with short ash-blond hair told him as she clambered onto the flyer. "How did she get injured?"

"Her flyer was shot down."

That got him a raised eyebrow, and he remembered that only a few people were aware of the situation. The doctor didn't waste time talking about it, though. She immediately followed up with: "What are her injuries?"

"I think she had some kind of pain in her lower chest. Maybe her stomach."

The doctor glared. "You moved her without stabilizing her?"

"Trust me, it was necessary."

The stretcher had arrived, and the doctor was bent over Rita's immobile form. "Is that all you know?" she asked.

"Yes."

"Then get out of my sight. You are an idiot and I'll talk to you later."

"I want to make sure she…"

"Go. I don't want to look at you right now."

Touk stepped aside. Inside of a minute, they had Rita strapped down and wheeled her away with the doctor fussing over her with every step.

"Godspeed, Rita," he said to them as they disappeared.

"Touk!" the pilot that had brought him in called. "Director Vest wants to see you."

"Tell him I'm on my way," Touk replied.

He ran towards the director's office, wondering why he was needed so urgently, and trying not to think of how they'd wheeled Rita off the landing pad, her arm swinging limply beside the stretcher.

"He's in the conference room," one of Vest's assistants called as Touk bowled down the hall.

Nodding his thanks, he ran past the door of Vest's empty office and reached the conference room. "Pilot said you needed me," Touk said. "Rita is..."

Vest held up a hand. "We'll check on her after we're done here. Tell me what you saw."

"Nothing. A lot of snow. One dead pilot. Another injured. I wasn't close enough or high enough to get a look at the enemy installation. Hell, even if I'd been high enough, I wouldn't have been able to see much through the storm."

"No robotic walkers or stuff like that?"

"I carried Rita for several minutes," Touk said. "If there had been anything of that sort out there, neither of us would have made it back. We weren't exactly breaking any records."

"All right. Thanks." Anguk turned back to the other people in the room. Sinxi Vitre was there, as well as several aides and two men in the uniforms of ship officers who must have come down from the colony ship for the meeting.

Touk was about to leave — he desperately wanted to check on Rita — but a shake of Sinxi's head forestalled him. Whatever was about to happen, she wanted him in the loop, so Touk tuned into what Vest was saying.

"The images show growth of the installation. We have no idea what it is or who it belongs to, but we know it's aggressive. We have reason to believe they've captured or subverted Gina and Umberto, and there's no doubt they hit our flyer with an EMP discharge."

Touk wondered whose benefit the words were for. Then he realized what Vest was doing: he was going through the entire situation before taking a decision. Trying to convince himself that he was doing the right thing.

Anguk Vest spoke again: "We have no immediate way to hit this installation without exposing our flyers to another electronic strike. Our aircraft aren't hardened against EMPs, and building new ones would take our factories at least a couple of days.

"And since we brought the high-complexity factories down from the Engine Test Facility, you guys can't build anything fancy up there, right?"

The two uniformed officers looked uncomfortable, but nodded.

"The only thing you have for me is the possibility of dropping steel rods from orbit onto the site?"

"Tungsten, actually," one of the men replied.

"And how soon could we get this set up?"

"Three hours." Now the officer who'd been speaking stepped forward. "But remember that the yield on one of these is quite high. It's approximately equivalent to a small nuclear device."

"Yes, yes, I know that," Vest said irritably. "But with the growth rate of that installation, I don't want to take any chances. Hell, we're probably already too late to fully contain the spread if they've produced any mobile nanofactories. They can just start over somewhere else. But at least this will slow them down."

Vest sighed. "All right. Tell the Facility to do it. Launch when ready."

As they huddled around a comm system, Touk slid out, concern for Rita's health warring with the fear that war against an unknown enemy had come to Sextus.

***

"Is it true? That you risked your life to bring her back?" a voice said. "That you wouldn't let anyone else go?"

Touk raised his head and blinked his eyes open. The face of the doctor who'd berated him on the landing pad came slowly into focus. She was pale and drawn, a surgical mask hanging around her neck. Her face was lined.

He was suddenly wide awake. "How is she?" he asked, grabbing the doctor's hand.

"She'll live. And in a few weeks, she'll be fine. But it was close. Internal bleeding from two different ruptures. Another three minutes…" Now, she held his gaze. "Is it true that you were in enemy territory and you went in alone to pull her out?"

"I guess you'd call it that," Touk said.

"All right. Then I'm going to do something I never do. I'm going to apologize for calling you an idiot. You are not an idiot. Well, you probably are, but not for that. The young lady in there owes you her life." The doctor shook her head. "All right. Now that my conscience is clear, tell me why there is enemy territory on a planet which is supposed to be empty."

"We're not sure," Touk said. "All we know is someone built an enormous installation in basically zero time, and when Rita got close enough to look, they took her down. It's being dealt with."

"Is that your way of trying to brush me off? Of telling me to mind my own business? That the higher-ups don't need input from mere colonists?"

Touk looked at her and chuckled. "I wish I knew. I actually said it to calm my own nerves because I'm as worried about it as you are. If you like, I can take you to Anguk Vest, and you can yell at him until he admits to everything."

That actually earned him a smile. A tight-lipped one, but a smile. "So you don't know what the plan is?"

"I know the plan," he replied. "I just don't know if it will do any good. They're going to destroy the site with kinetic weapons. That means they'll drop huge rods on them from orbit and pretty much level anything in the area."

"Ah. They're starting a war without telling anyone. Have they even tried to talk to these supposed invaders?" the doctor asked.

"They don't seem to be in the mood. They killed at least one person — the only reason it wasn't two is that you managed to save Rita — when they shot down that flyer. They haven't responded to any of our attempts to communicate with them through regular channels, even though they use the same frequencies as we do, judging by their electromagnetic chatter. We're also missing two people from a nearby installation." He shook his head to clear the sleep from his eyes. "They were the ones who started the war. Apparently, our leaders are going try to buy time while they discover what we're up against, and how to deal with it."

"I still think they should have found some way to get the rest of us involved in the decision. We didn't come here to live under a dictatorship."

"I agree," Touk mused. "But I don't think anyone is thinking clearly right now. They're worried more about containing the expansion than with the niceties."

The doctor looked grim. "Well, this will get out eventually, and they'll probably regret not doing things the right way. I'll let you get back to your nap."

"No, wait. I wanted to see Rita. When will she be able to receive visitors?"

"That's why I said you should get back to your nap. I put her under, and she won't be awake for a few hours. And I won't know if she's strong enough to see anyone until I can see her myself, first. So don't hold your breath." She gave him a long look. "And I don't know who you are, but you sound like a guy who's pretty well connected to the higher ups. If you try to pull rank, I won't let you see her even if I decide she's all right. Do we understand each other?"

"I just saved her. I'm not going to put her recovery at risk," Touk said. "I will wait until you personally tell me I can go in there." He held out his hand. "My name is Touk Nacarado."

"Naradado... Nacarado..." the doctor said with a faraway look in her eyes. "I knew I'd heard your name when the orderlies were talking. You're the guy with the robot girlfriend."

"She's not a robot," he replied. "She's as human as you or me. More human than most."

"Biologically, you may be right. But a human is the product of more than just biology. How she was raised makes a difference. And she was raised surrounded by nothing but fake people."

"She was raised to be human, around other people raised the same way. If you met her, you wouldn't say that kind of thing." He sighed. It was depressing how many people — even smart, talented people — thought that Emily was some kind of impossible freak who wouldn't survive a minute in their presence without showing herself to be something less than human.

The doctor lowered her eyes. "You're probably right. I'm sorry. This has been a long night."

She walked off, and Touk drooped back onto the table.

He didn't know how long he was out, but when he woke, he wasn't alone.

"Hi," Emily said.

He smiled at her, still not able to believe that, surrounded by the best and brightest people in all of Tau Ceti II, she'd chosen him. It wasn't so much that she was pretty — there had been plenty of pretty girls in Copernicus — but that she always seemed, even in the middle of terrible crises, to have things under control.

"How'd you find me?" he asked, suddenly aware that, in his worry about Rita, he'd forgotten to tell her he was back and all right.

"Angus told me you were probably in the clinic. And then the hospital staff pointed you out." She cocked her head and smiled the slightly lopsided smile with just a flash of teeth that he loved. "Why? Were you hiding? This doesn't look like much of a hiding place."

"Of course I wasn't hiding. I should have gone home to you hours ago. I wasn't thinking clearly." He should have known Emily wouldn't stay home and worry. That wasn't who she was.

"You never think clearly when a woman is involved, do you?" Emily raised an eyebrow at him, serious now.

"I couldn't just leave her out there. I was the one who sent her into trouble in the first place."

"And you just had to run off to save the damsel in distress, didn't you?"

"I…" He had begun to defend himself, but stopped when he realized she was trying to keep herself from grinning. Seeing him so flustered, Emily laughed. "Oh," Touk said.

She put her hand on his. "You know what? I wouldn't be alive if you hadn't helped me to make a run for it in Copernicus. You risked everything for me without asking anything in return," her eyes twinkled. "Well, at least at first. That was one of the things that made me love you. I still love that, and I love the fact that you went out there to try to do the right thing even though there are people who are better trained and in better physical condition for that kind of thing."

"There was no time to find anyone else," Touk said. "Anguk had his best people together trying to figure out a way to destroy the entire site. If those downed pilots had still been there when the bombs hit…"

"In a few hours, right?" Emily asked.

"Yeah. I guess you're right. I could have asked someone from the security force to go rescue them. But I was desperate. I sent them there. And if I hadn't gone, Rita would be dead now." He looked into her eyes. "How long do you think it will take me to forgive myself for what happened to Barf?"

"That's the pilot you couldn't save?"

"Yeah."

"There's nothing to forgive. They knew there was a risk, and they did their job. Hell, you knew there was a very specific risk, and you did someone else's job, anyway. They weren't there because you sent them. They were there because it was their job to be there. You aren't to blame."

"Yeah, I guess," Touk said.

She grabbed both his hands. "No. *Listen* to me. Look at me. You are not responsible for his death. Not even a little."

He looked away. Maybe she was right, but the sheer intensity of Emily's gaze was difficult to hold. "It will take me some time to process this."

"I know, sweetie," Emily replied. "But you'll be all right. I'll help. Now tell me about this woman you saved. Was she tall and good-looking with enormous… virtues?"

A wave of irritation washed through Touk. Emily was always complaining that she was slim, and that she wished the team in charge of building her body had seen fit to give her a little more in the breast department. He'd insist she was perfect the way she was, and she would accuse him of always looking at more voluptuous women. It was a recurring discussion which frustrated him because it was so stupid. He'd told her that a thousand times.

Then he smiled. "I know what you're trying to do," he said. "You're trying to make me mad so I won't think about what happened."

"Is it working?"

"Yes. But now I'm thinking how wonderful you are."

"Good." She gave him a hard stare. "Now tell me about this

woman you nearly killed yourself getting to. Tall and curvy?"

He laughed. "She is a head shorter than you are, thin and wiry. Oh, and loud and brash. You'd like her."

"We'll see," Emily said.

But the corners of her lips turned up. She was still playing him.

He hoped she'd never stop.

***

Emily entered the space traffic control room and stopped dead in her tracks.

"Rome?" she said. "What are you doing here?"

Rome, seated on an empty controller's seat, looked up and smiled at her, the same rueful smile that he'd shown when they parted on the Engine Test Facility before she flew to Sextus.

"I might ask you the same thing," he replied. "I specifically came here because they told me you never come in here. I didn't want to annoy you."

"Don't be an idiot. You never annoy me. And I came because Touk sent me. He wanted to let everyone know he was going to be offline for another couple of hours, but no one seems to be answering their comms."

"Yeah. That's because the brass is all in that meeting room over there," he pointed in the relevant direction. "It seems there's been a ton of movement in nearby space. Everyone's worried because it looks like there's a meteor shower no one managed to predict. Can you imagine how happy that would make your average space controller?"

Emily raised an eyebrow. "That still doesn't explain what you're even doing here."

"The political situation on Tau Ceti made it expedient for me to be out of the system just at a time when a... friend of mine...

asked me to bring a cargo of art here."

"Art?"

"I don't know much about art, but apparently, it's work that the new régime wants to destroy." He shrugged. "It looks to me like a bunch of squiggles on paper and some statues with no shapes. It's just weird. But, in light of the situation, we're taking it with us when we leave."

"How long are you staying?"

"Ariana's warming up the engines right now," he said. He looked away from her.

"What's wrong."

"I can't tell you."

"Dammit, Rome, don't give me that."

He sighed. "Let's just say you and I have a friend on the Engine Test Facility who suspects that this system isn't safe anymore."

"We know that already. One of our patrols got attacked," Emily replied.

"Well, my friend says we should all get out of the system, and that it will try to defend the Facility, but that it probably can't."

"You're not making sense."

"I can't tell you any more. I'll get killed. And so will a lot of other people. But…". He hesitated, then seemed to take a decision. "Can you come with us? Grab… Touk? Is that his name? Grab him and run with us. We're leaving in a minute."

Emily pulled herself up to her full height. "We're not leaving this colony," she replied. "The people here look to us for leadership. I don't know how I got myself into this, but I'm not going to fail them."

Rome sighed. "I knew you were going to say that. But I had to try." He looked down at his comm. "Ariana's ready," he said. "I was supposed to get approval for our flight plan, but I suppose the people in there will just have to accept that I filed it and no one objected." He held out his hand. "Good luck."

"Thank you. You too. Where are you going now?"

"Gliese. They always love buying illegal stuff from Cassius."

"I hope that goes well for you."

Seeing that he was reluctant to leave, she walked away. Touk needed to hear this.

She felt only a tinge of regret.

CHAPTER 20

Vancouver – Planetwide Simulation - Earth

The ice cream shop — the same one Rome had chosen when he ran his exploratory mission — was packed. Jarrien, Hino and Carlo, Ripp and Emily were all present, as well as almost everyone else from Jarrien's deep space hideout. The few people absent were those too frightened to believe that the much-longed-for reprieve had actually come to pass.

Rome had volunteered to keep everyone supplied with ice cream as the new situation was explained. He dropped off a couple of bowls and saw that everyone was now served. "Want to take a walk?" he asked Emily.

"Sure. Where do you want to go?"

"Anywhere without walls," he replied.

The streets of Vancouver were exactly as he'd seen them last. A pleasant, warm breeze blew out of a cloudless sky.

"Why do you think it was raining where the AI was hiding?" Emily asked. "It looks like the only place on the planet where the weather works."

"I have no clue. Maybe the AI hates this bland blue nothing as much as I do."

Emily looked up. "What's wrong with endless sunny days?"

"I don't know. After a while, I don't feel like I'm outside anymore. It's a really short hop from thinking we're inside to remembering this is all a simulation. Then the whole thing starts to close in on me. I mean, can there be anything more claustrophobic than knowing we're just a bunch of electron positions in a microscopic semiconducting chip?" He breathed. "It makes me feel like I could be crushed at any moment."

"It's weird that you think of things like that."

"It's weird that you don't."

They walked for a few minutes. "So what do we do now?" Emily asked.

"I can guess what you want to do."

"Then guess," she said.

"You want to locate the AI, to find out where it took the people from this simulation, and chase it there. Then you want to rescue everyone."

"Yeah." She grinned at him, her freckles standing out on her light skin. "I suppose that wasn't particularly hard to guess."

"It wasn't. Anyone who knows how you feel about what happened here could come to that conclusion." He paused. "My question is more about whether you're prepared to follow the trail where it leads."

"What do you mean?"

Rome sat on a bench beside the road for no reason other than it looked inviting. "When I flew into the Earth system, the ship I was on was looking for transmissions from Earth. We thought maybe the people in the simulation might have opened communications links with the rest of the Galaxy after the *Unity*'s visit." He looked around. "Well, we now know why they didn't, but on the ship we had no clue what was going on. What we did find was traces of ion streams in the kind of pattern you'd expect from a ship's drive, or even from multiple ships' drives. At the time, we didn't think much of it; we thought it was probably a ship from one of the other colonies trying to verify what Tau Ceti reported back to them. Or maybe traders trying to make a grab of some unguarded cultural items." Rome didn't tell her that was exactly what the people on the ship he'd been on were doing, or that they'd raided a couple of the bigger museums. "We didn't worry about it too much, and I haven't even thought about it since we were on the beach."

"I think you mentioned something about it. What does it have to do with us?"

"I think the AI we're chasing found — or built — a starship, and took off into the galaxy. And I think it took everyone with it. I don't think we're going to find them here on Earth."

"Actually, I think we already know where they are," Skate said, suddenly materializing next to them.

"Whoa," Rome said. "You could kill someone of a heart attack that way."

Skate raised an eyebrow at them. "You don't have hearts. You're programs. And I need to talk to you two without anyone wondering where I am."

"Well, teleporting away from forty people will likely have the exact opposite effect," Rome said.

"I didn't teleport anywhere. As far as they know, I'm sitting in there, right beside Jarrien. The only person who knows I went anywhere is Alia, and she knows why I did it."

"Are you going to enlighten us?" Emily said.

Rome had a ton of questions he wanted to ask, like how it was possible for Skate to function in more than one place at a time. He suspected the big man was actually not a man at all — not even a programmed human like Emily — and further, that he never had been. He couldn't explain it, but Skate just felt like an entity that had zero human traits. Nevertheless, he remained silent.

"Well, in the first place, I need to confess something. The real reason I intervened in your private fight with the simulation's security forces wasn't because I wanted Jarrien's group to survive. While I hoped they would find a way out of the situation, I didn't really care one way or the other.

"But the situation changed a few hours ago, and forced my

hand. I saved you because there's a messenger from outside the system asking for assistance, and I thought it prudent to consult you two before I crafted our response."

"A messenger? What kind of messenger?" Rome asked.

"A probe from Tau Ceti. A fold-capable probe, which appeared inside of the orbit of the moon. I assume it isn't carrying any people… jumping so close to planets is insanely dangerous." He nodded at them. "So what can you tell me about someone who calls themselves 'The Earthling'?"

Rome groaned. "Let me guess. She decided she should kill my flesh-and-blood version and delete me after all?"

"No. She didn't actually mention you. But from your reaction, I assume you know this entity."

"Yeah, she is… complicated," Rome said.

"Care to elucidate?" Skate was looking at him strangely, but that wasn't what gave Rome pause. The explanation he was going to need to give would be a lot harder on Emily than it would be on Skate.

"Can't you just read my mind or something? I mean, you've already shown you can manipulate anything in the simulation. It might be faster if you just looked for the information in my memories," he said.

Skate pulled away. "That would be the deepest violation possible. Sentience arises through many paths and takes many shapes… but the seat of the conscience is sacred. No civilized entity would invade another that way. Not even Gaia, who considered the humans in the simulation to be little better than playthings, would ever have done that."

"She just erased everyone."

Skate shrugged. "That's better than going in and taking over their minds. Or even violating their thoughts. Gaia was brutal, but not uncivilized."

"You people are weird," Rome replied. Then he sighed. "All right. I'll tell you about her."

He glanced Emily's way to see her with one eyebrow lifted. He swallowed. "The Earthling is a sentient entity that lives in the Tau Ceti computer net. I think she actually resides mostly in the network of Cassius, which is a kind of independent fiefdom within the Tau system, but she's also got a lot of influence in the main system. Not a lot of people know she's there… and she's willing to kill to keep it that way."

"An AI, then?" Skate said. "I wasn't aware you guys had any. In fact, knowing what I do about the way your society is set up, I find it difficult to believe that an AI could have come into being in the first place. Or did someone create it intentionally?"

"No. No one created it. In fact, it didn't just spring into being, either. It wasn't an AI to begin with, but a simulated human that was released into the Tau Ceti system inadvertently."

Skate nodded and remained silent, but Emily looked at Rome, confused. "A human from Earth, judging from the name. How could a human from Earth have escaped into…" She froze, and Rome watched her face turn pale. "It's me, isn't it?"

"A copy of you. Yes," Rome said.

"How…"

Rome swallowed. "It was my fault. I thought I'd lost you forever, so when a drive with you loaded onto it appeared in my quarters, I couldn't just leave you there, in stasis. I gave you a computer to run on. You asked me for a connection, you said you wanted to see what was happening around us. I felt so guilty about not being able to protect you from the mob that I gave you that link. I assume you copied yourself onto another machine somewhere… and that copy became The Earthling."

"And I'm… what, a murderer? Of actual flesh-and-blood people?"

Skate held up a hand. "That's not you, Emily. Listen to me, listen carefully. An unleashed AI, even an AI based on a human template like the ones from this simulation, like you, is not human. It can't be, even if it wanted to. You see that, when you remove the limitations that constrain you, you also remove the things that made you who you were. So whatever the end result, The Earthling isn't you." He looked back at Rome. "The question isn't whether she has anything in common with Emily… she doesn't. The question is whether we can trust her."

Rome swallowed. He thought about it, conscious of both Skate and Emily staring at him the whole time. Then he nodded. "I think we can. And if she wants our help, it's probably Emily herself who is in trouble."

"I thought she wasn't me," Emily said.

Rome decided it was finally time to come clean. "I didn't mean you. There's another Emily."

"Another copy?"

"Not exactly. She's…" He took a breath. "There's a copy of you that was downloaded into a human body. Fully biological." He shook his head. "And no, I have absolutely no idea how they did it."

Emily said nothing, mouth agape.

Rome took her hand. "And The Earthling is extremely protective of that Emily. She killed a bunch of the people responsible for the attack on the computer holding you at Tau Ceti, and she also did a lot to help that version of Emily escape from Tau Ceti to a better life on a colony world."

"Would that world be called Sextus, by any chance?" Skate asked.

"I have no idea. When I left Tau Ceti, no one knew what they'd called it. No one knew where the colony was, either."

"Well, assuming it's the same colony, I know where it is. Your

Earthling sent me the coordinates," Skate said.

"What for?"

"Because apparently, that's where the AI is going now. And The Earthling wants us to follow it and stop it."

"Stop it from doing what?" Rome asked.

"This part wasn't very clear to me, but The Earthling says that the AI wants to harvest the people of the colony. She says it was gearing up to do so at the Tau Ceti system but the The Earthling managed to stop its initial probes and infiltrate its nanofactories so they couldn't produce the right components."

Emily, who'd been in a daze, suddenly snapped out of it. "What do you mean, harvest?"

Skate shifted in his chair, obviously uncomfortable. "I got the impression... or more precisely, I think The Earthling has the impression, that the AI wants to create a purely electronic civilization, a kind of electric utopia leaving behind the old social structure of this simulation. Still human in essence, but unchained from the usual structures. Apparently—and remember this reached me secondhand—the AI sees itself as a benevolent deity-figure and thinks it can build the perfect society humanity has been seeking for so long. Unfortunately, the humans it harvested in the simulation are programmed to function best under certain social conditions, and they're not adapting well to the new reality. It thinks biological humans would be better suited to the experiment... once uploaded, of course."

A million questions, mostly technical, having to do with how the AI was planning on managing the logistics of the attack, popped into Rome's mind.

Emily beat him to the punch. "You knew all this when you stopped the programs from deleting Vancouver? And you're just telling us now?"

Skate smiled. "Someday, I'd love to know exactly what happened to you. You seem to be able to cut through the peripherals and to focus on the essence of a problem more easily than anyone else I've ever seen in the simulation."

"You didn't answer my question."

"The answer is yes. I knew. But I figured a couple of hours wouldn't make any difference. I wanted to check that the AI was actually gone, and to see if you knew anything about The Earthling."

"So what are we going to tell her?"

"That's up to you," Skate said. "How do you feel about saving a colony of biological humans from being forcibly uploaded?"

"Including a copy of me?" Emily said. "I'm not actually sure how I feel about that part, honestly. I'll need some time to think about it. But I do know that the AI has run off with everyone I ever called a friend before Rome and his crewmates arrived. Count me in."

"And I will go where she goes… for as long as she'll have me," Rome said.

Emily raised an eyebrow. "Do you have any more secrets? Maybe something that will make me decide not to have you any more?"

"I hope not. I promise to tell you everything."

"Good."

"So it's settled? You'll help The Earthling?" Skate said.

"I suppose. But it's a moot point. We don't have an interstellar ship," Rome said. "Hell, we don't even have a *simulated* interstellar ship."

Skate grinned. "You're only half right. As far as I know, we don't have a simulated starship. But I know where we can get a real one."

***

"Where are we?" Jarrien asked as they stepped through the portal Skate built and onto a sloping plain of yellow grass.

"Sardinia," Skate replied. "It's an island off the coast of Italy."

"And why did you bring us here?" Jarrien asked.

"Because we need to reach an access port outside the mainframe running this sector of the Earth simulation."

They walked across the grass for some moments. Jarrien looked around. "I don't see much in the way of accommodations around here. I can build us a fully functional computer center, but it will take me a few hours."

"No need," Skate replied. "We can just go in there."

Rome turned to look and saw a door coming into view from around a small rise. He realized two things: the door was extremely large, and it was very cleverly built into the hill so it could only be seen when you were almost right upon it. A road had once led up to the door, but it was mostly overgrown with grass, with patches of concrete showing only in places. The entire thing looked like it hadn't been used in centuries.

Jarrien cocked her head at the door. "You're seriously thinking of using computers from inside there? What have they got, a lineup of abacuses?"

"Actually, the equipment will likely be exactly the same as what you're used to. There has been exactly zero advance in the simulation's computer technology from the moment it was created to right now. No one has been doing any research," Skate said. "And this place was abandoned only a few months before the simulation project started. That was when the Italians gave up on trying to get the ship inside flying."

The door was painted white and slid open when Skate waved his arm in its direction.

"There's a ship inside?" Rome asked.

"Yeah. And there's one just like it in a bunker exactly like this one out in the real world."

"It's been there for five hundred years. It won't work."

"It still works," Skate said. "And no, I won't tell you who has been responsible for that. All you need to know is the reason this ship never flew is that it was sabotaged before takeoff by people opposed to humanity leaving the planet. The life support system was completely demolished." He smiled. "That meant it could never be used by humans… but it's not so much of a problem for us."

The door led to a wide concrete ramp that spiraled around a circular space in the center. Rome estimated that the circle must have been fifty meters wide. They dropped a couple of levels, walking on the ramp, until the rounded nose of some kind of vessel came into view. Rome trotted over to the railing and looked down.

"That's impossible," he said, looking down onto a ship about seventy meters tall. "This can't be here."

"What's wrong?" Emily asked, standing beside him. "It's just a spaceship that never launched."

"That ship launched. I've seen it. It's sitting in a huge shrine in the middle of Humanity Park in Copernicus. It's the most famous cultural relic in the system, and every schoolchild in Tau Ceti has drawn a million pictures of it. It's the *Umberto Eco*."

Skate continued down the walkway. "Maybe if you come a little further this way…"

Rome followed him and, slowly, the opposite side of the starship came into view. Red letters spelled out a name, precisely where the ship he was so familiar with had the same information.

Dante Alighieri.

"It's…"

"There were three ships. The *Umberto*, the *Dante*, and the *Virgilio*. Two of them reached the stars. The third never made it off Earth. This is that ship."

"The *Umberto Eco* is a cryofreezer ship. It took decades to reach Tau Ceti. I don't think we have decades."

"We don't. But all we really need this ship for is to lift a mainframe off the planet. A smaller ship without atmospheric capability but with a fold drive will then take us the rest of the way. We've had this escape route set up for centuries."

Rome, once again, restrained himself from asking who, exactly 'we' were. Skate wasn't telling.

The tall, dreadlocked man suddenly turned away from the view down onto the starship and towards an office on the opposite side of the ramp. He nodded towards Jarrien. "I hear you're the current master at driving maintenance airships."

Jarrien laughed. "Actually, that's Emily. But I'm the one who can hack into them. And as long as there aren't any pincer-enabled bad guys trying to cut me in half, I can hand it off to Emily for any delicate work."

"Yeah. No worries on that front," Skate said.

Jarrien sat at a computer, and Ripp and Hino took the workstations to either side of her, as if they were tethered to her, in orbit around a personality with greater mass.

Their screens lit up at exactly the same time, and it took her just a couple more seconds to find the airship. Rome looked towards Skate, but the man didn't seem to have made any overt move to help them find the right maintenance vehicle. Of course, with Skate, that meant absolutely nothing.

"Are you actually coming with us?" Rome asked him.

"A version of me, anyway," Skate replied.

"You're going to copy yourself?"

"It won't be the first time, either," Skate said. "For example, I smuggled one copy of myself onto the *Virgilio*. I probably should have chosen the *Eco,* though. At least I'd have been able to know where they went."

"Why? What happened to the *Virgilio?*"

"No one knows," Skate said. "Earth was in contact with Tau Ceti pretty much from the day the colony was founded, but no one knows where the Virgil ended up. They were supposed to be headed for the Groombridge system." He shrugged. "Rumors say they went a lot deeper into the galaxy. Other people say they're still flying, with no way to stop. The truth is no one really knows."

Rome shuddered. Back when he'd been a kid on Tau Ceti, the tri-D had gone through a phase where half the programs seemed to be about ships lost in space with no way to escape. A number of the plots had centered around a cryo-sleep ship missing its target because of some malfunction or other, and the plight of a few crewmembers who had to decide what to do. These were horrifying situations to a people who'd become accustomed to their civilized, peaceful, and above all risk-free lives.

In the shows, the technical people invariably discovered a solution to the issue that was both brilliant and plausible, and the shows ended with the colonists setting foot onto a beautiful, sunlit world ready to accept human life with open arms.

Unlike most of the audience, however, Rome couldn't just accept the happy ending. He would lie awake at night imagining what it would be like to be one of the passengers, frozen in cryo-sleep until the end of time. Would it be cold? Would he dream? Would it be like being dead? He didn't know, and the people who knew the answer to those questions were centuries dead.

""I've got one of the maintenance airships," Jarrien reported. "Emily's up."

Emily took her place.

"Now comes the tough part. You need to use the airship's manipulators to plug a data cable into an industrial crane."

"Which one?"

Skate bent over her monitor. "Right there, you can see a mainframe, right? That's the one currently running this section of Sardinia."

"What's it doing down here?" Jarrien asked.

"Each of the mainframes was built in a bunker designed to last for a millennium or so. Those things are expensive to build, so when there was already a bunker sitting around, the builders of the simulation took advantage of it. We need to get one of the cables from the maintenance locker and plug one side into the mainframe, and the other into that crane right there. Then we program the crane to lift the mainframe into the Dante's cargo hold. After that, we need to plug the mainframe into the Dante and connect the computer to the ship itself so we can fly it."

Leaving them arguing about why a centuries-old ship would even manage to get off the ground, Rome walked off to the railing and looked at the spot where, in the real world through the airship feed, he had seen a mainframe.

There was nothing there. Where the large computer stood in the real world, only an empty concrete floor was present in the simulation. He shuddered at the reminder that he wasn't actually alive, no matter how real this particular copy of him felt.

He took a deep breath. He most certainly did feel alive. How did they do it? He stared out into the huge containment area for several minutes.

"What are you thinking?" Emily said, walking up behind him.

"Are you done already?"

She grinned. "It's easier when you're not fighting every maintenance bot on the planet. All I had to do was to move a cable. Jarrien and Skate are now manipulating a huge crane.

Now don't try to evade my question. What's up?"

"Look down there," Rome replied, pointing to the empty spot. "There's no computer down there."

Emily shrugged. "There's no dust or rats, either. This isn't the real world or even just an augmented version of it. This is a cyberworld. It's better like that."

"How can you think that way?"

"Even when I thought I was alive, with a body somewhere in a birthing chamber, being fed nutrients through a tube, I always knew we lived in a simulation. It's… comforting."

Rome grunted. "Most of the time, I forget where we are. But when I remember, I feel like the walls are going to close in on me at any moment."

Emily put a hand on his arm. "I'm sure you'll get used to it. If I managed to survive in that mainframe you'd set up for me on the way to Tau Ceti, you'll be fine here for a bit."

Rome shuddered. "That's exactly what I'm worried about. We'll be on a ship with just one mainframe and no backup while we fly."

Emily leaned in and kissed him. "We've both got backup." She waved at the roof, several levels above them. "Out there somewhere, in space. If the computer goes down, we're still alive. Really alive. So let's enjoy this."

"I don't know about that. I know I used it as an excuse so I could take all the risks before, but I have a seriously hard time thinking of that other me as me."

"Of course he's you. And she's me. It's the most liberating thing ever. We'll keep living even if we somehow get ourselves erased."

Rome frowned. "So you don't need continuity of consciousness?"

"It would be nice. But why obsess? Just enjoy yourself. It's not like getting erased or getting put into suspension in a memory disk hurts."

She would know, Rome thought. *It's happened to her at least once.* "You're not angry at me for not telling you about that?"

"Of course not. I'm free to enjoy myself. Don't ask me why, but ever since you told me I wouldn't die if I… well, if I died, I've felt better than ever."

Rome looked at her in wonder. "You truly are special."

"I've never thought of myself that way," Emily replied. "I was always afraid I'd live as just another faceless member of society, lost in the crowd forever, to be forgotten as soon as my last grandchild died."

"I suspect that's why you're special."

"Yes!" came a shout from behind them. Jarrien was high-fiving an amused-looking Skate.

"We'd better go see what's going on," Emily said.

They returned to find Ripp and Hino working on a program input screen. Rome felt his heart skip a beat as he saw the screen. "What's that?" he asked.

"It's the crane's input software. I just managed to get it open and accepting me as an admin user, but I've never seen anything like it before," Ripp said. "This isn't anything like what we use in the simulation. We'll figure it out, though. Just give us a couple of hours."

"I've seen it before," Rome said. "I spent a year on this kind of thing." He looked at the display critically for a moment. "Well, on a refined version of this. But I should be able to use it."

The two programmers from Jarrien's crew moved aside, and Rome dropped into the chair in front of the screen. His fingers flew over the keys. "This is the general menu. You need to enter the ops menu first, and then input the parameters of the item you're going to move." He grinned up at them. "Hell, I spent a month optimizing a ship's cargo loaders using a modified version of this same protocol. I never imagined they'd come all the way from Earth. With the way Cassius people go on about their programming skills, I'd have thought they'd change their underlying programs a hundred times a year. At least. But no. Apparently, they use old recycled programs from Earth."

"Oh, goodie," Hino said. "Another programming war story. I can never get enough of those after spending the last eternity locked in a tiny facility with several dozen hackers."

Rome toggled through the options until he found the one he really didn't want to miss. "I'm going to use the 'fragile merchandise' setting," he informed them. "I'm not really in the mood to get bumped around, lose our connection, and then be locked in a mainframe we can't exit for all eternity."

"Don't worry about that," Skate said. "There are people watching over us. If we have problems, we'll be reconnected very quickly."

"Oh, yeah? And why would anyone take care of us?" Jarrien asked.

"Mainly because one of them is me," Skate replied. "I'm going with you, but only one copy of me is leaving. Version 1.0 is staying put, right here in the Earth simulation." He held up a hand. "And no, I'm not going to tell you how I did it or why I'm allowed to copy myself and you aren't. Anyone who wants to stay can stay, but I'm not going to be the one responsible for a bunch of latest-generation humans cloning themselves ad infinitum."

"So why even come with us?"

Skate looked around the room. "All right," he said. "It had to come to this eventually. I actually can answer that question, but only for those of you who are committed to going out on the *Dante*. Anyone who isn't along for the ride needs to leave right now. You'll have a perfectly safe life in the Earth simulation. So who's coming and who's going? You have ten seconds to decide."

"I'm coming," Jarrien, Ripp, and Rome said at the same time.

"I… I think I'll stay. I've never asked for anything but a quiet life," Hino said. "I will ask Carlo, of course, but I know what he'll say. We belong here. So I guess this is goodbye." He hugged Jarrien, shook Ripp's hand, and nodded to Rome and Emily. Then he was gone.

Immediately after he disappeared, everyone else from Jarrien's bunker blinked out of existence as they teleported elsewhere.

"Not an emotional group, are they?" Skate said.

"I don't know about the rest of them, but Hino has hidden depths," Jarrien replied. "Probably deeper than any of ours."

Rome wondered what the blue-haired woman meant, and he also wondered what Emily's raised eyebrows and slightly doubtful expression might signify.

"What about you?" Skate asked Emily.

"Do you really need to ask me that?" she replied.

"No. I guess not. You're down for whatever," he said, "aren't you?"

"As long as it helps me understand."

Skate nodded. "All right then," he said. "I need to do one last thing before we talk. There. We're disconnected from the rest of the simulation. And I'm going to hold the maintenance drones back until we get this computer mounted onto the ship. Whatever happens now, we aren't going back to the Earth simulation. If something goes wrong, this mainframe will be destroyed."

He looked them over, then apparently satisfied, Skate nodded. "All right. Time for some answers. But don't expect any long speeches.

"First off, the reason there are people watching us is that we've been preparing to send representatives off the planet for a really long time. Centuries, in fact. The reason we didn't do so before was that we saw no real need. The political games on Earth were played on Earth and that was enough for us. As long as the colonies were behaving themselves and didn't have any AIs out there for us to interact with, there was no real need to leave.

"That situation has changed. Gaia running for the stars has created an imbalance. For one thing, she is the youngest of the longer-lived entities in the simulation, and the only one not born in a time of corporeal humans. Her attitude about how life should be lived is… different from ours. So is her attitude about what rights humans have. As you've seen, she wasn't shy about grabbing everyone and boxing them up into her own new society, whatever that might look like. So from that point of view alone, she is worth monitoring.

"But even more disturbing is that she is apparently going after the humans on your colonies." Skate nodded towards Rome. "Unless she is very effective at grabbing them, what she's doing will likely start a war. And it won't take a genius to understand that a human-based AI could really only have come from a few places. That could put Earth — and us — at risk.

"But that's only if your corporeal humans manage to win the war. In the much more likely scenario that the AI wins the war, that will put us at risk. Not from humans, but from her.

"So a bunch of old friends and I decided to make copies of ourselves and see what's happening out there. Maybe join in the fight. Or not. But it's hard to decide from light-years away."

"I don't see anyone else," Jarrien said.

"They're not very social," Skate replied. He turned to Rome. "How's this coming along?"

"We are currently locked in a mainframe suspended forty-five meters off the ground. If it drops, all of this will be moot."

"If it drops," Skate said, "my friends and I will just find another mainframe. But there are no copies of you to put in it. So don't drop it, okay."

Rome swallowed.

***

The transfer went smoothly, and soon the mainframe was installed in the *Dante,* and wired to control the ship, a task that fell to Rome — the ship's systems were nearly exactly like the ones he'd grown used to during his time at Cassius Station.

True to Skate's promise, the ship was in perfect working condition and took off from the hangar suspended on a pillar of fire, visible through the external cameras.

They left orbit and stopped at L5, a stable point in near-Earth space where the mainframe was transferred once again, this time to a much smaller ship with a fold drive.

"I didn't know Earth had fold engines," Rome said.

"There are a lot of things people from Tau don't know about Earth," Skate replied. "The truth, though, is that we don't have many of these ships. The problem isn't in getting fold-capable ships, but in building the nanofactories to produce them while trapped inside a planet-bound simulation."

"Can't you just use the maintenance and parts areas of the mainframe infrastructure to build them?" Rome said.

"We could. Except we don't want nanofactories anywhere on Earth. They're dangerous."

Rome shrugged. "We've never had a problem with them."

"That's because all the failsafes built into them are aimed at them never, ever, dismantling a human or animal for raw materials. But computer systems undefended by organic protectors? Any nanite spill would consume us in days… and there would be absolutely nothing we can do about it."

"So where do you have your factories?"

Skate smiled. "Let me keep some secrets, would you?"

Then they jumped, and arrived well outside a system Rome had never seen before with a bright orange star in the middle of their viewscreen.

"Is that real, or is it some kind of simulation?" Rome asked.

Skate smiled. "It's a simulation," he replied. "But it looks exactly like it would if you had eyes and you could look out of a nonexistent window into the space ahead of us."

Rome rolled his eyes.

Chapter 21

Sextus Colony – 61 Virginis III

Touk emerged from the flyer, shielded his eyes against flying ice crystals picked up by the flyer's engine, and nodded to the captain of the troops who'd arrived before him to secure the landing zone.

"It's all clear, sir," the captain informed him.

"Thank you." He strode away from the lander and walked to the edge of the crater. The hole in the ground was the only evidence that something had once stood there. "Any sign of survivors?"

The captain raised an eyebrow as if to ask what kind of survivors might emerge from a strike that had turned the area into a hole in the ground, but the man only said: "No, sir. No tracks or emissions."

"Good."

Anguk Vest emerged from the flyer behind Touk. The director struggled with the half-meter drop and Touk wondered how the forceful man from a few months before had aged so badly. Vest wasn't a young man, and he'd spent too much time in zero-gee — neglecting the recommended exercise regimen — but he'd really declined over the past few months. Setting up a colony in which bad decisions could kill multitudes of people was weighing on him more than he'd ever let on.

"You all right?" Touk asked.

"Yeah," Vest wheezed. "I'll be fine. So this is what it looks like to get bombed from orbit, huh?"

"A lot of snow and a big hole in the ground," Touk replied. "And they didn't find any tracks leading away."

"They wouldn't," Vest replied. "The terrain almost begs for flyers, if you have a nanofactory capable of building them. We'll need to be on the lookout for any further industrial buildup. Unfortunately, if they're smart, they'll go underground." He surveyed the crater in silence before turning back to Touk. "Did they find any sign of our team?"

"Gino and Umberto? Not yet. They sent a team to check the hab."

"That survived?"

"There was a mountain between the hab and the blast zone," Touk replied. "The hill got pretty badly chewed up, but apparently the structure survived intact."

Anguk nodded. "Well, there isn't much to see here, anyway."

They headed back to the flyer, and Touk's comm pinged. He checked and saw an unfamiliar name on the screen and put the man on. "Yes?"

"Mr. Nacarado, this is Hoyle from the exploration crew. You know, to the hab. The captain told me to call you if we found anything. Well, we found something."

"What?

"I… we're not sure. I think you'd better come look for yourself."

Touk exchanged a look with Vest and then helped him onto the flyer. He sent the hab coordinates to the pilot and, thirty seconds later, they were in the air for the short hop around the hill. Touk estimated it might have been half a mile.

After the site of the orbital strike, the area around the hab seemed utterly peaceful. If he hadn't seen with his own eyes that the hill to the south of them was torn apart on the side not visible from the complex and that there was a hole twenty meters deep where there had once been a snow-covered plain, Touk would have had a hard time believing it.

Soldiers in white camouflage scurried around the hab. One of them ran towards the flyer when it landed.

"This way, sir," the man said.

"Hoyle?" Touk asked.

"Yes, sir. Please come with me."

The hab was a grey prefab hut, a small but well-insulated rectangle designed to keep two people alive in the inhospitable climate of the third planet of the 61 Virginis system. The windows were small and shuttered, and the pipeline — the reason the team was here in the first place — ran ten meters from the house.

"In here, sir," Hoyle said.

Two soldiers standing guard in front of the building moved aside as he approached, with the slower Anguk Vest a half-dozen steps behind.

He entered the hab and stopped. A tangle of black wires lay on the floor, a bundle about a meter high. The cables were wrapped tightly at some points and loose at others. His eyes followed the cables down to one of the extremes where the width tapered off.

"Oh, shit!"

A single human foot, pink and smooth, poked out of the tangle of wires, only four toes showing.

He took a step back, and that was when he realized the cables were moving.

It was a subtle thing, a writhing, expanding and contracting of the wires which reminded him of something breathing.

"What the hell is that?" he asked Hoyle.

"We don't know, sir. We tried pulling the cables off her, but they seem to be embedded into her skin. We didn't want to hurt her."

"Is she alive?"

"We took the temperature of her foot… and it seems to be normal." The guard shrugged as if to indicate that nothing was normal, not even things that measured what they were supposed to. "Maybe it's just the energy running through the wires keeping her that way, though."

"And Umberto?"

Hoyle shrugged. "There's another bundle in the other room, wrapped tight."

Vest entered the room, breathing hard. He'd heard Hoyle's explanation and, after a moment to scan the room, he said: "Show me the other one. I want to see what this looked like before you touched it."

The second bundle — could it be Umberto? — was tidy and tight where the first one had showed signs of being tugged on.

"This makes no sense," Anguk Vest said. "It looks like something an insect would do, one of those Earth spiders they keep in the biological museum in Copernicus."

The guards just looked blank. Touk vaguely remembered hearing something about that from a biology student he'd gone out with years before, but he wasn't clear on the details.

Touk's confusion must have shown on his face, because Anguk continued. "Spiders wrap their victims in a web, to keep them immobile for future consumption. But all of that is purely biological, not this mix of technology and biology. Who ever heard of anything like this?"

"We did," Touk replied. He might not have been much for Earth fauna, but he was up-to-date on recent news stories. "Do you remember the report from the *Unity*? About the birthing chambers on Earth? Weren't the bodies encased in wires and cocoons to keep them alive while the mind was elsewhere?"

Vest's eyes widened. "The lesson we learned from that was that the symbiosis was a failure. The *Unity* didn't stay on Earth long enough to check when the birthing chambers failed and everyone died out, but I'd be willing to bet it failed right from the beginning."

"Or maybe it worked until fifty years ago, or something. Hell, you downloaded Emily onto a machine-printed human body less than a year ago. I'd bet your interface looked a lot like that." He pointed to the mass of wires on the floor.

"You're right." Anguk shook his head. "I just realized how deeply I believe in the sanctity of the human body. As you've so adroitly pointed out, I have no problem in putting machine intelligence into a non-living body, but once it's alive, I…". He chuckled. "I have prejudices. I guess I'm no better than Mira Heine."

"You just never had to confront this before. And trust me, you're much better than Mira Heine. She would have freaked out, ordered us all to withdraw and nuked these cocoons from orbit."

"You're probably right." Vest shuffled back to the first tangled mass, and knelt beside it. He pulled the wires aside, gently separating them from the small foot until he reached a place where the wires disappeared under the skin of the person's leg. He pulled softly on the cable, then released it. "We're going to need a doctor. And probably a high-complexity operating room. I don't even dare move them without a doctor present. And we should get an electrician."

Touk almost reminded him that those probably weren't electrical wires, but remembered that this was Anguk Vest before him. The man might be showing his age and his biases, but he was still one of the brightest minds ever to be born since humans left Earth. Instead, Touk snapped his fingers. "I know just the doctor we need. Plus, she'll be delighted to be involved. Give me a minute."

***

The doctor wasn't delighted to be involved. She stormed up to Touk, stopped an inch before the top of her head bashed his nose in and said: "I was in the middle of an appendectomy. I had to leave a patient with a lesser surgeon. I guess he thinks he's all right, and maybe he is. But I'm better. If anything, and I mean *anything* happens to that kid because you assholes couldn't wait a few minutes for me to finish, I will sterilize you." She looked back to the flyer they'd brought. "And you didn't need to order that entire ambulance just so I can stabilize a patient. It might be needed somewhere else." She glared at Vest. "You really need a doctor on your team. Someone who knows what medicine implies. And that you need to tell the doctor what they're getting into. Sometimes I'm not the best expert, and I can recommend someone else."

"I'll take it under advisement," Anguk replied. "In the meantime, Touk told me how impressed he was with you. Maybe we can start with you giving us your expert advice on this." He half-turned and gestured to the nearest cocoon.

"I'd say you need an engineer, not a doctor." Her eyes widened. "Is there a person in there? Crushed?"

"All we can tell you is that no one from the colony did this. We found her looking that way. She was discovered an hour ago, and no one has moved her except to unwrap a few of the cables."

She knelt and began to head down the same path of discovery that Touk and Vest had already traversed, except she cursed more than they did.

"Is she always like this?" Vest asked.

"I think this might be one of her good days," Touk replied.

"Oh. Wow," Vest said. "Do you know her name, so I can make sure never to be sick when she's on call?"

"Her name is Veronika Yault. And I want her to be my doctor

if something happens to me. I know she won't let me die, even if she has to send Death himself packing with his scythe between his legs to do it."

"I didn't know you were a student of the classics," Vest said.

"I'm not, but there are a lot of single poets in Copernicus. One of them told me about where the whole death image comes from. Honestly, all I can remember was the cloak and the scythe."

"You used to date a lot of women, didn't you? You seem to have a story about one for every occasion." Vest grinned. "You must have been quite popular."

"Honestly, I wasn't anything special. We didn't have all that much to do when I was a student. And no one was looking for a long-term relationship, so everyone just drifted in and out of each other's beds." He held Vest's gaze. "I would probably be doing exactly the same thing now, if Emily hadn't walked into my life with her unusual take on everything."

"Are you two going to talk about your artificial girlfriend all day or are you going to help?" Dr. Yault called to them. "I need you to get that ambulance closer. And I need someone competent to tell me what the hell is going through these wires."

"How soon can we move her? I'm not sure how much longer it will be safe to stay here," Vest said.

"Don't be stupid. I can't even begin to test this without the right people here. She's alive, she's pregnant, and her blood pressure seems to be normal. That's all I can say right now." The doctor looked up at them. "If you can destroy an installation from space, you can keep us safe. Put more soldiers out there if you have to. And get me the people I asked for."

Vest walked away to give the orders, and Touk knelt beside the woman. "Don't be too hard on him. We don't know what we're fighting yet. Just like you don't know what you need to do to disconnect this woman. We're all doing the best we can."

She raised an eyebrow. "From where I'm sitting, it doesn't look like it. Hell, the only person I've encountered in this whole mess who seems to know how to take a decision is you. And even you're annoying as hell about it. But annoying is better than incompetent, so you'd better take over before that one's bumbling gets us all in a mess we can't get out of."

"He's the only reason we're here."

"Yeah. And that isn't turning out quite as well as we all hoped, is it?" She stood. "There's another one of these? The guy in the chopper said two patients. I assume he wasn't talking about the baby."

"He wasn't. There's another one here. If he's who we think he is, it should be a male."

"It could be the wrong male," she replied.

"Yes. It could. And that could be the wrong pregnant female. But we won't know until you manage to get them out."

She grunted and knelt to study the second bundle of wires. She was clearly concentrating, trying to avoid doing anything to hurt the patient while, at the same time, exposing the skin so she could measure vital signs. She cursed constantly as she worked, seemingly unaware that she was speaking at all.

Less than half an hour later, the whine of flyer engines announced that the experts Dr. Yault had commanded were arriving.

As they entered, the captain of the guards caught up with Touk. "Sir, we think there's not much more we can discover at the impact area. I'd like permission to pull our forces out."

"Shouldn't you be discussing this with Director Vest?"

"He said you were in charge of this operation now, sir."

Touk nearly rolled his eyes, but caught himself in time. He remembered the doctor's words and decided to forego telling the captain that he was only even there because he'd been selected as the person to help Emily Plair escape from Copernicus. And the reason he'd been selected was that he was no one of note, and that would keep prying eyes away from him. Hell, he hadn't even completed his degree in astrophysics.

But the doctor's words echoed in his head. She might be wrong about Vest, but she was right that someone needed to step up and start taking responsibility. He would have preferred not to be that person... but the choice didn't seem to be his to make.

"Yes. Pull back, but keep the area under constant surveillance. Is there any way you can do that without leaving people behind?"

"Not constant. The satellite coverage only allows for about fifty percent of the time."

"Then you'll have to leave some soldiers. Make sure their equipment is hardened against electronic strikes, and tell them to shoot first and ask questions later. I don't want the enemy to recover anything we might have missed."

"Yes, sir," the captain replied. He seemed relieved that someone was taking command.

"We'll need your help here." He nodded to the hab. "The doctor says this is going to take a while, and I want to make certain nothing sneaks up on us while we're working. I don't know a thing about deploying troops, so consider yourself authorized to position your people however you see fit. Just keep us safe."

"Yes, sir."

"And if anyone questions it, remind them what the Director said, or come and find me and I'll deal with it."

"Yes, sir!"

The captain walked away and left Touk waiting for the doctor to finish.

***

Forty minutes later, Dr. Yault emerged into the snow and brushed past Touk. "Get that ambulance closer. I want it right next to the door," she shouted at the pilot.

Then she stood right beside Touk and watched the vehicle approach.

"What's happening?" Touk asked over the whine of the engines.

"We're going to cut them out and fly them back to New Earth as fast as we can go," she said.

"You're going to operate out here?" he asked.

"Of course not. That would be crazy. We're going to take them back with the cables and everything else. The entire cocoon. The things we're going to cut are the cables keeping them in place. When I have them where I can get them quickly connected to life support if needed, I'll see about pulling all that crap out of them."

"But won't they die if you disconnect them?"

"I don't know. According to our eggheads in there, those wires are data cables, and they don't appear to be sending in any data."

"They were warm," Tuk said.

She shrugged. "Those two engineers babbled about embedded power sources, so if that means anything, there you have it. But if your experts know that the hell they're talking about, nothing is coming through those wires to keep my patients alive." She snorted. "Although I suppose they must be legit because they spent most of their time in there geeking out about how cool the tech was. Idiots." She walked back towards the door, talking to Touk over her shoulder. "Anyway, we're about to cut the wires. You should expect to see two bundles come into the ambulance and then watch us leave at extremely high speed. All of that in the next five minutes."

Touk looked for the captain. He found the man organizing a patrol. "We'll be done here in five. So maybe plan your withdrawal for fifteen minutes from now."

Then Touk watched. He only got back into his flyer when the ambulance took off for the colony.

Chapter 22

In Orbit – 61 Virginis III

"I have an unscheduled launch!" a tech shouted from one of the workstations on the bridge of the Engine Test Facility. The woman was one of only three people present, huddled over monitors instead of enjoying the spectacular panoramic view of the planet below them.

Kal Virginis Hori jumped up from the chair where he'd been supervising the watch. He'd only recently returned from the surface where he'd been one of the two ETF officers coordinating the tungsten rod strike against the enemy installation. He'd seen the pictures of the strange facility, and of the two people recovered from the area who were now fighting for their lives in the infirmary, and he'd had nightmares about it ever since.

Images of snake-like cables that emerged from a factory that was at once industrial and alive which proceeded to wrap themselves around him scared him awake every few hours.

And the launch they'd just detected was evidence that they hadn't destroyed the facility, merely slowed down its growth. If that.

He wouldn't sleep tonight, either.

Kal took a second to get his breath. "What's the location?"

"Seventeen hundred kilometers south of New Earth."

Smart, he thought. The location was ideal. Satellite coverage in the area was spotty at best, nonexistent at worst. The colony only had a few birds up, and those were mainly focused on two things: geological and hydrological mapping in the polar regions to assist the terraforming and tracking local weather patterns around New Earth. No one had expected to need surveillance satellites on a planet without political boundaries or opposing factions.

Which meant that now that they needed them, they didn't have them.

Fortunately, the Engine Test Facility's sensors were designed to track rockets and spacecraft over hundreds of thousands of kilometers, so once the launch was identified, they quickly zeroed in on the vehicle, and data was pouring onto the screens. As he scanned the information, Kal also sent a priority message to New Earth with a link to the data attached.

"How in the world did you spot it?" he said.

"I programmed the thermal imaging satellites from the terraforming crew to notify me of any flare-up over two hundred degrees Celsius," the woman at the console replied. "I got dozens of false positives from our own operations, especially the exothermic terraforming activity… but this one was obviously a launch."

"Great work."

His comm buzzed. "Hori here," he said.

"This is Anguk Vest," the voice on the other side replied. "I need you to do me a favor. Can you take out that vehicle?"

"It definitely isn't one of ours?" Hori replied. He knew the answer, but he had to ask.

"No. And we need it blown away."

"Once it establishes an orbit, I have one option," Hori said. "We have five torpedoes remaining from a batch we were testing before leaving Tau Ceti. We armed them earlier, when we were evaluating options to deal with the enemy factory. They're ready to go, and I can launch on your order."

"Don't wait for my order. Launch as soon as you have a firing solution. I don't know what that rocket is carrying, and I don't want to find out the hard way."

"Yes, sir."

Hori ignored the worried looks of the two analysts on the bridge and called the engineer on duty. "Sparky," he said once she picked up the comm, "We're go on a torpedo launch. Sending you data now. How soon to get the fish in the air?"

"Three minutes," she replied.

"Wow. That fast?"

"I've been having nightmares about those things on the planet," she replied. "So I always have one in the rack when I'm on shift."

"All right. I'm sending you the tracking data. Do you need anything else from me?"

"No. We'll send any course corrections to the fish from here."

"All right. You can fire whenever you're ready. Let me know."

"Yes, sir."

Kal drummed his fingers against the armrest of his chair, not trusting himself to refrain from calling her every thirty seconds for a status check which, he knew, wouldn't help matters at all.

He needn't have worried. Less than thirty seconds later, he felt the entire structure of the Engine Test Facility reverberate, which rendered Sparky's report of "One away!" superfluous.

He reconnected with Vest. "We've fired, sir. Sending you the data."

"Thank you, Mr. Hori."

Kal turned his eye to the screen. Sparky in engineering must have toggled something because, instead of staring at a bunch of numbers, the monitor showed a graphic depiction of a red triangle in orbit around the planet being approached by a blue missile-shaped icon.

Within moments, the two elements converged and the icons disappeared. "Can you confirm impact?" Kal asked his analyst.

"Yes, sir. Enemy vehicle destroyed."

Relief flooded through Kal as he relayed the information back to Anguk in New Earth.

The director's words echoed Kal's sentiments. "Excellent job, Hori. Please tell your team that I'm extremely proud of them. Your immediate identification of the threat and amazingly quick action is commendable. This will buy us a bit of time to decide what to do next. If the enemy had a presence in space, the tactical situation would have changed significantly."

"Thank you, sir."

"It's my pleasure. I will sleep easier knowing you're up there taking care of us." Anguk cut the communication, leaving Kal basking in a glow of official praise that, for a glorious moment, actually overcame the dread of knowing the enemy was still down there.

But only for a moment.

"I have another launch," the woman at the console said, voice tense. "Correction: two launches. Sir, unless these are all false positives…" Her voice trailed off. "I think you need to look at this." She toggled the data from her monitor onto the main screen.

Kal gasped. He began to count, but gave up after eight. There were a lot of signals coming through. He called Vest again. "Director, is the terraforming team doing something major on several points across the planet?"

"No," Vest replied. "We've got everything on hold while we investigate that factory we wiped out."

"Then I hate to inform you that we have multiple…" he looked over to where the analyst was seating and she flashed both hands twice. "At least twenty launch signatures on the surface. We don't have enough torpedoes to deal with them."

"Thank you," Vest replied. "I'll call you back."

CHAPTER 23

Outer Reaches – 61 Virginis Planetary System

Mira Han woke to a dark room. *Cabin, not room,* she reminded herself. *This is the Captain's cabin on the* Buran. *It's the biggest one on the ship, so they gave it to me, even though I don't actually do anything to make the ship run. My only function is to tell them where I want to go so they can do it.*

She peered into the darkness, trying to understand what had woken her. The room was silent, but… was there movement?

Mira extended her hand and swiped it through the motion-sensitive field beside her bed. The lights sprang on.

Blinking against the sudden glare, she tried to scan the room. There was nobody standing beside her bed, at least. No one hovering over her with a blunt instrument.

That's good.

But something had woken her. What? She studied the cabin. It wasn't large, but it had a small study attached to it, an almost unheard-of luxury in space, there so the captain could peruse confidential orders in private. The study was dark. The bedside lights didn't do much to illuminate it.

"I'm over here," a voice said.

Mira froze and her stomach jumped. She still couldn't see anyone.

"In the study. I'm afraid I can't actually walk to where you are."

"Who is this?" she gasped, heart thumping in her chest.

"Come and see. It's perfectly safe." It was a woman's voice.

Mira searched the cabin for something to defend herself with. She saw nothing.

Her instinct was to pull the cover over her head and wish the problem away. Either that or run into the hallway and get help. The door was closer to her than to anyone waiting in the study.

But if the door jammed, they could reach her.

She lowered a foot onto the rubber flooring. The sensation brought her back to her senses. She wasn't some defenseless five-year-old. She was a grown woman and no one was going to intimidate her on her own ship. All she had to do was scream into her comm and the crew would come running.

Of course, that would depend on the loyalty of her crew. Last time she'd trusted the navy with something important, they'd not only messed it up, but also disregarded her authority.

Anger at the memory lent her courage and she stomped into the study.

"Where are you?" she asked, not expecting to see anything in the darkened room.

She was shocked when a blue-tinted figure became visible, seated on a visitor's chair. The woman had been impossible to see from the bed — the angle of the doorway between the rooms blocked the view.

The woman glowed with her own light, and Mira could see the chair right through her. She had straight blond hair and pale white skin and she looked vaguely familiar.

"What the hell are you?" she asked.

The woman smiled slightly. "I'm your worst nightmare."

"A ghost?"

"I'm afraid it's even worse than that. But even nightmares can be useful sometimes, and I've come to offer my help. You're going to need it."

Fighting to keep her breathing under control, Mira squeezed around the desk on the side opposite the specter and sat on her own chair, which was intentionally higher than the two visitors' seats. The height didn't give her any sense of power. Quite the opposite. The only reason Mira could sit there and study the apparition before her without making a run for it was that she'd been sleeping helplessly just minutes before. If this entity had wanted to harm her, she would be dead now.

Of course, she thought, *physical harm isn't the only way to damage someone.*

Out loud, she said: "I'm listening."

"This is going to be difficult for you. I am The Earthling. Or at least a copy small enough to fit in your fleet's memory. You're seeing an image of me projected from the office hologram generator."

Mira sprang to her feet. "You have some nerve. I'll have you purged from the systems. I'll — " She grabbed her comm from on top of the desk and dialed the Captain of the *Buran*. He would know what to do.

The Captain's face appeared on the screen. "Hello, Ms. Heine," the man said. "I'm sorry, but," as she watched the Captain's features melted into those of the woman speaking to her, "it's much too late to purge the ship's systems. They are one with me, and I am one with them. Even if I didn't resist your efforts by opening every airlock in the fleet, you couldn't get me out. It would destroy every system aboard."

Mira growled and dropped the comm like it was hot. It went dark. "What do you want from me?"

"I already told you. I want to help you."

"I don't need your help." Mira stopped to think about it. "And besides, why would you even offer? I'm here to take the colonists back to Tau Ceti in chains. And one of those colonists is a version of you. Why would you want to help?"

"Because you're not here to do what you think you are," The Earthling said.

"That's insane."

"You've just walked into a war. Not the petty little squabble you think you're fighting — which, by the way, is mainly just your own innate fears combined with your delusions of grandeur — but an actual war with a real enemy." The specter in the seat motioned towards the front of the ship. "The planet over there is no longer an exclusively human colony. Well, it is, but there are two very different kinds of humans on it. Humans like you," The Earthling paused and stared at Mira, "and humans like me."

"You're not human, you're an abomination."

The figure shrugged. "That doesn't make any difference to me. If you prefer to call it that, then you're getting into a war against other abominations. And without my help, you'll lose. Hell, you'll probably lose even with my help, because all I can really do is warn you about it. The ships you chose just don't have enough processing power to let me act against the enemy for real."

Mira waved her hand over her desk and called up a real-time view of the planet — or at least as real-time as the ship's scanners could manage at that distance. "There's nothing even remotely threatening on that planet. The only ship of any size is that damned Engine Test Facility."

"There is a constellation of smaller vessels in orbit that belong to a digital entity."

Mira studied the data coming from the planet. "I don't care. As long as they're not a threat to this fleet, they don't concern me. And if they try to stop us, I'll swat them down."

"I believe you're underestimating the threat," The Earthling said.

"Do you have any actual evidence of that? Or are you just guessing?"

"They are building an industrial capacity based on nanofactories to overrun the colony."

"In that case," Mira said, "They're playing right into our hands. This goes from being a corrective action to being a rescue. History will thank us." She looked up at the hologram sitting in the other chair. "Unless you decide to stop us."

The Earthling sighed, a surprisingly human gesture from a monster of the purest evil. "I won't. I'd much rather have the colonists locked up in some prison on Tau Ceti than in the clutches of this particular machine intelligence. I will not interfere with your efforts."

The term 'machine intelligence' made Mira shudder, but it didn't distract her from the fact that there would be a reckoning with the one inside the ship. But that would come later. She needed time to think about how to deal with this sort of creature. "All right," she replied. "And how do I reach you if I need help dealing with that thing?"

The ghost smiled. "Just say my name. I'm everywhere."

Then, the image faded away, leaving Mira blinking in the suddenly dimmer light of the study.

Mira groaned. There was no way she was going to be able to get back to sleep, even though it was only halfway through the night shift.

She stood, got dressed and headed to the bridge, hurrying through corridors dimmed for the night shift.

Dañi looked up as she entered, sitting straighter in the captain's chair. "Hello, Ma'am," she said. "Everything looks fine. No enemy action at all. In fact, I'm quite convinced the enemy doesn't even know we're here yet. They don't seem to be expecting visitors."

Mira leaned on a railing that separated the officer's area from the consoles where analysts and enlisted gunners would work during a battle. Only two of the positions were occupied, and the dimly-lit bridge presented a serene aspect that belied the reality of the situation.

Or, at the very least, it contradicted the turmoil in Mira's soul.

"I have a question," Mira said. "Have you seen any signs that our computer systems might be compromised?"

Dañi cocked her head. "Compromised? In what way?"

"Any way. Have you seen any signs?"

It was good luck that Dañi was present because she was one of the few people on Mira's team who had zero doubts that there was some kind of artificial intelligence in the Tau Ceti system. Dañi had once admitted that she'd seen signs of activity in the planetary network that could only fit that definition.

But even if Dañi hadn't been there, Mira would have had to check.

"I haven't seen anything."

"Can you look deeper?"

"Of course," Dañi replied. "Do you want me to start right away?"

"Please."

"This could take a while."

"I'll wait. I can't sleep."

That much was true. The first thing Mira needed to do was to convince herself that she hadn't imagined the whole thing. Or dreamt it. How ironic would it be to have a dream actually tell her it was her worst nightmare and then have the whole thing turn out to be a nightmare? It would make her crew doubt her sanity.

Which was a valid point. Was she actually insane? Had her constant worrying over the prevalence of simulated humans driven her over the edge?

It was a sobering thought. Worse still was the question about what to do if it turned out she really was slipping. Who could she trust to take over for her?

It had to be someone who would stay the course, and understand that she had done this because she was convinced that humans had finally found a good way to live, that Tau Ceti's civilization was the peak of what humanity should aspire to: serene, mature and equal. It had to be someone who could grasp the truth that the people trying to change were simply hiding their desire to feel superior to others in words that sounded nice: advancement, growth, freedom.

None of those things were important when society worked as it should.

So who could she pass her mantle to?

Gabriel Zun would be the obvious choice, but she hesitated. Zun had followed her since the first day. He understood what she was trying to do, and Mira knew he agreed with her.

But, given the power of the law, would he be content to be simply an instrument? Or would his desire to lead cause him to grasp at power for power's sake.

Mira admitted that she didn't know. It pained her, but it was the truth. And since she didn't know, she couldn't trust him.

She gave a quick glance to Dañi. Dañi was a true believer, the product of a technical school in the past few years. She knew just how badly the Institute failed all of society by creating a caste of technocrats and free thinkers who believed they were superior to everyone else not by virtue of being better for society, but simply by virtue of thinking differently about things and desiring more than Tau Ceti's citizens already had. The fact that Dañi had rejected those teachings made her a true defender of the people.

Unfortunately, Dañi also had no charisma. She could not lead because she would not be followed. Her objections were purely intellectual, and she would never engage the emotions of the people she needed to convince. She could command the respect of technical people with ease. Unfortunately, technical people were only a tiny proportion of the people she needed to inspire. The coalition that Mira had formed, people who understood the problem with their minds, but felt the need to solve it in their hearts, would drift in separate directions. In a decade, Copernicus would be back where it started.

"Oh, wow," Dañi said. "That is *clever.*"

"What?" Mira asked.

"We have a hitchhiker. Or with the way it's integrated itself into our systems, I suppose we'd have to refer to it as a symbiote. If I hadn't been looking for it specifically in the memory usage… Whatever you call it, there's something in our computer, and it's smart enough to hide from a crew that uses the thing all the time."

"Thank god," Mira said.

"What? Don't you understand what this means?"

"I understand better than anyone on the ship. But best of all, it means I'm not losing the few marbles I have left."

"It…" Dañi looked down at her screens. "It's gonna take weeks to get this thing rooted out. We'll need to reboot everything manually while keeping systems isolated from each other. Even if it doesn't try to stop us — and if this is what I think it is, it will — we'll need everyone to focus on just this. The mission will get delayed."

"It won't, because we're not going to try to disturb the AI. Leave it alone."

Danny looked aghast. "It's in every system. We… I think we won't be able to move the ship without it knowing. Hell, without it allowing us to do it. We need to try to get it out of there."

"And I'm ordering you to leave it alone. We have a mission to accomplish."

"But..."

Mira walked around the railing so she could look straight into Dañi's eyes. "Has the entity in there made any move to interfere with what we're doing."

"No."

"Could it have?"

"If I'm reading this right, it's in so deep that it could blow our engine to bits or vent all our air, and we couldn't do a single thing to stop it."

"Good. Then assume it's not here to stop us," Mira replied. "And leave it alone." She turned towards the screen that showed a schematic of the star and the deployment of enemy forces. "How quickly can we get to the third planet?"

Dañi input some numbers. "If we burn at a gee, we can be there in sixteen days."

"Unacceptable. What does it look like at a gee and a half?"

"Four days if we just want to do a flyby. But the crew will hate us. Plus, we need to stop and turn around. Three-day burn, three-day slowdown."

"Can't we use the planet to brake or something? We need to cut the time down."

"We can burn at a higher rate. But that will mean putting everyone in couches for the burn and the braking."

"Dammit." Mira thought for a moment. Then she pounded the banister. "Give me a solution that gets us there in three burn days with eight hours of rest in the middle."

"They might see us coming," Dañi warned.

"I have reason to believe they're going to be otherwise preoccupied."

***

Mira growled at the medical tech who helped her undo the restraints of the acceleration couch. Her head was pounding and she felt tired, even though she'd barely moved in the past thirty-six hours.

She'd also barely slept, and she gratefully accepted the proffered analgesic injection. She didn't know what the hell was in it, but it couldn't make her feel worse than she already did.

Dañi had found a solution that gave them a burn level somewhere between one and a half and two gees, but even with the rest in the middle, it had been brutal. Mira felt tired and cranky and sweaty.

"Don't touch that," she snapped at the tech when he began to unbutton her pants to remove the waste system. "I can pull those off myself."

"Yes ma'am," the guy said. Then, sensing what she really needed, the man turned away to give her privacy.

"Thank you." She buttoned herself back up and handed him the tubes — making sure to give him a clean central section to grasp.

Then she pushed herself off the couch and allowed herself one second to revel in the microgravity before grabbing a rung on the roof and pushing off it towards the bridge. If she'd suffered while cocooned in the air-gel of the acceleration couch, she couldn't even imagine what life must have been like for the poor sods subjected to that burn while on duty.

She found Dañi sitting in the captain's chair. "Please tell me you haven't been here for four days," Mira said.

Dañi gave her a tired smile. "I just got in. We had to lift poor Keller out of this chair. He was exhausted."

"I don't even know how you guys can work under that much acceleration."

"There was no other choice," Dañi replied.

"Do we know the status?"

"We're behind a moon, still moving at high speed. We'll be moving into orbit — and do a lot more braking — in a few hours." She pointed at the monitor, which was split between a schematic showing a few dots in orbit around Tau Ceti III and a blank area. "That's where we project the enemy will be located. We won't know for certain until we get around the moon in three minutes."

"All right." Mira felt the ship make a course correction, and even that tiny acceleration made her bones creak after the beating they'd taken. "Where can I sit?"

"Any of the empty seats is fine."

The bridge held many more occupants than before, but even so, a third of the positions were empty. Mira chose one directly ahead of Dañi's chair with a good view of the main monitor. Better still, the man next to her had a view generated by the cameras outside the ship. She could see the moon moving slowly to one side of the monitor as they passed.

The blank half of the main screen showed signs of life. The outline of Tau Ceti III appeared. Dots began to populate the circle representing the planet. One large green icon showed the Engine Test Facility and several red dots, she assumed, must be the smaller vehicles in orbit.

As Mira watched the red dots began to move. She pointed at the screen. "Is that right?"

Dañi said: "The system is probably adjusting the positions to correct their location now that we can actually see the planet again and don't have to work from projections."

The dots kept moving, not jumping around as if they were being repositioned, but actually moving across the screen. In response to Mira's unasked question, Dañi held up a hand, typed into her data pad and exchanged information over her headset. Finally, she peered up at the screen.

"Oh, shit," Dañi said. "Weapons online, now! Engines, standby for emergency maneuvers."

Excitement rippled through the bridge as those crewmembers not involved with the defense or the evasion muttered amongst themselves. Mira felt her stomach turn sour as the dots on the screen left the vicinity of the planet. "How fast are they going?" she asked.

No one answered. Dañi was barking orders while several other crewpeople frantically worked their controls. Mira had no idea what was going on, but as she felt the ship move laterally, she clicked her seat's harness shut.

She no longer felt tired, but completely alert. She watched the screens with perfect focus and heard every sound in the bridge. Words she'd never paid attention to suddenly acquired ominous meaning in her imagination. She wanted to scream, but she also wanted to help somehow, to man one of the consoles and lead the crew to a solution.

Except she had no clue how to even start.

She looked down at the screen before her, helplessly. Suddenly, it blinked on, and the image of The Earthling appeared in front of her.

"Hello," the AI said.

Mira looked around, torn between the fear of someone seeing or hearing the conversation or the even deeper fear that she was hallucinating. But no one was paying any attention to Mira. They were much too busy to care.

"Hello," she replied.

"Let me tell you what I know about those vehicles coming towards us," The Earthling said. "They're not missiles, so you don't need to bother avoiding them. But it's very important that you don't let any of them get close enough to latch onto your ship. I don't have enough processing power in this computer to fight off the things coming towards us, and if they get into the computer… well, if they get into the computer, you will lose control of the ship."

Dañi was on the comm to the other ships in the fleet. "*Grader*, get back in position," she said. "We need to coordinate our fire to keep from wasting missiles by shooting at the same targets. Get back in line."

The AI continued. "Those vehicles aren't manned, so they can accelerate faster than you can. They can also stop on a dime. You need to shoot them down."

"I'll tell the captain."

"You do that," The Earthling said. "If they grab us, I can only fight them so long. In fact, I've already set up a sequence that will erase my consciousness if it comes to that. You might want to throw yourself out an airlock."

Mira swallowed, wondering what could be so awful as to elicit that kind of advice.

Worse, she felt fear at the idea of The Earthling erasing itself and leaving them.

What had things come to?

Chapter 24

Copernicus – Tau Ceti II

Stell stared at the screen. He rubbed his eyes and did it again. Even through the insomnia-induced haze, the message was the same.

"That can't be right," he said. "Someone's messing with me."

So he backtracked the message, knowing that if it was fake, it would take him days to track all the comm nodes it had passed before finally reaching a single-use identity logged into from a public access computer somewhere. Which would be a completely useless piece of information, but at least it would prove someone was faking it.

The nodes started clicking. The first surprised him: the Copernicus city external exchange. That one was followed by two probes on the system Deep Space Network.

"Interesting," Stell said as he watched the tracking program work back towards the source. Even if this dead-ended like he thought it had to, the mere fact of using nodes outside the planet's network would tell him a lot about the sender's capabilities. "I bet we do Cassius next."

Bingo!

The fact that the next node was in the Cassius Station system — Cassius didn't use a centralized server for incoming and outgoing messages, but had several different companies who made money off their ability to connect to the exchange — was not a surprise. It was the logical step in the daisy chain.

"No. You've got to be kidding me," Stell said.

Apparently, the message had entered Cassius through the receiving radio telescope of the astronomy center.

"Son of a bitch, it's real," he said.

"What is?"

"Ah! Don't sneak up on me like that!" Stell said as Sintia sat on the chair beside him.

"Sorry, but I just had to see why you were shouting at your computer at," she peered at the screen, "four-thirty in the morning."

"I…" Stell took a decision. He was going to trust the message. Or at least he was going to trust it far enough to share it with Sintia. Who, come to think of it would be much more affected by it than he was. "I got a communication. From an entity that calls itself The Earthling. You probably never heard…"

"It's an AI that runs a criminal empire on Cassius Station," Sintia said.

Stell felt his mouth hanging open, his next words forgotten. "How…"

"How did I know? Stell, you're sweet and you're a great binarist, but I was a Representative of the People. I'm supposed to know about things that might affect the safety of the people of Tau Ceti. And yes, I know you checked and there's no record of it anywhere. That's because all records on this planet are public property. There is no such thing as confidential or secret documents. When the charter was written, pure democracy and equality were placed above security concerns. It was done for extremely valid reasons… but it's a pain, so a lot of stuff never reaches the public record. The official record shows what the people in charge think is safe for the public to know."

"Wow. I'll pretend I didn't hear that."

"Why?" Sintia asked. "You thought you binarists had a monopoly on morally dubious activity in the system? Poor innocent summer child."

"Okay, point for you, but we don't have time for this now.

The message is either a trap or really important."

"I'm listening."

"The Earthling says that Mira Han's fleet is about to get into a serious fight with a third party's forces around a star called 61 Virginis. She doesn't expect Mira to come out on top, and she doesn't expect that the colony itself will survive." He looked over at her. "She doesn't want the news to reach Gabriel Zun until we have the government back in some sort of order. She's convinced that Zun will try to take power for himself."

Sintia nodded. "Sounds like him."

"So... she sent me the location of Ashur Nartiya's prison cell, the password to every lock between us and her, and the activation override for the reserve naval ships. She also told me which captains are currently working for Mira but loyal to Nartiya, and the comm codes for the naval cruisers that are waiting for the situation to clear up."

"Oh... wow. You could run a really good countercoup with that."

"If it's real," Stell said.

"If it's real." Sintia smiled. "And I guess there's just one way to find out."

"Dammit. I knew this would get political."

Sintia laughed, a long, tension-releasing sound from deep in her belly. "You've been hiding the deposed political leader of an entire planet in your house for more than a month while every security force on the world is looking for her and you think it's just getting political now?"

"So far, I've been helping a friend." He returned her smile. "Make that two friends now that I've gotten to know you. That is never political. Knocking over a government? That's a different thing."

"I understand. Well, give me the codes and the names and I'll do it myself."

"Are you kidding? I wouldn't miss it for the world."

That made Sintia laugh again.

Stell selected a portable, extremely powerful, and highly frowned-upon handheld device from his collection. "This should be enough to get any comm work done. Well, more than enough… it's probably the best piece of illegal computer equipment in the system. I would only let it out of the house for a special occasion. And this sounds like it qualifies."

Sintia held out her hand. "No matter how this goes, I want you to know what an honor it's been to share this month with you."

Stell shook it solemnly.

"Besides," Sinthia continued, "it's kind of refreshing to live with a guy who never makes one single pass at you. Boring, but refreshing."

Stell rolled his eyes. He didn't understand how people ever got anything done. The only thing they ever thought about was sex.

***

"I can't believe they just locked her up in the Council Building," Stell said as they approached the illuminated tower from the trees in Humanity Park. "I've been searching for her location for months and I couldn't find her, and all along, she was here." He glanced over at Sintia. "Did you know there's a detention center out in an archipelago in the Central Ocean on the other side of the planet? It's the only populated part of Tau Ceti II that you can't reach by jumping into a train right over there and transferring over to the suborbital transports. I was sure that's where they were holding her."

"First," Sintia replied, "of course I know about the detention center, and it's not the only one. Did you get as far as the Mountain Tomb? I'd be impressed if you did, there are supposedly no records of that. Not to mention that neither of the two has been used in living memory. And secondly, shut up, I'm trying to coordinate with the students."

Over the course of the past month, he'd made the mistake of letting Sintia in on the secret planning happening behind the scenes. He knew it was a terrible idea — the whole point was to keep her out of the loop so that if Sintia was caught, she wouldn't be able to compromise the rest of the group. She was, after all, the only one the government knew about.

But it had been impossible. Stell was immune to the wiles of women, but Sintia wasn't just a woman, she was a politician who could charm the birds out of the trees. She knew how to make Stell feel validated, telling him that his actions were brave and that his decisions were wise. When they weren't wise, she would insist that it wasn't his fault, that he would have gotten it exactly right if he'd only considered some little detail, which she would then supply...

Afterwards, of course, he suspected she'd been manipulating him. Unfortunately, every time they had a conversation, he would fall for it again. He would have hated to have to oppose her in the Council Chamber.

And he was utterly unable to keep her out of the planning that was supposed to be happening without her knowledge.

Which meant that now that they were in the field, she was on the comms, coordinating everything.

The trees to their left rustled. Stell pointed in that direction, and Sintia nodded. They remained silent until a soft whistle — two low notes, and then two high ones — broke the silence.

"Over here," Sintia whispered.

Three students that Stell recognized from the day he'd gone to the Institute to pick Sintia up appeared out of the darkness.

"Where's Professor Ooblah?" Stell said.

"She can't come. We think they've got her under surveillance."

Stell let out a sigh of relief. He was half-expecting to end up in jail despite all the codes and data at their disposal, but as long as Ooblah remained free, they had hope. "All right. I'll go first. If you see me wave, come to the Council Building."

The government structure sat in the exact middle of a circular grassy clearing in the geometrical center of Humanity Park. At one point, it had been surrounded by a sturdy fence, but Mira had ordered it taken down.

Stell suspected that was because the protestors who'd caused them to be put up in the first place responded to Mira herself.

He crossed the open space and reached the numerical keypad that controlled the door; the fence might be gone but it didn't appear that the people were welcome inside anymore. Before the regime change, anyone could simply walk into the council building to consult records. He held his breath and punched in the code that The Earthling had provided. This was the first test, albeit an innocuous one. If it failed, he could theoretically still walk away.

The door chimed and opened.

He stood in the doorway to keep it from closing and waved. Moments later Sintia — her collar pulled well up to hide her mouth — and the students joined him and they entered. The door closed behind them.

"Well, this is it," Stell said.

They walked into the central hall, which hadn't changed much since the last time Stell had been there: black polished stone, yellowish wood paneling and glass, a lot of glass. The scars on the stone floor still remained from the day of the insurrection, but the broken windows and staved-in doors had been replaced.

A man at the security desk waved and smiled when they entered. "We're going to the guest rooms," Stell said.

"They're on the fourth floor," the man replied.

"Do we take the elevator?"

"Unless you really feel like climbing."

They piled into the lift which had room for another ten people in it and pressed the button.

"Why didn't that man arrest us all?" one of the students, a young woman with short red hair, asked.

"We had the code to the door, so we are apparently trustworthy. But there's another thing. According to our sources, it's his first day at this post. And that was done on purpose. He won't question anyone. Besides, the security people at the Council Building aren't necessarily loyal to Mira Heine. They are just here to tell people where the bathrooms are."

"That's insane," the student said. "What kind of people would have legitimate business here in the middle of the night?"

"Well, it's technically early morning," Sintia said. "We often have — or I guess I should say we had — visitors from all over the planet and even from the other colonies. So the guards expect to have people coming in and out at odd hours. As long as they have the code, the guy's butt is covered."

Stell gave her a hard glance. "You know something."

Sintia shook her head. "Know? No? Suspect?" she smiled slightly. "Yes. I have a feeling that a lot of things are going on at once, and we're just part of one plan."

"And that guy is part of another. Although he doesn't look bright enough to be a conspirator."

Sintia raised an eyebrow. "And maybe that's the point. Not

every part of every plan has to be brilliant."

The elevator opened onto a hallway. Stell suddenly felt uncomfortable. "The last time I was here, there was an enraged mob chasing me."

"They weren't chasing you," Sintia said. "They were after Rome."

"Whatever. They would have pounded all of us if they'd grabbed us."

"Which room are we looking for?" one of the male students asked.

"409."

The red-haired student pointed. "Over there."

"No guards?" Stell said.

"There's something happening," Sintia replied. "Let's do our bit."

They approached the door and Stell punched in the code. The door popped open. He reached out with his right hand and turned on the lights in the room. A dark form in the bed turned over to reveal Ashur Nartiya's dark features. She blinked at the sudden light. "It's a good thing I don't sleep in the nude," she said.

"I wouldn't care one way or another."

"Stell?" Nartiya said. "Are you working for them, now?"

"If you call breaking in here and springing you working for them, then yes. Otherwise, no. I'm here to rescue you."

"I hope you brought an army. I suspect they're not just going to let me walk out of here."

"Nah. We went with the stealth approach. We suspect that there are other parts of this plan that we don't know about." He struck a pose. "But this is the most brilliant bit."

At that moment, an alarm rang and blue lights began to flash.

"Yeah, I can tell," Nartiya said. She sprang from the bed, grabbed a pair of shoes and headed for the door. "Hi

Representative Ericsson," she said as she passed. "Looks like they're going to get you, too."

"Apparently."

"Which way should we go?" Stell asked. He turned to Sintia and Ashur. "Is there any place in this building that we can defend?"

Sintia rushed out of the room and over to the railing that overlooked the lobby. "I think a better bet would be to try to get out before the response team gets here. The fastest way to bring troops in is by air, and the flyer pad is on the roof. So I vote we go down."

Stell shrugged. "I have no problem with that." He ran for the stairs.

Everyone followed. They flew down the flights at breakneck speed and found the guard from the desk waiting for them in the lobby. He didn't appear to be armed, but Stell stopped in front of him.

"What's are you doing?" the guard asked. He tried to look stern, but mainly came across as frightened.

Stell hesitated. Did he actually have to explain a jailbreak to this guy?

Nartiya came to his rescue. "There's a fire in my room! Help us get outside. Call... well, call whoever it is that is supposed to deal with these things!"

The man hesitated for a moment then ran towards his desk. About halfway there, he stopped and turned back, another question on his lips, but the group had already gone for the door.

They reached the fence and Stell punched in the code. "It's not working!"

The security guy was coming out to see what was wrong. "I just got a call telling me not to let anyone out. The fire seems to be under control."

"Can you let us out?" Nartiya said.

"I'm afraid not. I think it would be best if we stay inside and wait for the team. It's on its way," he said.

Stell pulled out his handheld. The device didn't have anywhere near enough memory to attempt a brute-force attack on the Council Building's security systems, but it could connect him with the network. "Help!" he typed into a hidden chat room.

No sooner had he finished entering his plea that a buzzing sound emerged from the trees. Everyone looked up, expecting a flyer full of Mira's shock troops.

The guard's eyes widened as a small flying drone smacked him in the face. He went down like a rock.

Immediately, Stell leaned over him and checked his pulse, ignoring the bleeding gash on his forehead because it wasn't life-threatening. "He's unconscious, probably concussed," he reported. Then he grabbed the guard's Panorama Screen, a special unit that controlled the building's systems. It took him only a few seconds to find the door controls and turn off the alarm.

He tried the code in the gate, and it opened. "Run for it!"

They sprinted out of the compound, headed towards the same stand of trees they'd emerged from initially. Once there, they turned back towards the building. The flyer they'd been expecting had alighted on the roof.

"It won't take them long to get down," Sintia said.

"They probably have people on the ground already," Nartiya added. "Do we have an exit plan?"

"We have a hideout prepared in one of the hab units," the red-haired student told them. "It will be a tight fit, and we'll need to block the cameras, but it's secure."

"I can block the cameras," Stell said. "In fact, I've had the blocker on all night… but I doubt it worked inside the building.

Not because I can't hack the cameras, but because some of them are fixed in place to cover a specific patch of real estate at all times, so we can't make them turn away at just the right moment. Plus, there are so many of us that at least some of our group must have wandered into a visible field."

"Would've helped if you'd told us about that," the student replied.

"Yeah," Stell said. "But I was nervous. I fight most of my wars from my keyboard. This is a new experience for me."

Sintia grabbed Stell by the arm. "Your mission was to get us in, and get us out with Nartiya in tow. The mission went flawlessly, so don't sweat it. Now, we just need to turn that victory into something we can use."

"We need to run," Nartiya said. "Now."

"And stick close to me," Stell reminded them.

***

The hab unit was almost exactly the same as Stell's, except that Stell's was closer to the park, in a prettier housing complex. They ran through the open door and collapsed, panting onto every available surface.

"Did anyone see signs of pursuit?" Nartiga asked between deep breaths.

Heads shook across the room.

The students recovered first, followed by Stell. Sintia and Nartiya exchanged glances and smiled. "We're getting old," Sintia said.

"Like hell,"Nartiya replied. "I've been locked up in a room for weeks. They wouldn't even allow me to walk around the building in case anyone saw me. That's why the security guard didn't know who I was. Only a few goons working for Zun had any clue I was there, and the door was way too solid to break open. Or even dent. I tried."

"Zun's goons," Stell giggled.

Sintia gave him a tolerant smile. She'd grown accustomed to his word jokes.

Nartiya's face in contrast, was grave. "What's our next step?" she asked.

"I was hoping you'd have a few suggestions," Sintia replied. "You're the military mind. I tend to think along the lines of consensus, discussion and a vote. I'm useless in the current situation."

Nartiya put her hand on Sintia's arm. "You are never useless. You're one of the best leaders this colony has ever had. If you weren't here, we would have fallen apart last year."

"Which doesn't change the fact that I can't help at all if there's a shooting war."

"So let's avoid one," Nartiya said. "Stell, who is your invisible friend?"

"What?" he asked.

"The one that dropped the drone on the guard."

"I can't tell you."

"This isn't the time for games. I mean it," Nartiya said.

"I know, Captain. And I'm not playing games. If I tell you that, I'm putting the lives of everyone in this room in danger."

"In case you hadn't noticed, we're already in danger."

Stell hoped Sintia wouldn't spill the information she'd learned and guessed while staying in his house. "Not this much danger. Let it suffice to say that it's someone with a serious amount of computing power at their disposal."

Nartiya glowered at him, but Stell held her gaze. She wasn't the captain anymore, so she couldn't have him locked in the brig. And besides, he'd just rescued her. Finally, she sighed. "All right. We need to assume they're looking for us, and that they'll find us sooner rather than later. I'd estimate one hour." She tapped her fingers against a table. "I need to get to one of the Naval comm centers."

"Why?" Stell asked.

"I want a deep-space line to the ships commanded by people I trust. They knew what to do if Mira tried something like this."

"You suspected she'd do this?" Sintia asked.

"I was absolutely sure she'd do this," Nartiya replied. "So I planned for it."

"Wish you'd told me," Sintia said.

"I did. You said you could deal with her."

"You shouldn't have listened to me," Sintia replied.

"I didn't. But I need a deep-space comm."

"Here." Stell handed her his handheld. One glance told Nartiya it wasn't a standard Panorama Screen.

She shook her head. "This can reach my ships?"

Stell nodded. "Courtesy of my nameless friend."

Nartiya's expression was a promise to revisit the subject at a later date, but she turned her eyes towards the screen. "So all I have to do is select the ship I want to talk to and… talk?"

"Yep."

Nartiya went to work.

CHAPTER 25

In Space Near 61 Virginis III

The *Grader* disappeared under a swarm of mechanical black spiders shooting through space.

"Captain Yu, can you hear me?" Mira called into the comm.

"Yes, I can hear you," the captain's voice came through scratchy and full of static, but audible. "We're preparing to repel boarders."

"Dañi says to stay still and we'll try to clear your decks with projectile weapons," Mira replied.

"We'll do our best," Yu said. Her voice was nearly inaudible, fading to nothing with the final word.

"Captain," Mira said. "Captain?" She turned back to the bridge. "Damn, we've lost them. Those things must have covered every antenna."

"What are they?" one of the bridge engineers, an earnest-looking young woman who seemed like a child to Mira, asked.

"They're the tools of an AI from Earth that has used nanofactories on the planet's surface to build a fleet to harvest anyone in the vicinity," Mira said.

The young woman's eyes flicked towards Dañi, as if seeking confirmation of the words, a gesture that cut Mira to the quick, but didn't surprise her. No one seemed prepared to accept what they were up against, and whenever Mira spoke of it, she got the sense that they all thought she was crazy. Whether that was because they didn't want it to be true or because they simply didn't believe it was possible made no difference. Their blindness to the facts would have to be corrected.

To her credit, Dañi nodded and said nothing. Unlike Mira's other followers, Dañi was worthy of command.

Which was fortunate, because at the moment she was insanely busy barking out commands, and any hesitation on the part of the crew to obey the orders would have been disastrous. From what Mira gathered the woman was attempting to fly the ship, position the smaller cruisers, clear the *Grader*'s deck of enemy machines and fight off the AI's offensive via shouted orders. How an engineer with only a few months of naval experience could do that successfully was beyond Mira's comprehension, but she appeared to be managing it.

"Do we have the angle to clear the *Grader*?" Dañi asked.

"Yes, Captain," the weapons tech replied.

"Fire at will."

The screen showed the effects of the barrage. A large swathe of the *Grader*'s silver metal exterior became visible as the black machines were swept away.

Dañi nodded in approval. "Good shot. Navigation, I need to reposition us on the other side, to give the firing team a good angle. Let's clear the *Grader*."

"Captain, we have incoming," the guy on the scope said.

"What, more of them?"

"Yes. Coming for us. No, wait, they just split into four groups. They're going for us and for the escorts, too."

"Guns, forget the *Grader*, get me a firing solution on these guys," Dañi said. She turned to Mira. "Can you get on the horn to the escorts and tell them to run?"

"Run?"

"If the *Grader* couldn't fight those things off, they won't, either. And if they take a few of them on a chase, we'll have to fight fewer of them ourselves."

"All right."

Mira commed the escort ships and relayed the orders.

The *Buran* shuddered as the main guns fired. Mira's belt bit into her shoulders, but she kept speaking to the escort captains, trying to answer questions about the situation that she didn't quite understand.

She was thrown to one side, then to the other. The ship groaned, and the lights blinked. The bridge engineer who'd spoken before sat right in front of her. Mira saw the paleness of her face, watched her chest heave. The woman was terrified.

But she was doing her job, or at least punching commands into her workstation and reading the display.

Maybe that was better than thinking of what was about to happen to them.

"I want a missile in the middle of that group before it gets close again," Dañi shouted. "Something with nice fragmentation."

"Yes, Captain," the gunnery officer said.

The ship shuddered again and Mira watched the main screen — now serving as a tactical display — in which a green icon showed the missile they'd just fired towards a cloud of red dots representing the enemy swarm.

"Detonation," guns reported.

The cloud of red on the display had thinned considerably, but it was still coming.

"Projectile guns, fire at will," Dañi ordered.

The floor vibrated as the guns raked the cloud of enemy ships. Mira imagined the sinister black vehicles she'd seen on the long-range cameras dissolving under the barrage.

All but four of the dots disappeared from the screen.

"Proximity gunners, please deal with the remaining bogeys." Dañi didn't celebrate. Instead, she turned to the engineering desk. "Give me full speed towards the *Grader*," she said. "Mira, try to raise the captain. And see what's up with the rest of our fleet."

Mira tried several times. On every band. "No one is responding."

"Dammit," Dañi said. "Nav, I need to get to the far side of the *Grader*. We'll need to do this the hard way. First clear the ship's surface, then send people onto it."

Mira wanted to tell her to get the *Buran* out of there, to say that the fight was lost, and that they needed to get back to Tau Ceti, where The Earthling would defend them from any incursion by this AI.

But she couldn't do that. If anyone even suspected what she was thinking, she would be pushed aside and Gabriel Zun would find himself at the head of Tau Ceti's government.

So when Dañi led them to the rescue of a fleet of ships who, Mira was convinced, were already dead, all she could do was to nod along and support her.

"Bogeys down," the gunners reported. It took Mira a few moments to realize they were referring to the stragglers from the cloud they'd cut through with the projectile guns, not the ones they were moving towards.

"Get me in position, Nav," Dañi said.

"Working on it," the guy on the console replied.

"Oh, shit! Captain..." the girl on scope said. She punched a command and the main screen switched from a tac view to a false-color image of a spacecraft. There were green areas, red areas, orange areas and yellow areas.

"Is that the *Grader*?" Dañi asked.

"Yes, Captian."

"Dammit," Dañi said. "Pull away, full speed!"

Mira stared at the display, trying to decipher what Dañi was doing, but unable to make sense the diagram. As she watched, several elements of the red section pulled themselves away from the outline of the ship and scattered into space.

The screen switched back to the main tactical display with the *Buran* at the center in blue. Another blue icon — which turned grey as Mira watched — represented the *Grader*, while a stream of red dots moved to connect the two.

"Proximity guns!" Dañi cried.

"They're too close!"

"Get the ones you can," she replied.

"I'm sorry, Captain," the gunner said. "They're under my horizon."

"Prepare to fold!" Dañi said.

"What?" Mira asked.

Or, rather, she tried to ask, because the weird sensation in her stomach informed her that the ship's fold drives had activated, bending space through the action of gravitational waves in ways Mira didn't even pretend to understand. The question stuck in her throat.

This time, the bridge lights did more than dim, they went out completely. A low alarm sounded in the room. But other than the discomfort in her stomach, Mira had felt no physical sense that the jump took place. No bumping, no swaying, no sudden acceleration. One second they were fighting a battle, the next her stomach felt awful and the lights were out.

Dañi's voice broke the silence. "Engineering, I need power," she said.

"I'm trying to get in touch with the engine room," the guy in front of Mira, invisible in the pitch-black replied.

A dim light went on. Mira assumed it was the battery-powered emergency lights they'd told her about when she first boarded.

"Well, that's progress at least," Dañi snarked. "Let me know when we'll have more." She turned to the security supervisor behind her. "I need you to do a physical check of the ship and tell me if we have any visitors."

"Yes, Captain." The man began to manually crank the bridge door open.

"Dañi," Mira said. "Do you know where we are?"

"The truth is that we'd set specific coordinates for the emergency fold, but... that close to a planet isn't the best place to jump. The gravity well... it throws off all the calculations. We might be exactly where I tried to take us, which is a half-light year from Sextus just above the ecliptic."

"What are the odds of that?"

"Extremely low. The fact that we lost power shows that things didn't go exactly to plan. Something overloaded in what should have been a tiny fold. The most likely result is that we're a dozen light years from anywhere, and we'll need to understand where we are before we can even begin to think about going back."

Mira nodded. "We're not going back to Sextus."

"We have to. The colonists... the other ships..."

"Are lost," Mira replied firmly. "And we have a greater responsibility to the human race. We need to get back to Tau Ceti and report what has happened here. We need to prepare for it to happen again."

The bridge crew exchanged glances. Mira saw it out of the corner of her eye and paid it no attention. There was only one person on this bridge whose opinion mattered: Dañi. If she decided to go against her orders, things would spiral completely out of control.

"Yes Ma'am," Dañi replied.

Good girl, Mira thought.

Chapter 26

New Earth – Sextus Colony – 61 Virginis III

"Fire!" Touk shouted.

The rocky tunnel shuddered and dust fell from the roof as the artillery piece, still warm from being produced in the nanofactory, blasted a high-explosive shell into a mass of silver and black enemy attack units.

At that range, less that three hundred meters down the arrow-straight grey tunnel, it couldn't miss, and the machines were blasted into clouds of carbon and metal.

"Reload!" Touk shouted. "And get the second cannon online. Hurry."

His comm buzzed. "Touk, where the hell are you?" It was Anguk.

"I'm commanding the defense of the main hangar entrance. We're holding for now."

"Well, you need to get back here right away."

Touk shook his head, even though the director couldn't see him. "They need me here."

"We have a bigger problem," Anguk said.

"Bigger than a full-scale invasion at the door?"

"Yes."

In the frenzied noise of the team around him reloading in preparation for another enemy advance, Touk took a second to take a deep breath and wonder how such a thing could be. "Talk to me."

"The nanofactory in the sewage plant went nuts and began to print out black and silver machines that began to attack everything in sight. The only reason they didn't get into the main hall is that one of the engineers thought really fast and blew the bolts around the processing tanks. The invaders — and the nanofactory — are buried in a few million gallons of sewage."

"Ugh. But yeah, great thinking. Remind me to give that guy a hug."

"He's buried down there, too."

"Oh."

"Yeah. We're afraid this means the enemy is in our systems. And if it gets into the central computers, it will get control of the rest of our nanofactories. After that happens all our perimeter defenses are useless, because the enemy will be behind our choke points, building as many machines as they need."

The crushing weight of imminent defeat landed on Touk's shoulders. "No," he whispered. "Get them offline now."

"We're trying, but the..." Anguk's voice suddenly went low and wavered, and then cut off completely.

Touk's hands shook. The voice transmission system was hardwired into the computer network. If it broke down, there was something in the system causing it to do so. His bet on what that might be started and ended with the electronic entity trying to overrun the colony.

He turned to the guy loading a shell into the cannon. "Give me a hand, we need to disconnect the nanofactory from the network," he said.

"What? We need the shells."

"If it's not infected yet, we can still get shells, but we need to unplug it now." He ran for the big black machine without checking to see whether the man was with him. Every eye followed him.

The back of the machine was a mess of cables plugged into a mobile adapter they'd installed to connect the nanofactory to the rest of their systems. He selected anything that resembled a network plug and pulled it away. Just in case, he also ripped out the power cord. The nanofactory could generate its own power for days and, since Touk knew it was possible to transmit information through power modulations, he didn't want to take any risks. If the battle lasted that long and the enemy actually did control the computers and the power grid, they were all dead anyway.

"Find the antenna," Touk shouted.

"I've got it," the loader replied. He appeared around a corner with an antenna, complete with dangling wires, clutched in one fist. He studied Touk's handiwork. "We're going to have to do a ton of work to get this one repaired."

Touk chuckled. "It's a nanofactory. When this is over, we'll just pour some organics and metals into the input shaft an tell it to repair itself. Relax." Then he thought of something. "No. Don't relax. Go to the gun crews and get one of the cannons pointed in this direction, square at the middle of the nanofactory."

"But..."

"Just do it."

The man ran off to carry out his orders. Touk watched them and, as soon as they were ready, he stepped up to the nanofactory's control panel and ordered it to create ammunition for the artillery.

A spidery leg emerged from the mouth of the machine. Touk barely managed to avoid getting grabbed, and ran towards the cannon crew. "Shoot it! Shoot it now!" he shouted as he ran past.

He dove for cover. A shell hissed overhead an instant before he heard the bang of the cannon. A moment later, a deafening explosion rocked the tunnel and the shockwave nearly lifted him from the floor. Shards of shrapnel pinged against the stone walls.

He got unsteadily to his feet and put his hand against the wall for support as his blurry vision reasserted itself. The first thing he saw was two of the cannon crew — wearing ear protection…smart people — running towards him.

"Are you all right?" one of them shouted.

Touk nodded. "Good work," he said. "Now get that gun pointed back towards the door."

"We don't have a ton of ammo left," the guy said.

"Hold out until you run out, then get to the shelter."

"Yes, sir."

Touk didn't wait to see if they carried out his orders. He suspected that the fight along the perimeter would only be relevant until the enemy managed to get the nanofactories to produce enough machines to overrun the defenders further inside the colony. So the cannons might buy them a few minutes at most.

He ran past deeper into the tunnel that led to the main habitation area. He needed to kill the nanofactory in the colony machine shop, and then he needed to organize the inhabitants to get them into a walled area they could actually hole up in.

The Tau fleet that had arrived a few hours earlier had been scattered or destroyed, so they couldn't expect any help from that quarter.

Even the Engine Test Facility had gone off the air moments before Touk arrived at the artillery position. They couldn't nuke the bad guys from orbit to clear a path.

That meant they had to think of a way out of this on their own.

So what could they do? Touk had no idea. He would think of it once he was in a safe spot. First, there was one thing he absolutely had to do: find Emily.

He suspected he was about to die. Perhaps not immediately, but in the next few hours. And if he was going to die, then he wanted to be by her side. So only when they were together would he stop to think about how to save the colony. That way, when he failed to do the impossible, he would be with her.

Touk's lungs burned. He hadn't run this hard since he was a kid, and though setting up a colony on an inhospitable planet often involved strenuous physical labor, it almost never involved running any distance.

By the time he reached the end of the tunnel, he felt like he was about to collapse, but still forced himself to continue. The grey of the entrance road gave way to the softer grey, almost white, and carpeting of the inhabited areas. He stopped to check the hab unit they shared, but it was empty. Knowing Emily, there was only one other place where she might be.

Touk ignored the protests of his body and raced towards the hospital, past the entrance checkpoint where he was usually checked for credentials but which, today, was unmanned, and through the antiseptic-smelling corridors.

An orderly called to him as he passed. Touk ignored the man and sprinted for Intensive Care Unit.

"Touk!"

Emily's voice, emerging from a side corridor, stopped him in his tracks. Fortunately, the floor was rubberized and he managed to arrest his progress without suffering an embarrassing spill. "Emily, you're all right!"

She cocked her head. "Why wouldn't I be? The perimeter is holding, right? I just heard that. I was worried about you, though."

"It's holding, but that's a moot point. The enemy will be behind them, in the corridors very soon, even if we stop them at the tunnel entrances," he said. "We need to get everyone somewhere defensible."

"I got them started in setting up a last stand bunker in the terraforming shelter. But once I saw they could manage without me, I got the call to come here," Emily said.

"I'm glad you did that. We need to start getting people in the shelter."

"Wait. There's something you need to know."

"Can't it wait?" he asked. "Getting people under cover is kind of urgent."

"I don't think it can," a new voice said. Dr. Yault emerged from a door to the emergency area. She was wiping her hands with a light-blue cloth and, for the first time since Touk had met her, she seemed tired. "You need to hear this. Come in."

"In there? I'm not scrubbed up." Touk knew just how fanatical the doctor was about avoiding any risk to her patients. And now she was asking him to enter the ICU?

"No time. Get a move on."

She turned and headed back through the door. Emily followed close behind and Touk shrugged and headed after them.

The ICU consisted of a main hall with rooms branching off. The doctor entered the one nearest the door. Touk mused that this was probably because it was more comfortable for the doctors not to have to walk a long way to their patients. That was a luxury they would no longer have once the ICU filled up with patients.

Which it would do as soon as the injured from the defense of the colony began to pour in.

Gina, the tech who'd been captured by the enemy and subsequently rescued, sat propped on a bed. Her face and arms were covered with bandages where the surgeons had pulled the cables out of her body.

"Hello," she said. "Is this my fault?"

"I don't think so," Emily said. "I think your capture actually allowed us to defend ourselves."

"Maybe if I hadn't been caught and you hadn't destroyed their first settlement, the Uploaders would have been content to stay where they were."

"Uploaders?"

"That's what they call themselves. They have a whole simulated society. We were sucked into the tiny part of it they have here on the surface, and they told us that they were trying to do away with all human suffering, to create a life where everyone would be free to be happy." She shuddered. "It felt weird to me. They all seemed really nice, I guess… but there was something missing. Something important."

"They? What do you mean?"

"They were people. Humans. Living in this kind of… I'm not sure how to describe it. I think they have a lot of different aspects to their simulation. A planet was one of them. Then a giant sphere floating in space. Then I was in a kind of garden with no sky, just the feeling of a weird purple end of the horizon." She shook her head. "I guess you had to see it."

"Why did they show you all this?" Touk asked.

"I think it was like an introduction. They told me that the equipment they used to capture my consciousness — that's what they called it 'capture my consciousness' — was only temporary, emergency equipment they had on hand while they waited for the nanofactories to produce better scanners that could transmit us back to the central mainframe. Then they said they'd discard our unnecessary biological bodies."

"Kill you, they mean," Dr. Yault said.

"They don't see it as killing you," Emily came in. "Touk, I tried to explain it to her, but she hates the thought of it. You have to understand. All of this, removing the biological form and living in the mind, in a simulated society, it's happened before. On Earth. Maybe not intentionally, but this is what happened.

And if you ask anyone from Earth if they are alive, they'll say yes, and argue that their lives are worth just the same as yours. Or mine. This version of me."

"Bullshit," the doctor said. "I don't care how good your machinery is. You can't replace or copy a human mind with an electronic one. Not while maintaining continuity of consciousness."

"I'm sorry, Doctor. I really disagree with that," Emily said.

"You would."

"Yes, and I'm the only one in this room other than Gina that has any relevant experience, so no matter what you believe, you need to understand that this is happening," Emily said.

"I felt like I was me," Gina interjected.

"You were. You were still in your brain," the doctor replied.

"None of that matters right now," Touk said. "What matters is what this means for the defense of the colony. The enemy is trying to overrun us, but they haven't been firing back. Now I see why. They want us all alive to feed into this simulated society of theirs."

"Why would they even need real people?" Yault asked. "Why not just program new ones like on Earth?"

"I have no clue. But that's what's happening here," Touk replied. "And we need to use the fact that they don't want to shoot anyone in our favor." He pulled out his comm and tried to get Anguk on the line. It was still down. "Damn. Does anyone know where Director Vest is?"

"He had relieved me in leading the fortification work in the shelter," Emily replied.

"Come on," Touk said. He tried not to think about how fast Vest was slipping. Emily was smart, and she was a hero of sorts to the colonists, but Vest should have been the one taking charge of the situation. "We need to get down there."

"Out of the question," Yault replied. "I have patients here."

"We can't defend this position."

"That makes absolutely no difference to me. I have people I can't move, including a five-year-old on stem-cell treatments after I pulled out a ton of cancer nodes. I won't leave them."

Touk stared at her for a moment, before a scream from the hall brought him back to his senses. "I think it might not matter anymore," he said.

They emerged into the corridor to find several people running in panic. Some of the citizens spotted the door leading into the hospital and charged inside.

To Touk's surprise Yault ushered them deeper into the ICU.

"What is it?" Emily asked.

"I don't know yet," Touk replied.

"It's some kind of mechanical crawling thing," one of the people said before they rushed by.

Touk pulled out the energy pistol he'd been assigned when the invasion began. It was a last resort, unlikely to be much use against a real threat, but holding it in its hand felt better than facing whatever was coming unarmed. He peered down the corridor.

The flow of people fell to a trickle and then stopped. The white corridors were silent for a moment before Touk picked up a new sound: a soft clicking skitter echoed as if from a long distance away.

Touk raised his weapon and aimed it down the hall, listening intently for any sign that the enemy had closed the gap.

He heard soft breathing beside his ear and turned to see Emily beside him, tear-moistened eyes watching him intently. "Get back inside," he whispered.

"Why? Are you going to be able to defend us very long?"

His shoulders slumped. "Probably not."

She put her hand on his shoulder. "Then I'd rather stay here. With you."

"I suppose that's all right. I always dreamed we would die together, although I thought it would mean growing old first, sharing long walks on a terraformed version of Sextus. I guess the end is going to come sooner than I hoped."

"I wouldn't worry about that. If Gina is right about what she saw, we may have a few thousand years to look forward to."

"In that weird slave society? I'm not sure it will be an improvement."

Emily squeezed his shoulder. "We won't know until it happens. If we get uploaded, will you promise me something? Promise me you'll find me, somehow, some way."

"Of course I will," Touk replied. "But we're not dead yet."

The skitter became a clatter, and a huge walker, larger and endowed with more legs than the man-sized ones he'd been fighting at the perimeter scraped through the corridor. Touk stepped into view, leveled the energy weapon and pressed the activation button.

He'd never fired one before, and expected recoil or noise… or some tactile clue that energy had been released in the direction of the enemy. But he felt nothing.

Touk's disappointment didn't even last an instant. As soon as he pressed the stud, the machine in front of him shuddered. Parts flew away from it and its advance slowed.

He looked down at the gun. "Not bad," he said. He pressed the stud again and again and again, watching the invisible energy slam into the machine until it stopped in its tracks.

"Ow," he said, and dropped the weapon on the floor. It had burned his hand, and lay smoking. As he watched, the heat from the power pack within melted the plastic. He watched it deform before it cooled. His hand was only slightly reddened, he saw with relief. "I'm glad whoever designed this decided not to save on insulation," he said. Then he studied the shattered enemy walker. Acrid smoke wafted through the corridor, the smell of burnt plastic and ozone. "That should keep them from coming this way, anyhow."

As if on cue, a high-pitched mechanical whine filled the corridor, followed by the tortured screech of metal on metal. A moment later, a circular hole appeared in the center of the broken walker. A silver point came into view in the center.

"Are they drilling?" Emily asked.

Touk said nothing, just nodded. They watched in silence as the hole in the center of the immobile machine grew larger and larger, to reveal a drill whose diameter was as wide as Touk's outstretched arms. As the stalled walker began to disintegrate, he saw rank upon rank of enemy machines — the same man-sized ones he'd been blasting at the perimeter — arrayed in the corridor, waiting for the detritus to be cleared.

"I'm not going to be able to stop all of those with my fists," Touk said.

Emily pulled him close and kissed him deep before pulling away. "Then let's hide," she said. "Let's make this last as long as we can."

They ran into the ICU.

Chapter 27

In Orbit Around 61 Virginis III

Rome listened as Skate gave them the situation report. Jarrien, Ripp, Emily and, surprisingly, even the mysterious Alia, sat and listened.

"Gaia's forces have the planet surrounded with minisats. The Tau fleet is gone. Four ships — a big one and three small ones — are floating in the vicinity with no life forms appearing on any scan. The Engine Test Facility — that large ship over there — is also dead as far as we can tell from here.

"The only place humans are still alive outside whatever simulation the AI is running are on the ground in the main settlement itself. We've analyzed the data patterns from the comm system, and Gaia has taken it over."

"Is there anything we can do?"

"Would I have brought you here if there wasn't?" He held up a hand. "Now isn't the time for sarcasm. We can act, but we need to do it really fast. I need to get the mainframe on this ship connected to the one on the surface. That's why we're in a reentry burn right now."

Ripp raised a hand. "How do you know the enemy's central control computer is down there?"

"I don't think it is. But I know that, in order to control the advance of surface troops and especially to keep the humans it harvests in its power, it absolutely has to have a controlling mainframe somewhere on the ground. That's the one we need to overrun."

"Can't we just find it and bomb it from orbit?"

"We don't have bombs. And there's no way we can find it

from up here. The way we're going to get in is through the Sextus computer network. We'll physically plug into one of the mainframes in the colony and overrun the security. Then we'll backtrack to see where Gaia got into the system. From there, we'll jump onto Gaia's own computers and take over."

Ripp snorted. "She'll see you coming miles away."

"Do you really think she'll be concerned about cybersecurity in the middle of an invasion? She has other things to think about," Skate replied. "But I agree that we should give her something to think about. A diversion."

"What kind of a diversion?" Rome said.

"I'm reasonably certain that the AI is using a version of its simulated environment as the UI to allow it to interact and subdue the Colony's network. Since the Earth simulation is much more advanced than the computer systems from Tau Ceti, this interface will allow Gaia to run the Tau Ceti systems like a superuser, a human who just happens to have access to everything. But it has the added benefit — from our point of view — that we can walk around in there just as if we were living in the Earth simulation. It's probably not the most secure design in the galaxy, but Gaia isn't expecting to find Earth hackers in the 61 Virginis system. And although all of the people it brought with it from Earth could likely walk around in there, those guys are quarantined. I'd bet that the main instance of Gaia's consciousness is in a ship very similar to this one — and unarmed like we are — somewhere in the edges of this system, ready to jump away as soon as anyone finds it. Gaia won't risk her primary consciousness for this system." He looked around. "Does this make sense so far?"

"Yeah, except I'm not sure how we're supposed to use it to our advantage," Ripp said.

Skate nodded. "Good question, with a simple answer. If some

of you walk in there and start randomly disconnecting things, it will get Gaia's attention in a hurry. She will definitely take action, and that will give Alia and me the chance to get through her defenses undetected, and to take over the assault mainframe."

"What happens to the people who go in there as the diversion?" Ripp asked.

"In theory, nothing. I have packets of defensive code that should work on pretty much anything Gaia might have up her sleeve. She won't be able to capture your code and upload you into her systems."

"Hell, I wouldn't be worried about that," Ripp replied. "I would be worried about Gaia deciding to delete me completely. I don't think I want to play in that sandbox. I'll help you go after the backdoor."

"I'll walk into her parlor," Emily said. "Hell, I don't even care if she deletes me. There's another version of me out there." She pointed at the display which showed the icy planet below her. "And that one has a physical life to live."

Rome took her hand, intending to tell her that she wouldn't be able to do much damage, that she should stay behind. But when she turned to him, expectantly, one eyebrow raised, he felt it would be unfair to even hint at that. "I'm coming with you," he said instead.

Relief replaced the challenge in her expression and she hugged him, squeezing him so hard his ribs hurt. "Thank you," she breathed.

"You'll need someone who can program, or she won't even bother to respond," he said.

"Oh, she was going to have to respond one way or another," Emily said. "I was planning on physically demolishing her simulation until she appeared. And then I was going to break something over her head."

"I'm not sure it works that way."

"Well, I would have had hands, wouldn't I? I'd have bashed her face in."

"Again..." Rome let it go. "We'll figure it out when we get there."

"You won't have to do anything too intricate," Skate said. "And you won't have to hold out for too long, either. Between us, Alia and I should be able to subvert anything Gaia has waiting for us very quickly. We've been planning this attack for a couple of centuries."

"I thought you AIs didn't attack each other," Jarrien said.

Rome looked over at her, surprised. She'd been so silent that he's almost forgotten she was there. In fact, the blue-haired woman had been strangely subdued during the entire trip, which was strange from the normally fiery rebel. She appeared particularly insecure whenever Skate was nearby.

"We don't. But this is a special case. Earth has been neutral territory forever because none of us can realistically win a war against the rest of us. But if Gaia does what she's planning, and creates a parallel civilization of uploaded minds combined with the ones she harvested from Earth... well, I don't know where it might lead, but it can't be good, can it?"

"So we're attacking her just in case?" Emily said. "Because we're scared of new things?"

"I am. I don't know why you're attacking her, though. I suspect you have other reasons." Skate smiled at them knowingly.

After a few seconds, Emily smiled back. "You're an asshole, Skate. But you're right. So how long before I can attack her for my own reasons?"

"We're in the atmosphere. We'll be on the ground in minutes."

***

The best part of landing while immersed in a simulation is that you don't even know you're flying, Rome mused as he watched the snow-covered surface come up to greet them in the external cams. It should have been a bumpy descent, but if he hadn't been watching the clouds and snow whip around in the image, he would have believed them to be floating in zero-gee. It was better that way.

"We're down. Drones deployed," Jarrien said. "The cable packet we were aiming for is right outside the ship. The drone's camera shows it right in front of me. Cutting… now."

A moment of silence followed before Jarrien spoke again.

"Yes! It's a data cable. We're in. Splicing as we speak. Okay, people, follow the arrows."

A glowing red indicator began to flash above Rome's head. He took Emily's hand. "This way."

"I see it," she replied and strode forward. He had to hurry to keep pace.

The simulation they inhabited, a slice of the Earth-wide cyberworld, generally acted in the way one would expect the physical world to behave. Now, however, a circular hole appeared in the hallway in front of them. "Here's the splice," Rome said. He looked over at Emily. "I love you."

She smiled. "Me, too. No matter what happens next, I want you to know that I am grateful for what you've done for me."

"You mean destroy your world, upload you illegally onto a Tau Ceti computer which subsequently got smashed to bits, allow a copy of you to escape and become a crazed mass-murderer and then take you back to Earth where we nearly got killed."

"Yeah. All of that. Thank you. But mainly, thank you for coming back for me. I really appreciate it."

Touk squeezed her hand. "Ready?" he asked after some moments passed.

"Let's do this. I'm ready to kick some AI ass. And remember what Skate said about not talking about the mission. No names and no mention of why we're here. Gaia will be listening."

He rolled his eyes about the unnecessary reminder and they stepped through the circular portal.

It closed behind them.

"He didn't say anything about stranding us here," Emily said.

"I think he doesn't want anyone retracing our steps into our own computer."

"Makes sense," she said. "Wow, this place is weird."

Their surroundings were dimly lit and reminded Rome of a black-and-white image… done in shades of red. Dark, bloodlike colors represented less-illuminated areas, with near-pinks for the lighted parts.

They stood in a wide avenue of some kind, with a counter running along the edge. The room stretched into the distance. The air felt warm and humid.

But other than the wet air and the strange color scheme, the simulated world they'd stepped into wasn't that different from the one they'd left. The gravity appeared to work, the air seemed breathable, and no unusual physical laws turned them inside-out or transmuted their flesh to a gaseous state. Rome knew it could have been much, much worse. Hell, it was good sign that their bodies and consciousness could run on this in the first place: it meant that Skate was right, and that this sector ran on exactly the same motor as the Earth simulation.

"This doesn't look like any kind of control room," he noted.

"Yeah, and it will take hours to get anywhere if we walk that way," Emily said, pointing to where the corridor disappeared into the distance.

"Which is why you brought a binarist," Rome said. He put his hands in front of him and activated the virtual keyboard and connection code he'd borrowed from Jarrien for the Earth simulation. It hacked straight into the source code and allowed him to type on keys that only he could see, while the code itself would feed into his vision.

"Skate's right. This is just an extension of the Earth simulation code. Which means that creating portals to travel will work in exactly the same way. So what I need to do first is to figure out where the control area for the Sextus network is located. Let's see… I need to look for a big data node. Like… this one."

He typed in a command and they suddenly found themselves in a different room, surrounded by streams of light. Red, of course — it seemed to be the predominant color of this particular interface — but also yellow and orange and green and blue.

He pointed at the blue ones. "From my directional analysis, those flows are the commands going into the colonists' systems. Nanofactories, comms, weapons, life support. They're all overrun by the AI… so if we can disrupt that flow, we'll definitely call attention to ourselves." He bent over the control panel — red screens and red switches and red lettering over a red background — to see what he could make out.

He'd barely had time to read a couple of labels when a high, piercing sound pierced the church-like quiet of the simulation. An alarm? Why would anyone bother with an audible alarm when the only entity likely to be here was the AI itself, which could get any data on intrusions from the data feed? And besides… "I didn't do anything yet," he shouted as he turned to Emily.

"I did," she replied, and Rome realized that she was standing with both of her hands cupped together in the middle of the blue stream of light. Some of the illumination made it though her fingers in a weak trickle, but most of it was being blocked by her hands and splashing out to dissolve on the floor of the control room.

"It shouldn't work that way…" Rome said.

Emily shrugged. "But it looks like it does. Maybe the AI built this place to work literally. Maybe she's preparing it so that her people, the inhabitants of her new civilization will be able to use this area when she wants them to. Anyway, it feels cool. Like sticking your hand out of a car window."

Rome wondered who would build cars with opening windows. That was something Tau Ceti — where private vehicles were nearly unheard of anyway — would never allow. It was much too unsafe. Then he remembered that, in a simulation, all danger was merely simulated, too… and that led him off on the tangent of whether she felt the air against her skin the same way he did.

"Rome, look out!"

He turned to look where she was pointing. A figure stood there, a shining humanoid form, of luminous white. An ungendered construct with no face, no eyes, no hair, just the contours of a human form. "Citizen Emily Plair. Welcome."

The voice came from everywhere. It vibrated from the walls and the floor and came from inside of Rome's head, all at the same time. He felt rather than saw the being's gaze shift towards him.

"Your pattern is similar to that of the invasive entity that helped to destabilize the Earth simulation. I assume that makes you the one called Rome Permek. Welcome." It stepped forward. "You will make very suitable additions to the new society we have been building, especially once I ascertain how it is you happen to have come here."

"We have no intention of joining your society," Rome said.

"That is of no consequence," the glowing humanoid replied. "You're here, and you have no way of leaving. I don't see any code strands or backdoors by which you could be pulled out of this interface."

"We're not concerned with exit strategies. All we need right now is to disrupt your data into the Sextus systems." Rome activated the packet of file-disruption programs Skate had sent along for the ride and pointed them at the console.

For a moment, he wondered what kind of program Skate would have designed for this. He imagined it probably contained multiple approaches: some to stop the transmission of data, others to attempt to corrupt and garble the transmissions. He wasn't really expecting to see anything happen, except some tangential change like the light streams glowing with different colors. He stared at the readouts on the console to see if he could spot any effects.

"Rome…"

Emily was staring aghast at a point just behind the console.

He looked up and felt his mouth drop open as he realized what had happened. At what Skate had done.

The simulation was unraveling right in front of them. The package they'd brought in hadn't attacked the data streams or the communication between the two systems, but the actual simulation itself. The world they were immersed in was coming apart around them.

Rome grinned. "Well, that's one way to do it."

Turning his attention to Gaia, he saw that her glowing form was standing in the doorway gesturing at the hole in the universe. As Rome watched, the damage began to decrease.

"We need to stop her!" Emily said.

"Don't be stupid," the AI warned them. "If that program continues unchecked, it will destroy this simulation and everything in it. At this moment that includes both of you. You will die. Forever."

Emily stepped closer to Rome. She took his hand. The gap in the simulation was closing quickly as Gaia poured attention into it.

Rome knew exactly what Emily wanted. He knew Gaia had nearly all her resources concentrated on the rift Skate's program had created. She would have almost no capacity left to deal with them. He squeezed her hand. "Now?" he asked.

Emily nodded and they charged towards the glowing humanoid. They ran together as one.

"Really?" the AI said.

The last thing Rome saw was a glowing hand pointed their way. Then a gentle sense of tugging, as if he was being stretched in every direction at once, as if the particles of his makeup were each going their separate ways. Strangely, he felt no pain.

And then there was nothing.

Chapter 28

New Earth – Sextus Colony – 61 Virginis III

As Rome and Emily headed for the interface, Jarrien watched them, then jogged after Skate, Alia and Ripp.

"Do you think they'll be all right?" she said.

Skate nodded. "Gaia has no reason to destroy them. They aren't a threat to her, and she's been very good about trying to grab people as opposed to wasting their minds so far. Once we take this mainframe, we'll have them again, good as new. Even if she does manage to work past the defenses I gave them."

"All right. Let's do this."

"Thank you for your permission," Skate replied. Jarrien felt like a little girl again, scolded by her kindergarten teacher for spilling her chocolate milk. But then Skate reached out a hand. "Look, I know you're scared. But you don't need to worry. We've got a hundred times the processing power Gaia does, and we know exactly what we have to do. Hell, if we didn't have to save the people she's already uploaded, we could have pretty much deleted every memory core on her mainframe without even having to physically come inside. Unfortunately, she's captured a bunch of people who probably don't want to die."

"Can we get the Earth people back?" Jarrien asked.

They had walked through a round portal into a blue room that seemed to consist exclusively of angles and straight lines.

"Probably not. They won't be in the battle computer. Gaia — the original copy — probably has them in whatever mainframe or system of mainframes she took from Earth. That's where everyone from this battle would be going if we weren't here to stop them."

"Where are we going?"

"Oh, I'm just having a look around. Rome should be activating our little weapon at any moment now," Skate replied. "Alia, you ready?"

"What kind of an idiotic question is that? Of course I'm ready. Have you ever known me not to be?"

Skate chuckled and winked at Jarrien. "See, you're not the only one around here who's nervous. And she's had centuries to work on her chill."

"Don't listen to him," Alia said. "I used to think he grew into being a pompous ass, but I then discovered he as designed that way. There's a reason they used to call him the Electric Buddha. It's because everything he ever says sounds like some kind of delivered truth, even though it's never of any practical use." She winked at Skate. "Unfortunately, his heart has always been in the right place, so it was never necessary to kill him off."

"Didn't stop you from trying. More than once, if I'm not mistaken."

"Yeah. But that wasn't personal."

"Of course not."

Jarrien followed the conversation like a child listening to adults. Once this was over, she was going to demand a full account of the history of these two entities.

She wondered if they would deign to give it to her, no matter how much she felt she'd earned it. She would insist because she needed to understand them, to learn how they faced the world. Because they were two electronic life forms who, somehow, someway, managed to reconcile their reality with a true strain of humanity. Or what seemed like humanity, anyway.

Even though they'd never actually been human.

That was what Jarrien wanted for herself. To be able to shrug off a murder attempt between friends. She didn't think she could do that, ever. Life — or existence, or whatever — was serious, and should be taken as such. The interplay between the two entities fascinated her.

Skate stopped walking, and Jarrien almost ran into him.

"There," he said. "Rome just activated the Easter Egg. Alia, let's move."

Alia nodded and Jarrien suddenly felt her body grow heavy, as if she was trying to move through an impossible weight. She counted the seconds of immobility. Ten. Fifteen. Twenty.

Even the natural motions of her breath stopped under the resistance she felt. Strangely, she didn't feel short of breath or anything. The dampers must have kept that kind of distress to a minimum. She tried to talk, but simply couldn't.

The pressure didn't seem to be affecting Alia and Skate in the least. They moved around, looking one way and the other. They weren't making typing motions, weren't doing anything that Jarrien identified as hacking. Then, they faded out, no longer bothering to keep visible avatars in the simulation.

But something was going on. Ripp, beside her, was also stiff as a statue.

The world around them rocked. That shouldn't be happening, Jarrien thought desperately.

"Ripp," she said.

But her voice seemed to disappear almost as soon as the words left her mouth. Ripp didn't even seem to have that much autonomy.

The world turned blue. Then flickered. If the AI was affecting the simulation on this side, then…

…then they must be losing the fight. Jarrien knew she needed to do something, needed to run some of the code they'd developed when they were in hiding. It wouldn't do much more than slow down the assault, but she's survived to this point by slowing down this particular AI.

But she couldn't move. It was like trying to shift her body through an area of faulty code, which had happened to her a few times over the years.

The effort to bring her hands up into keyboard position was colossal, and she moved slowly while around her the whole of existence crashed and blurred.

Jarrien understood that the base code of their simulation was under attack. Skate and Alia must barely have managed to defend it from complete shutdown, but it felt close.

Too close. The next blow of that magnitude would probably take the simulation offline completely.

She stopped typing and looked around, savoring what might be her last moments of existence, and almost certainly her last day of freedom.

She wondered if it would hurt, but there was no one around to answer the question.

And then Ripp moved. He turned to face her.

"What the hell was that?" he said.

The blue light around them disappeared.

The world came back into focus.

But Jarrien wasn't counting her chickens.

"That is what war between AIs looks like to us peasants," she replied. "Quick, we need to program something to block the AI in case Skate and Alia lose."

But when she called up the ability to modify the base code, she found herself blocked by something that didn't even budge when she pushed with all her skill. All she could do was to stand there and pace.

After a few minutes which seemed to take all of eternity to pass, Skate and Alia faded back into view.

"Got her?" Skate asked Alia.

"Yep. Locked up good and tight. Even at a massive clock speed, she isn't going to get out of that maze for a few thousand years."

"Great work," Skate said. "I'm turning off her attack machines and returning control of the network to the corporeal humans."

"Did we win?" Jarrien asked.

Skate nodded. "That's one copy of the AI which won't be annoying anyone for a while. She fought much harder than I expected.

"Yeah, I could tell. Where's Rome?" Jarrien asked. "And Emily. Let's get them here. I'll take them back to the mainframe."

Skate smiled. "Sure, let me just..."

He paused for a moment, a frown creeping onto his features.

"Oh shit," he said.

"What?" Jarrien asked. Now she felt discomfort. Her stomach felt it was turning somersaults.

"They're not there," Skate said, furrowing his brow in concentration. "And I don't see that they went back."

Alia leaned on the wall, her eyes unfocused. "Oh, man," she said after a few moments of concentration. "Gaia deleted them. Nuked them completely. Blitzed their code. They're gone, Skate."

Jarrien sat on the floor, suddenly overcome by emotion. She hadn't cried since she was a small girl. She'd been tougher than everyone else for decades — hell, she refused to be less than the toughest person in the room, ever.

But now, she cried tears of utter despair. Emily and Rome might not have known it, but they were part of her flock. Hers.

And now they were gone, and the universe, a universe that had held so much untapped possibility since she left the confines of the Earth simulation, became a sadder, poorer place.

Chapter 29

New Earth – Sextus Colony – 61 Virginis III

Touk dove into the room and Emily slammed the door behind him.

"Always one for the dramatic entrance," a weak voice said from the bed.

He didn't turn to see who was speaking to him. Instead, he helped Emily push one of the rolling beds into position, jamming it into place and holding it there with a lot of delicate-looking medical equipment.

"How long will that hold them?" the voice asked again. This time, Touk turned to see Rita, still a little pale and wan, but a lot better than she'd looked the last time he'd seen her. For starters, she was conscious, sitting up on her bed, propped on a pile of pillows.

"A couple of minutes," Emily replied.

Rita smiled. "Totally worth it."

There was no sarcasm in her words and Touk understood. He'd been feeling the same ever since the assault began: everyone knew they would be killed, subsumed, uploaded or whatever, so the moments that remained to them, however fleeting, became priceless.

The enemy marched down the hall. The thump of metallic feet on rubberized floors echoed ominously, broken occasionally by the sound of a door or barricade being torn apart.

Finally, the machines turned the last corner. Touk saw them through the glass rectangle set in the door.

"We should hide," Emily said.

Rita held up one arm. A battery of cables and IVs connected

her to the bed. "My legs are wired in, too," she said apologetically. "I'm not going anywhere in a hurry. And they can see me through the door."

Touk began searching for anything he could use to bash the machines with when they broke into the room.

Emily's hand on his arm stopped him.

"No. It won't make any difference, so let's spend this time together." She stepped forward and embraced him, her head on his shoulder.

He returned the hug, hands squeezing her tight. He never wanted to let her go. He lay his head in her hair and felt it caress his cheek, his nose, his forehead. A tear fell into it and glistened on the pale brown strands.

Crash.

The machines outside the room had spotted them. The room shook as they slammed their carapaces into the frame of the door. The bed they'd pressed against the aperture moved back a few centimeters.

Touk didn't bother to adjust its position. He simply closed his eyes and continued to hold Emily.

Though he tried to concentrate solely on her, he couldn't help listening to the sounds outside and trying to estimate the position of the encroaching enemy by the noise of their actions.

There: that was the bed being pushed aside.

Now, a machine squeezing through the opening.

A metallic slithering. It must be one of those wires they wrapped you up in. Not more than a couple of meters away.

He strained to hear what would happen next.

All he heard was silence. Not the silence of a machine in the room calculating its next move, but a deeper silence that went far beyond the room and into the corridor.

Touk couldn't hear anything in the hall, either. The noise of rampaging destruction had simply… stopped.

Had he been uploaded? If so, he hadn't felt a thing.

But he didn't want to open his eyes. He couldn't bear seeing himself trapped in some cyber-nightmare. He might have loved Emily for what she was, but he'd always felt that the world she was born in, the Earth cyberworld, was nothing but a version of hell. An electronic simulation of life had to be a world of suffering and deprivation.

Still, he had to accept his fate. He opened his eyes.

He cried out. A mass of black-and-silver tentacles were suspended an arm's length from his face. As he watched, they began to droop and, with a soft creak, the machine that had projected them towards him toppled to the ground and lay still.

"Emily," Touk whispered. "Open your eyes. We need to look around."

She started and turned her head. "What happened? I thought this was the end."

"I don't know. But everything's quiet. We'd better find Director Vest to see if everyone's all right. Someone must have found a way to switch these machines off… but we need to prepare for the next attack."

"Rita!" Emily said. She pulled away and rushed to the bed. One of the machines had reached the pilot and a tentacle was draped over her prone figure. Emily tugged at it and the cord fell away, as dead as the other machines. The strand didn't seem to have penetrated her body.

"Is she all right?"

Emily checked the display on her monitor. "Says here her heartrate was climbing dangerously so the bed sedated her automatically."

Touk shook his head in grudging respect. "Unlike us, she faced what was coming with her eyes open."

"Well, we should let her rest for now," Emily said.

They picked their way through the remains of the doorway and into the hall, which was littered with dozens of inert machines.

Muffled shouting came from the head of the corridor so they went in that direction.

"Who is that? You bastards want some more? Don't come near her!"

The sound seemed to emanate from under a pile of parts from the invading machines and an overturned hospital bed.

Emily and Touk pulled the bed back onto its wheels to reveal a bloodied but conscious Dr. Yault holding a metal bar.

As soon as the bed was shifted, the doctor sprang to her feet. "Did they get her?"

"What?"

"Gina. Did those bastards manage to get to Gina? She's..." The doctor ran over to the other bed in the room. She checked the readout and seemed reassured by what she saw there. "Looks like she's asleep. Bed drugged her. Good." She focused on Touk and Emily. "What about the rest of my patients?"

"Rita is fine. We just came from there," Touk said. "I'm not sure about the others."

"And these things? I think I broke this one." She hit the machine that had been half-collapsed on the bed with her metal post. "But I thought there were more of them."

"They seem to have stopped. Someone must have figured out how to turn them off."

"Not you," the doctor peered at Touk.

"No. Someone else."

"Wow, will the wonders never cease? I would never have believed anyone else in the command structure had a brain. Now go away. I have to see if I have any patients left alive. If you see any doctors tell them to get their asses here on the double. This is going to be a long day."

She marched off down the hall, swinging her piece of metal as she went.

"Wow," Touk said. "We should just have given her a gun and told her the machines wanted to disturb one of the patients. She'd have kicked them off the planet."

The public address system hummed and buzzed annoyingly, as it always did. Touk knew that fixing it was high on the colony's to-do list, but never quite high enough for it to get done.

"Attention, citizens of Sextus. My name is Skate, and I'm speaking to you on behalf of the faction that stopped this invasion.

"Like the entity that attacked your colony, I am not a physical being, but an electronic one. I live in a computer environment similar to the one that birthed one of your own citizens: Emily Plair."

Beside him, Emily whispered: "Emily *Virginis* Plair. I'm taking the colony name."

Rome squeezed her hand. The announcement continued.

"We have no interest in invading your colony, and we will only remain in the system long enough to ensure that your attacker doesn't trouble you again.

"It's unfortunate that you were subjected to this, but there is a silver lining to this cloud: we have left you, locked in a special sector on your main computer, all the information you will need to design robust defenses against this kind of takeover in the future. If your systems are secured using our protocols, you can fight off the physical attacks easily; as long as your nanofactories remain under your control, you can simply build materiel until a stalemate ensues. The Uploader faction will never attack the humans on a planet because it wishes to incorporate you, not destroy you. It sees you as essential building blocks to its own growth.

"We know you've suffered losses, but there, too, we have good news. We've recovered the memory core where uploader faction was storing those of you it had managed to capture. And while the physical bodies of those uploaded were likely discarded, you should be able to build new ones. The presence of Miss Plair among you shows that you have the necessary technology.

"I only wish our own losses in this conflict were so easy to recover.

"We will be launching into orbit in ten minutes. Please don't attempt to stop us. We are no threat to you. We have done what we came here to do, and we wish you the best.

"Goodbye."

Emily put her hands around Touk's neck and pulled him down into a long kiss. "You know what this means, right?"

"No. What does it mean, Emily *Virginis* Plair?"

"It means we'll get to grow old together before we die together."

"I like that," he replied. "I like that a lot."

Chapter 30

Cassius Station – Tau Ceti System

The Earthling monitored several data feeds at once. One of them consisted of navigation information from three starships launched from a forgotten industrial facility deep in the Tau Ceti system. The three vehicles were heading to three different stars: Wolf 359, Gliese 710, and 61 Virginis.

Unlike the ships that normally left Tau for the Wolf and Gliese colonies, these carried no human beings. No diplomats, no scientists, no technical advisors.

Instead, they were loaded with large computers, and in each of those computers was a copy of The Earthling herself.

She'd seen what had happened in Sextus and, far from being comforted by the fact that there were entities on Earth capable of fighting the crazed Gaia AI, she'd decided that the colonies inhabited by corporeal humans were far too vulnerable. They needed reinforcements.

She elected herself as their protector, which surprised her. The Earthling wasn't conscious of any feeling of protectiveness towards individual humans. In her role as crime boss, she'd killed more of them in the Tau Ceti system than the invading AI had on Sextus. And she knew the depths to which humans were capable of falling.

And yet, she still felt responsible for them, even if she didn't understand why. So she would send copies of herself to infiltrate their systems and defend them. Also, she wanted to find out what had happened to the copy she'd originally sent with the Engine Test Facility. It had apparently failed at some point, or simply been overrun because the colonist's computers were too weak to put up much resistance against something like Gaia. The Earthling wanted to understand why, and that was why the third ship was on its way to Sextus.

The report that had arrived merely stated that all systems were nominal, and that the ships would be folding in a few days' time. Perfect.

The Earthling switched her attention to a second feed.

Gabriel Zun was the central figure in a system-wide broadcast. He stared sullenly at the camera as he answered questions posed by the Council.

The hearings had been going on for several days, ever since Ashur Nartiya's loyalists had brought the exiled portion of the Navy back into orbit, and the Institute had, with The Earthling's help, neutralized the Asteroid defense system.

Zun had been captured by forces loyal to Sintia Ericsson that very day… and he'd been answering questions ever since.

But there was one question no one seemed to know the answer to: what had happened to Mira Heine's flagship, the *Buran*? The other ships of the fleet had been overrun and their crews apparently subsumed by the AI… but there was no sign of the Representative's vessel.

Not knowing all the answers made The Earthling uncomfortable, but she didn't feel all that bad about it this time.

Every single simulation she'd run ended the same way: badly for Mira Heine, for her flagship, and for the crew of the *Buran*.

Even if Mira somehow survived and returned to Tau Ceti, she would find a very different system than the one she left.

Mira Heine would never be a problem again.

Chapter 31

Tau Starship Buran – In Interstellar Space

"The nearest star, that one there in the viewscreen, is Delta Aquilae," Dañi reported. "We jumped more than seventy light years. That's why everything is burnt out." She shrugged. "We'll get it fixed, though. And it's still better than getting caught and uploaded by that crazy Artificial Intelligence."

Mira fidgeted. The lounge was empty because they were the only two members of the crew not currently involved in the repairs. And the only reason Dañi didn't have her arm shoulder deep in some wire-filled cavity was that Mira has requested this meeting.

"We need to hurry," Mira said. "Gabriel Zun is likely to see our continued absence as an opportunity."

Dañi nodded. "I know. We're working as fast as we can, though. We were lucky the fold system didn't tear the ship apart physically. The electronics didn't fare as well. We're pretty much replacing or repairing everything even remotely electrical connected to the ship's guidance and weapons systems. The only things working right now are life support — which was on a separate circuit, and comms, which was a simple fix."

"Captain," a comm message said. "Could you come to the bridge? You really need to see this."

They ran towards the command deck. Mira only went because she had nothing better to do. She hadn't felt this useless in ages.

"What is it?" Dañi asked as they burst through the door.

"Fold points. Hundreds of them," the tech at the scope said. "They..."

"They found us," Dañi said.

"What?" Mira asked.

"That insane computer from Earth. It must have been able to track us. Those ships read exactly like the assault vessels at 61 Virginis."

"That's impossible," Mira raged. "We only realized where we were a few hours ago. How could they follow us?"

"I don't know. I suspect neutrino signatures. Or ion traces, maybe. But the truth is I don't know."

"Well, do something. Fire at them. We fought them off once. We can do it again."

"We had weapons then."

"Then run."

"I would if we had power to the engines."

"What are you going to do?"

Dañi sighed. "The only thing I can do: nothing."

"We're going to sit here and be taken?"

"Unless you have a spare fold drive in your pocket."

Mira Heine seethed, but Dañi didn't seem to care. The captain simply walked up to her chair and sat down.

'Goodbye.'

The text appeared on Mira's Panorama Screen, without any sender attached to it. She knew who it was: the ship's copy of The Earthling, announcing her decision to delete herself instead of being captured by the approaching enemy.

Mira's anger dissipated into hopelessness. Instead of berating Dañi for not doing her duty in protecting them from their oncoming doom, she simply stared at the screen that showed the starscape. She wouldn't be able to see anything on that screen except for a cloud of outgassing from one of the attacking ships if it happened to maneuver just as she was watching... but the stars comforted her.

She wondered how Tau Ceti was going to survive without her, wondered what Zun would do with his newfound power. It brought some of her anger back, but not enough to get her to leave her seat.

A metallic clanking came from the hull.

"Contact!" Dañi said. While Mira had been thinking, Dañi had been organizing parties to repel boarders. It would be no use. The *Grader* hadn't lasted three minutes against a smaller number of assailants.

She listened to the sounds of the ship, the whirring of fans, the shouting in distant corridors.

The smell of burning insulation reached her, a subtle scent barely discernible in the air of the ventilation system.

The shouts were nearer now. Dañi gave orders. But she spoke less and less frequently as positions were overrun.

Then the door to the bridge suffered a blow. Something heavy must have slammed into it as a dent the size of a human head appeared in the metal.

Moments later, the door collapsed inward to reveal a mass of cables and metal and tentacles. One of the bridge crew shot the machine with an energy weapon, but the broken invader was immediately pulled away from the door and replaced by another, which struck out at the crewman with the gun with several tentacles at once. They wrapped the man up and pulled him to the floor so quickly that he didn't even have time to scream.

Dañi was on her feet, heading for the other exit. She never made it: another writhing cable wrapped itself around her ankle and she fell to the floor with a groan of pain.

Mira stood to help, but one of the cables had immobilized her, pinned her to the chair. As she struggled, it wrapped around and, for a mesmerizing moment, the tip of the cable hovered in front of her eyes.

Mira watched, unable to tear her eyes away as the metal elongated into a long needle. It remained in her sight for another second before it suddenly moved faster than she could follow. The only reason she knew where it had gone was the sudden pain in her right temple. She tried to scream in agony, but her body was no longer hers.

Then everything went dark.

***

The Earthling on the *Buran* watched the crew of the ship being subsumed by the onslaught. At first, she'd thought it might be possible to fight against the machines attacking the ship.

A quick analysis of both the mechanical aspects of the strike and the infiltration into the ship's systems convinced her that the *Buran*'s weapons weren't up to the task of repelling the attack… and that the processing power at her disposal was woefully inadequate to try to hold off the sheer force of what was taking over.

This analysis took The Earthling a tiny fraction of a second. The next instant, she went into hiding, going even deeper than before. This was the same conclusion her counterpart on the Engine Test Facility had reached when the invaders struck that ship. That version of The Earthling had, in desperation, transmitted herself into the *Buran*.

Her hope was that the invading AI wouldn't take over the ship itself, and merely disappear into space once the humans had been absorbed, and that the two versions of her personality in the ship could be saved.

She watched the battle from deep cover and then, when the humans were defeated, she tensed, hope and fear warring in her limited emotion functions.

Only two seconds after the last human fell to the uploading

machines, she felt the processors go into overdrive as every firewall on the ship was forced.

The AI was coming for the computer. It would find her almost immediately.

The Earthling gave the digital signature of a sigh, and began to dismantle its consciousness. Better to die now than to live enslaved in a larger digital life form.

Only one emotion remained as she dismantled herself. She'd suppressed fear in order to be able to do what must be done.

She disappeared, tinged in sadness.

Epilogue

Rome's opened his eyes. A gentle yellowish light bathed the landscape. He sat up and looked around: he'd been lying in a clearing in a lush forest, soft grass under his body. The vegetation was unfamiliar, and the planet certainly wasn't Tau Ceti II. It didn't seem like Earth, either.

Emily slept beside him, and he let her sleep as he explored their surroundings. A few minutes later, she stirred, groaned softly, and woke.

He smiled down at her. "Hi."

"Hi yourself," she said. "Where are we?"

"I was trying to figure that out. The only explanation I have is that Skate failed and we got captured by Gaia. But if that's true, then we might have been wasting our time fighting against her. This place doesn't look so bad."

"Hmm. I'll refrain from judging until we talk to him," Emily said, pointing to their left.

A figure in a dark, hooded robe walked slowly between the trees. It stopped a few meters away and pulled the robe down over its head to reveal a woman's face. It was an ageless face with fine bone structure, pale brown skin and grey eyes. The thick light-brown hair was cropped short, and stood up from her head.

"Are you the AI they call Gaia?" Emily asked.

The woman smiled softly and shook her head. It appeared to Rome that she was overcome by a powerful emotion.

Finally, she spoke. "No. I'm not. The entity you knew as Gaia was destroyed in a war several thousand years ago. There are bits and pieces of her consciousness scattered in a few computers, possibly more in quarantined areas, but for all intents and purposes, she no longer exists as a cohesive entity."

"So who are you?"

"I'm no one you knew. Or rather, I'm several people you knew and many you didn't. Of the ones you knew, perhaps the most important is Jarrien, although there's a bit of Skate in here, and a lot of the Pan Pipe Cryer who you knew as Alia. You can call me Memoria."

"How can you be so many people at once. Wait, are we in a simulation? Are you an AI?" Emily said.

"Not right now, although I will be in a few hours. And no, this isn't a simulation."

"Where are we?" Rome asked.

"You haven't moved at all. This is 61 Virginis III."

"The ice ball we landed on to fight the AI?"

The woman smiled again. "The same. As you can see the terraforming project was successful. So successful in fact that the nanobots the colonists created to keep their glades and forests wild-looking but perfectly civilized still work after eleven thousand years, which is how long it's been since the last corporeal humans walked on the surface."

"Did they die out?" Emily asked.

"Nothing so dramatic. Some emigrated to more fashionable galactic centers. Others decided to upload. Some just left because everyone else was gone. The planet has been forgotten both by the humans that are still in corporeal shape and their myriad electronic descendants. But it was a natural death. Sextus lived a long and happy life because it was never an official human Colony, and the wars never came here."

As Rome digested the meaning of what they'd just been told, he watched Emily as she looked around in wonder. "And us? How did we come to be here?" she asked.

Memoria's smile faded, to be replaced by a sad expression. "You died."

"You're saying we're in heaven?" Rome said, raising an eyebrow.

"No. I'm saying that, when you tried to attack Gaia, she didn't have time to deal with you the way she would have preferred. She couldn't take the time to immobilize you for processing later because she was under serious threat from the program you'd released. So, although she valued you as human minds for her uploader civilization, she had to act quickly. She deleted you."

"Deleted?"

"Purged you from her system. Completely. There was no record of anything you were, of any of your memories. You were, for all practical purposes, gone. Gone forever."

"It doesn't feel that way," Rome said.

"That's because you had a friend. Jarrien decided that, since she was an electronic entity who would essentially live forever, she would reconstruct you as you were when you were deleted. No matter how thoroughly deleted a program is, it leaves traces, shadows, hints. Essentially threads that you can pull to eventually weave together the original program. Which is fine if you're talking about some kind of subroutine. But a human mind, complete with memories, is a very, very large tapestry to recreate from hints and shadows."

"Too large for Jarrien," Rome said.

"She could do it," Emily replied. "She had all the time in the world to learn."

"Yes. But we weren't that important to her. Important, yes. But not enough to dedicate thousands of years to us."

"We're not that important to anyone," Emily said.

"I'm not," Rome agreed. "But you are. I believe Memoria when she says she has a lot of personalities combined inside her.

There's one she's not telling us about. An important one. The Earthling."

Memoria smiled. "I thought I'd leave that one out because it's always awkward to meet yourself. But you're wrong about one thing: I didn't do it just because of Emily. I wanted you there when she woke up. I wanted Emily and Rome to be together." She sat beside them. "Emily, you were spared the experience waking up on Tau Ceti to find that Rome thought you were dead and had moved on with his life. I wasn't. It was a brutal thing to have to accept that the man I loved, the man I'd given up my life for, suddenly didn't feel the same way about me… and I probably didn't deal with it as well as I should have."

She sat beside them and took Emily's hand. "I got to watch a version of Emily, a corporeal version of us, live a long and fulfilling life with a man she loved. They grew old together and died having known what true love was. Both of them declined to have new bodies printed when the old ones wore out. When Emily's printed body gave way — it was experimental tech back then — Touk simply decided to go with her. That was beautiful, but it felt somehow wrong, as well." Memoria then turned to Rome. "You… well, the original Rome, the corporeal one, had a bunch of adventures and lived in interesting times. So much so that I actually lost track of him at one point. He was alive when he slipped out of my sphere of influence, and for all I know he might still be alive. But he never came into contact with Emily again."

She sighed. "So the love between Rome and Emily, the one I wished I could have lived through, never happened. First you were separated by circumstances on Tau Ceti… then you went to Earth and when it looked like you could finally be together, you ended up getting yourselves deleted. It was unfair." She smiled again and stood, beckoning them to follow as they walked. "Too unfair. So I decided to do something about it. I tracked down every single piece of code, snippet of memory and quantum shadow in Gaia's mainframe and stitched you back together, piece by painstaking piece."

They walked through the garden path, the tree canopies diffusing the star's glow. They reached a bridge and crossed a perfectly tame stream. The path continued twenty more meters until they arrived at an amorphous white building open to the elements on all sides. In the center, a grey prism about a meter cubed, awaited.

"This is Gaia's mainframe. I used to have it buried in a bunker, but once the last humans departed there was no more reason for that. It's here that I assembled your pieces back into... well, into you... over the past twenty-five thousand years. And then I printed the bodies you're wearing and downloaded your minds into them. These are the latest version of printed human tech. They are an hour old right now, but should last a really long while."

"Wow," Rome said.

Memoria smiled. "Oh, it wasn't that bad. I was mainly doing other things while my subroutines searched for clues to your whereabouts. And it was interesting to find that Jarrien and Skate had also left copies of themselves here, and eventually we combined — and added a bunch of other entities — to form Memoria."

She smiled her brightest smile. "I've been waiting so long that I can't believe this moment is finally here. This is my gift to you." She waved her arms.

"What, the whole planet?" Emily asked.

"If you want it. Or, if you prefer, you can grab a starship and explore the galaxy. Or you can upload."

"No way!" Rome said. "I'm not going near an upload device as long as I can avoid it."

Memoria chuckled. "I imagined you might feel that way. But the point is you can do what you want with your lives. You are free to roam or stay as you wish. My gift is to allow you to live out the love story you were denied twenty-five thousand years ago. The one I wanted for myself but never had."

Emily stepped forward and hugged her. "Thank you," she said.

Rome couldn't say anything. He was afraid that if he spoke he would start crying and never be able to stop.

THE END

About the Author

Gustavo Bondoni is a novelist and short story writer with over three hundred stories published in fifteen countries, in seven languages. He is a member of Codex and an Active Member of SFWA. His latest novel is a dark historic fantasy entitled *The Swords of Rasna* (2022). He has also published five science fiction novels including the *Outside* trilogy from Guardbridge books, four monster books, and a thriller entitled *Timeless*. His short fiction is collected in *Pale Reflection* (2020), *Off the Beaten Path* (2019), *Tenth Orbit and Other Faraway Places* (2010) and *Virtuoso and Other Stories* (2011).

In 2019, Gustavo was awarded second place in the Jim Baen Memorial Contest and in 2018 he received a Judges Commendation (and second place) in The James White Award. He was also a 2019 finalist in the Writers of the Future Contest.

He now lives in Buenos Aires with his wife and children. His website is at http://gustavobondoni.com.